The Catacomb Conspiracy

MARGOT ARNOLD

The Catacomb Conspiracy

A Penny Spring and Sir Toby Glendower Mystery

A Foul Play Press Book

The Countryman Press, Inc.
Woodstock, Vermont

Library of Congress Cataloging-in-Publication Data
Arnold, Margot
The Catacomb conspiracy :
a Penny Spring and Sir Toby Glendower mystery /
by Margot Arnold. -1st ed.
p.   cm.
"A Foul Play Press book."
ISBN 0-88150-208-1
I. Title.
PS3551.R536.C33   1991
813'.54—dc20
91-30527
CIP

A Foul Play Press Book
The Countryman Press, Inc.
Woodstock, Vermont 05091

Printed in the United States of America
on acid-free, recycled paper

To the Stusses,
Michael, Christy, Nathaniel and James,
with love

WHO'S WHO

GLENDOWER, TOBIAS MERLIN, archaeologist, F.B.A., F.S.A., K.B.E.; b. Swansea, Wales, Dec. 27, 1926; s. Thomas Owen and Myfanwy (Williams) G.; ed. Winchester Coll.; Magdalen Coll., Oxford, B.A., M.A., Ph.D.; fellow Magdalen Coll., 1949–; prof. Near Eastern and European Prehistoric Archaeology Oxford U., 1964–; created Knight, 1977; 1 dau., Sonya Danarova, m. Dr. Alexander Spring, 1991. Participated in more than 30 major archaeological expeditions. Author publications, including: What Not to Do in Archaeology, 1960; What to Do in Archaeology, 1970; Troezen Excavations—the final report, 1988; also numerous excavation and field reports. Clubs: Old Wykehamists, Athenaeum, Wine-tasters, University.

SPRING, PENELOPE ATHENE, anthropologist; b. Cambridge, Mass., May 16, 1928; d. Marcus and Muriel (Snow) Thayer; B.A., M.A., Radcliffe Coll.; Ph.D., Columbia U.; m. Arthur Upton Spring, June 24, 1953 (dec.); 1 son, Alexander Marcus. Lectr. anthropology Oxford U., 1958–68; Mathieson Reader in anthropology Oxford U., 1969–; fellow St. Anne's Coll., Oxford, 1969–. Field work in the Marquesas, East and South Africa, Uzbekistan, India, and among the Pueblo, Apache, Crow and Fox Indians. Author: Sex in the South Pacific, 1957; The Position of Women in Pastoral Societies, 1962; And Must They Die?—A Study of the American Indian, 1965; Caste and Change, 1968; Moslem Women, 1970; Crafts and Culture, 1972; The American Indian in the Twentieth Century, 1974; Hunter vs. Farmer, 1976; Feminism in the Twentieth-Century Muslim World, 1978; Voodoo and its Impact on Negro-American Society, 1980; The Changing Face of Polynesia, 1982; Pacific Studies: a Symposium, 1985; Trends in African Nationalism, 1987; Modern Micronesian Chiefdoms, 1989; The Marquesas: Today and Yesterday, 1990.

Chapter 1

"What we need is a complete change of scene, a change of pace—we're in a rut," Penelope Spring announced firmly to her morose companion. "I think we should go right away from Oxford, and now." They were sitting in Toby Glendower's large cluttered office in the Pitt-Rivers Museum as an insistent April shower tapped energetically at the window.

Sir Tobias squinted at her through an enveloping cloud of tobacco smoke and snorted in disbelief. "You've only just got back from six months at the ends of the earth! Wasn't that enough for you? All this go, go, go—what's the point of it at your age?"

"Let's leave my age out of it, and that's just what I mean. Six months of hard fieldwork in the Marquesas is hardly rest and recreation! I still have three months to go on my sabbatical and I could use some real rest and recuperation. This magnificent offer of the Redditches is just the sort of thing I had in mind—a free villa on the Appia Antica in Rome, where all we have to do is keep an eye on their servants and enjoy ourselves! I could use a large dollop of *la dolce vita,* so come on, Toby, it would be fun."

"Then you go. I'm much too busy," he rumbled. "I'm writing a book."

"You're *always* writing a book, and most of the time you never finish it. I wonder Oxford University Press doesn't shoot you on sight, the number of unfinished books you've left on their hands."

"Something has always come up. Besides, this is different—this is a textbook," he hedged.

"You writing an archaeology *textbook!* What on earth for?" She was completely sidetracked.

He cleared his throat. "Sonya has been taking a course at Columbia in archaeology—she's very interested, you know." He preened a little at this manifestation of good taste in his newly found daughter. "I saw her textbook when I was visiting them in New York—terribly written! Very unsound in parts, too. So I told her to pay it no mind and that I'd write her a good one. I also offered to go and see her instructor and put him straight on a few things, but for some reason she didn't think that was a very good idea."

Penny suppressed a grin. "Oh, I see, well that's different. But there's no reason you couldn't go on with it in sunny Italy, is there? It's all there in your head anyway."

"References," he said pompously, waving a hand at the crammed bookcases that stretched from floor to ceiling along two of the walls. "I need my library."

"Oh, nonsense, you can put those in at the end!—*I* always do. Anyway . . ." she played her trump card, "I thought you'd want to be there when they came through Rome."

"Who?"

"Why, Alex and Sonya, of course! I heard from Alex last night and Sonya's passport has finally come through, so as soon as he can arrange coverage for his patients they're off on their delayed honeymoon—Vienna, Paris, and ending up in Rome—the last week in May or first week in June, depending on when they can get off."

"First I've heard of it," Toby sniffed. "Last time Sonya called she made no mention of it."

"Well, it has only *just* happened," Penny retaliated. Since their precipitate retreat to America the young couple had wisely set up a schedule of calls to their respective parents: every two weeks Sonya would call her father with her news, and Alex would call his mother in the alternate weeks with his. As a result, Penny had heard more from him than she had ever done since he had first left for college. "So how about it?" she demanded.

"You're sure there is nothing more to it than that?" Toby was deeply suspicious. "No old student out there with some dire problem to solve? No bodies in the basement of the Redditch villa?"

Penny held up her right hand, "I swear it on a stack of Bibles! Nothing like that. I'm just as off all that as you are, after what we went through last time. Just a nice holiday in the sun, that's all!"

He grunted. "Well, I suppose I *could* make the time."

"You could give me the scholar's tour of Rome. We could explore it together. I'm sure there are places you've never seen," she tempted.

"I have seen *everything*," he stated firmly. "And most of it was not worth the effort. The Romans, to my mind, were a very dreary lot. Everything worthwhile in their culture they stole from the Greeks."

She was not about to challenge him and get him started on one of his favorite hobbyhorses, so changed tactics. "The villa has a marvelous garden, complete with swimming pool and sheltered patio, and Angela said it's only about a mile beyond the Aurelian Walls on the Via Appia, so it has all the delights of the country while being almost in the city. They love it."

"If they love it so much why are they offering it to you?" He was still suspicious.

"Because they are going to be on home leave, and Henry's

11

tour there is almost up so they'll be house hunting in England. His next assignment is to the Foreign Office here. Angela is a bit nervous about leaving the house untenanted for two months, because it is rented furnished and there are a number of valuable antiques in it. Rome is quite crime-ridden these days, so she wants somebody responsible staying there to keep an eye on things and to see the servants don't quietly make off with some of the smaller *objets d'art*. She says both the house and garden are stuffed with Roman antiquities, and the house itself is sitting on top of one of the unexcavated catacombs."

"I don't think that's even possible," Toby stated flatly. "All the catacombs have been looked at some time or another."

"In this case, no. That whole area of the Appia Antica has belonged to the Scorsi family for a very long time, and for some reason the Scorsis were anti-excavation, so the catacomb of St. Crescentia has never been opened." She was equally dogmatic. "The Redditches' villa isn't in the Scorsi family domain now—it was the dower of some female Scorsi way back, and I believe the present owner is a Barberini."

"St. Crescentia?" he muttered and, getting up, stalked over to a bookcase and extracted a massive, battered volume into which he peered. "Ah yes, here she is. St. Crescentia, virgin martyr, Diocletian persecution. That's when St. Agnes also got the chop I recall. Reputedly of patrician lineage. Relics in St. Margaret's Convent, Edinburgh, indicate she was eaten by lions. Small catacomb bearing her name on Via Appia Antica. Hmmph!"

"See!" Penny cried.

"If her relics are in Edinburgh, she isn't even in her own catacomb." He was not to be downed that easily.

"What does that matter?" She was getting impatient. "Anyway, are you or are you not *coming?* I have to let Angela know as soon as possible—they're leaving in a few days."

Toby capitulated. "Oh, very well. When?"

"How about the end of this week?"

He consulted his diary and shook his silver-thatched knoblike head. "I have to preside over a Society of Antiquaries meeting on Friday."

"Then how about Monday next?"

"All right, but don't forget it'll take a couple of days to drive down."

"You're not thinking of taking the Rolls!" she exclaimed. "It will be an albatross around our necks—you know what Rome traffic is like! Besides, one look at it and up go the prices. Why don't we fly out from Gatwick and rent a mini-car—a cinquecento or a little Fiat? Much more sensible."

He shuddered. "I hate small cars, particularly small, *foreign* cars. Still . . ." he sighed, "have it your way. Parking in Rome is, I recall, a bit of a problem."

Victory gained, she jumped up. "Then I'll let Angela know right away, and I'll take care of the bookings. All *you* have to do is pack. And don't forget it'll be a lot warmer in Rome than here."

"Spring in Rome can be bloody cold, so I shall pack accordingly," he replied, determined to have the last word for a change.

Angela Redditch, who had never got over a girlish tendency to gush, gushed in full spate over the phone. "Why that's absolutely *super,* Dr. Spring! You *and* Sir Tobias—we'll feel *terribly* honored to have you, although, of course, we won't actually *be* there, I'm afraid. We are starting the drive back on Saturday—and you'll be here Monday? No problem, none at all. The Lippis will have everything ready for you. Giovanni looks after all the outside work—not too reliably, I'm afraid . . ." she giggled girlishly. "But Rosa, his wife, is a *real* treasure. Does all the inside work and is a *super* cook. I've gained pounds and pounds! So has Henry. They both speak English of sorts. Oh, it will be *such* a relief to have you here . . ." and went on to give minute, if somewhat garbled, instructions to

13

the villa. Before ringing off, she added, "By the way, there's another of your ex-students on board at the embassy—Diane Grant? She does something in the Cultural Attaché's office, I'm not sure what. Do you remember her?" Penny did, albeit somewhat vaguely. "If you run into any problems I'm sure she'll be delighted to help out, and of course you can always contact us in Surrey at the number I gave you—Henry's parents' home. Have a *wonderful* time!" And with another cascade of giggles she was gone.

They had left England in a burst of April sunshine, only to be met at Leonardo da Vinci airport by a torrential downpour. Toby, a testy traveler at best, grumbled loudly as they passed through Customs and sloshed through puddles in the outer terminal. "You'd think after all these years they'd have figured out how to fix that damned leaky roof. Look at this place! In the Pantheon one expects to walk on water after a rainstorm, it was built with a hole in the roof; but here. . . ?"

Penny wisely held her peace as they sought the car rental agency, but Toby's mood was not improved when the only Fiat available was bright red—a color he loathed. "We'll look like the circus coming to town," he groused as he got behind the wheel and started off. "And the way this thing rides we'll be rattled to bits on those damn cobblestones of the Appia Antica."

She let him grouse on until they reached the great artery of Christoforo Columbo, then said mildly, "Oh, do shut up, Toby, we're here to enjoy ourselves. And look, the sun's out. Just keep your eyes peeled: we have to turn right at the Piazza di Navigatori onto the Via della Sette Chiese, then it's all the way down that and another right onto the Appia."

"Well, you've got the map, so you tell me when," he growled and gobbled into silence, taking the turns at a lunatic speed sufficient to satisfy the maddest of Roman drivers.

As they hit the uneven paving stones of the Appia Antica he slowed and muttered, "Now what?"

"We keep on past the tomb of Cecilia Mettela on the left and after that we'll pass the entrance to a big villa on the right, then there should be a restaurant right on the road—the Albergo del Sole—and after that the very next double doors we come to should be the garage to the Redditch villa, and the next single door is the main entrance. The Appia is too posh to have numbers," she muttered, peering at her scribbled instructions.

He slowed to a crawl to the vast displeasure of the drivers behind him, expressed with a cacophony of horns. Toby ignored them. "Well, there's the inn," he said. "And there's the double doors—and they're open. Shall I pull in?"

"Yes, *yes*. Obviously they're expecting us," she muttered, keeping a wary eye on a large Lamborghini that was camped on their back bumper. Toby swung violently across and in and the Lamborghini was gone with a final furious blast of its Klaxon horn.

"Sure this is right?" he asked, cutting the engine.

"According to what Angela said it should be, but we'll soon see." She scrambled out and went over to a small dark-green door at the rear of the garage. She turned the handle, but it was firmly locked. "Damn!"

"What now?" he enquired, uncoiling himself slowly and stretching.

"This is no go, we'll try the main entrance," she said, a pang of doubt shooting through her. They walked twenty yards along the busy, sidewalkless road until they came to a heavy, iron-studded wooden door. This time the massive iron handle turned and the door yielded with a creak, revealing a paved pathway leading to a long, low villa of grey stone with a roof of red terra-cotta tiles. The path was edged on both sides by flowerbeds in which jonquils, daffodils and tulips rioted gaily. "Yes, this must be it," she said with relief, looking quickly around. "See, there's the swimming pool and the glassed-in patio." With renewed confidence she went up and pulled the wrought-iron bell chain that hung beside a smaller version of the solid outer door. They could hear its harsh summons echoing through the house, but nothing happened. After another vain try, and avoiding Toby's accusing eye, she said, "Maybe they're out back. We'll try the back door." They followed a smaller paved pathway around to the side of the house nearest the garage. There was washing flapping on the line in a grassy wattle-fence enclosure, but pounding on the back door met with no more success than her previous efforts.

"Did you *tell* them when we'd be arriving?" Toby said acidly.

"Well, not specifically . . ." She was following the path which continued around to the back of the house. "I wasn't sure how long it would take us to pick up the car and get in, so I just said early afternoon." She peered in at the French windows of what had to be the living room. "But this is the right place—look, I can see Angela's wedding picture sitting there on the piano. Where on earth can the Lippis be?"

"The cat's away, so the mice do play," Toby sniffed. "No wonder the Redditches wanted someone around to keep an eye on things."

"I suppose we may as well explore the garden until someone shows up. Perhaps they just went out to do some shopping."

"Might as well." Toby got out his battered briar and lit up as they strolled across the large lawn at the back of the house. The garden rambled over the best part of an acre and, as specified, was crammed with antiquities: statues peered at them from bushes and were ranked like sentinels along the high wall encircling the villa. At every turn amphora and Roman urns sprouted flowers and hanging plants of bewildering variety, and an ornately carved Roman sarcophagus served as a watering trough for the vegetable garden, discreetly tucked away behind privet hedges along the rear wall.

"A motley crew to be sure," Toby remarked, his temper soothed by his first pipe since Heathrow. He looked around critically at the statues, some much weathered, others as pristine and sharp featured as when they had come from their Roman sculptor's chisel. "The gods cheek by jowl with emperors and sundry patricians, I see; all no doubt looted from the Appia Antica tombs." He looked up with approval at the high encircling stone wall, topped by jagged glass and, at the angles, by a ferocious *chevaux de frise* of iron spikes. "It certainly is private—it would take a courageous intruder to face that lot."

"Why would they bother when all they'd have to do is walk in the front gate like we did?" Penny said crossly. "A pane out of those French windows and they'd be in the house like a shot. I certainly am going to have a word with the Lippis about *that* when they show up."

"*If* they show up. Maybe they've hopped it," he observed.

Completing the circuit of the garden with no sign of the Lippis, they settled in chaises longues on the patio and contemplated the unruffled blue waters of the swimming pool that had evidently been newly filled, judging by its pristine cleanliness. Apart from the muted hum of traffic along the Appia Antica it was very quiet and very warm in the glass enclosure. "Could be worse," Toby said, lighting up again and puffing away contentedly. "The sun is nice." A companionable silence fell as they basked. As Penny started to drowse, their peace was shattered by an angry shout and pounding footsteps. They both sat up with a start and looked around to see a burly, dark-haired man, his face suffused with anger, running towards them. *"Que cosa che?* What is this, what are you doing here?" he yelled. "You trespass! I call the police. *Vai, vai!"*

Penny sprang up, followed at a more sedate pace by Toby.

"Signor Lippi? I am Dr. Spring and this is Sir Tobias Glendower. We are the invited and expected guests of the Redditches. Where have you been?"

As he came up to them, his hands curled into fists, his burly chest heaving, they could see his eyes were as bloodshot and as enraged as a bull's. A wave of garlic and sour wine reached out and enveloped them. "The Redditches are no here. They go," he shouted and pointed. "No can stay. Out, out!"

"But this is *ridiculous!*" Penny began, when there came a second interruption. There was a shrill cry, "Giovanni, *aspetti!*" and they all turned to see a short, stumpy woman drop a heavy shopping bag inside the front gate and come towards them at a stumbling run. Halting, she bobbed her head frantically and gave at the knees in a travesty of a curtsy, "*Scusi, oh scusi, signora, signor,* I beg a thousand pardons," she sobbed out and, reaching the belligerent man, wheeled on him and sprayed him with words like a machine gun. The pace was too fast for Penny's limited Italian, so she glanced quickly at Toby, whose face had settled into a bland impassivity as the woman's voice rose to an hysterical crescendo. The man flinched under her barrage, his eyes roving wildly between them and the enraged woman. As the tirade continued he seemed to shrink and wilt, until finally his fists unclenched, his shoulders slumped, and with a growl he turned and staggered uncertainly away.

The woman whirled on them, wringing her hands, "Oh, *dio mio,* what a terrible thing to happen! I am Rosa. I no expect you so soon, so I go for things for your dinner tonight. Oh, forgive me! All is *preparato*—all is ready for you . . . Please!" She bowed and waved at the house. "You come now, I show you. Everything just as Signora Redditch say to do. Please forgive!"

Penny made no move. "Your husband did not even seem to know we were expected," she said coldly.

"Oh that Giovanni!" Rosa's dark eyes slid away from hers

and the high color in her swarthy cheeks ebbed. "He get confused, he forget. No matter! All is well now, eh? Come please, I show you . . ." And she started back towards the house.

They followed her slowly. "Did you get what all that was about?" Penny muttered.

"Despite her frightful accent—Calabrian I think it must be—I gathered that Signor Lippi has been absent without leave for the past several days and so was unaware of our expected arrival. She's been combing the city for him. Further, he appears to be most unhappy at the prospect of our being here—I wonder why?" Toby rumbled.

"Well, welcome to your Roman holiday!" Penny said drily, and they followed the frantic Rosa into the cool dusky interior of the ancient villa.

Chapter 2

They soon found that the bad beginning had its compensations. Rosa Lippi could not do enough for them; she flew to do their slightest bidding and produced such exquisite meals that they even brought a gourmet gleam into Toby's usually uncritical eye, while Penny happily gained back all the weight she had so joyfully lost in the Marquesas. Even Giovanni, after two days of sulky withdrawal, came to them with an abject apology and from then on was fawningly deferential. He did his yard work—at least when they were around—with a frantic energy: mowing, digging, weeding, and skimming any leaf that dared to flutter on the surface of the swimming pool, with a diligence that verged upon the ludicrous.

Penny ascribed all this to her own firm stand on that first day. So that there could be no misunderstanding, she had roped Toby in as translator and then had laid down the law about the security of the villa and the necessity for locking the outer doors at all times. To emphasize her concern she had gone through the villa, room by room, with the inventory sheets Angela had left for her in the house folder, and had checked every single item. There was, she had discovered, an incredible amount of bric-a-brac, housed in glass cases of every shape and size in every room of the house; to her vast relief it was all intact and accounted for.

A case of Roman bric-a-brac in her own guest bedroom had caught Toby's eye. "Hmm, so much for the untouched catacomb," he remarked, peering into it. "If that isn't catacomb loot, I'll eat my manuscript. Although," he paused, "this lot looks like first-century loot, whereas St. Crescentia wasn't martyred until the fourth century. I see two very nice votive 'gold' glasses of St. Peter and St. Paul," and he indicated them with a long finger. "Tell me quickly, which is which?"

She peered in. "Why, I suppose the bald-headed man with the long beard is Peter and the curly-headed man with the short beard is Paul."

"Ah, and there you would be dead wrong!" Toby said with a gleeful chuckle. "We've all been so brainwashed by later Christian art into thinking of St. Peter as an old, white-headed man with a long beard that that's a natural assumption. Actually, all the *earliest* portraits of the two from the first century show them like this: it's St. Paul who is shown as the bald-headed one with a long beard, and Peter as the younger-looking one. When you think of it, they must have been about the same age and, since they both went in that first Neronian persecution in 64 AD, would both have been in their mid-sixties."

"So you think all this stuff in the house may be from the catacomb?" she queried.

He shook his head. "No, only the objects in this case." His brow furrowed. "There is one thing though. I wonder where this catacomb actually *is*. It certainly isn't anywhere under the house or in the front part of the garden adjoining the road."

"How do you know that?" she demanded.

"Because this house has a cellar, and the swimming pool, on a line with the house, is nine feet at its deep end. The catacombs, at least the first layer, would not be *that* deep, so if it had been there they'd have run right into it when they were building the villa or putting in the pool."

"So?"

"Oh, nothing. Just a bit odd, that's all, because most of them—like St. Sebastian or Praetextus or Vibia, which are just down the road from here—*are* directly off the Appia Antica."

"Well, anyway, we're not here to dig, but to enjoy ourselves," she reminded him. And this they proceeded to do.

For two weeks they basked, bathed, went sight-seeing and ate Rosa's delicious meals with hearty appetites, as showery April turned into a warm and beautiful May. It was indeed a *dolce vita* in which they were totally relaxed and content. It was only towards the end of the second week, while Penny was gazing dutifully at the mosaic-tiled "sweat-bath" where St. Cecilia had sung her Christian hymns while the soldiers of Diocletian had tried to suffocate her in her own house in Trastevere, that Penny finally admitted to herself that *she* was feeling a bit suffocated by all this ease and enjoyment and was just a tiny bit bored. She glanced quickly at Toby, who was rumbling on in his best lecturing style, and wondered if he also was beginning to get restless.

The past couple of days, during the early afternoon siesta when all of Rome shuts down with a clang for two hours, he had withdrawn to Henry Redditch's study adjacent to the living room where he had deposited all his notes for "the book." However, judging by the volume of pipe smoke that issued from the open French windows, she seriously doubted whether he was actually doing any writing. She half regretted not bringing along her own field notes from the Marquesas, which she easily could have transcribed into a more readable form, but then chided herself for the very thought. There would be plenty of time for all that when she got back to Oxford: this was her sabbatical and she was supposed to enjoy it, so enjoy it she was determined to do.

Following in Toby's learned wake around the church of St. Cecilia, she continued to reflect that, being a "people" person, she was not well suited for the role of dedicated sightseer. Since the only people currently around were the Lippis—she didn't count Toby—she had tried to zero in on them, but with little of her usual success. Rosa was that true rarity—a non-voluble Italian. She was always perfectly amiable, but tended to monosyllabic replies, at best, and any efforts on Penny's part to draw her out about her background or life were stone-walled by a rapid retreat into an Italian so thick that it baffled translation. Similarly, Giovanni, though ever ready with greetings and grins that verged on leers, tended to find something to do in a hurry whenever she tried to draw him into an actual conversation. Thwarted in her direct approach, she had had to retreat to the second resource of the field anthropologist: eagle-eyed observation.

What she had observed thus far had indicated very clearly that the Lippi marriage was far from idyllic. Giovanni obviously had a drinking problem, and by early afternoon was often semi-soused. Also, the minute his daily labors were over, he usually disappeared from the premises entirely, and often did not return until well after midnight. Although the drink was causing him to puff up and bloat, he still retained the vestiges of a Byronic handsomeness and was probably a womanizer as well as a drunk. That indeed would explain the raised angry voices that came from the kitchen quarters on the rare occasions he was around. It was a childless marriage—again an oddity in Italy—and a very evident mismatch.

From Rosa, her reluctant informant, she had extracted the meager facts behind it. Rosa herself, as Toby had surmised, was from a tiny village in Calabria at the very toe of Italy's boot; Giovanni, by contrast, was a Florentine. They had met when he was doing his compulsory military service in the area and he had married the seventeen-year-old Rosa in haste. His service completed, they had come to Rome and remained ever since—almost twenty years. The move had been Rosa's idea, and indeed, for all Giovanni's swaggering macho ways, it was evident that she was the driving force in the marriage. The peasant girl from rural Calabria *liked* Rome: the shops, the bustle, and, above all, the television. The only thing that brought a sparkle of delight to Rosa's dark eyes was anything to do with that magic box. The minute she was free of her duties, the television would go on in the Lippi's little living room that branched off the kitchen, and on it would remain until sign-off time. About the box and the people of the box, Rosa would wax enthusiastic, almost eloquent, but on her family, friends, or even Giovanni, she was silent and disinterested. Penny deduced that, like so many country Italians, Rosa had become a "city" girl and wanted no reminders of her humbler past.

It therefore came as a surprise when, the day after her ruminations in Trastevere, Rosa came to her in a state of high agitation. "Signora, I must ask great favor. My aunt—my aunt in Naples—she is very ill. She send for me to come quick—there is no one else. While I was out shopping Giovanni get this message on telephone. I can go please? Very urgent. I not stay long but must go see."

"Why, certainly!" Penny said quickly. "And I'm very sorry to hear it. I hope it isn't serious. You'll go by train? We'll drive you to the station. Don't worry about us, we'll be fine. Just let us know when you get there how things are."

"Oh,,yes, yes!" Rosa appeared in a fever to be gone. "And you very kind to drive me to Termini. I get first train out now. I call tonight. Plenty food here—in refrigerator, in cellar freezer. You manage?"

"Don't worry about that, just go and get ready. We are off to Ostia this afternoon and we'll eat out tonight," Penny soothed. "So don't bother to call until late—or even tomorrow will be fine."

When it came time to go there was no sign of the errant Giovanni, so they saw her onto the train at the central station

24

and then took off for a day of browsing through Rome's ancient port of Ostia Antica. It was such a beautiful sunny day that, having exhausted Ostia, when Toby suggested they go on and "do" Albano and the Papal summer residence at Castel Gandolfo in the Alban Hills, Penny agreed with alacrity. "Yes, we've no cause to hurry back and we can eat late at the Albergo del Sole on the way home."

They "did" Rome's parent town of Albano with Toby's habitual thoroughness, so by the time they drove back into Rome it was already dark. "May as well put the car away in the garage now," Toby observed as they bumped down the Antica. "We can walk to the restaurant more easily than parking there."

After parking the car in the garage, they tested all the outer doors of the villa and locked up the garage again, then walked the short distance to the Albergo, which, despite the late hour, was still crowded. "Makes a nice change, doesn't it?" Penny said, happily scanning the large menu. "It's almost a pity that Rosa is such a good cook; we haven't seen any of Rome's favorite eating spots."

"Yes, she is that," Toby agreed absently. "I suppose we'll have to keep an extra-careful eye on Giovanni with her away. He strikes me as a thoroughly shiftless character—I suppose the Redditches only tolerate him because of her."

"Well, at least he does his work, or most of it," Penny said magnanimously, tucking into her antipasto with zest. "So they probably overlook the rest."

They dined leisurely and long, so that it was well after ten-thirty when they emerged replete into the velvety-blue, star-spangled Roman night. As they walked contentedly towards the villa Toby remarked, with sudden testiness, "God! These Italians certainly love their horns. Just listen to that din, will you?"

"Sounds as if it's stuck," Penny said as the insistent bleat continued. "Probably a car in the parking lot of the restaurant." But, instead of receding, the noise grew louder and more insistent as they walked on.

"Good Lord!" Toby exclaimed, quickening his pace, "I think it's coming from *our* garage!" They hurried up to the double doors and stopped dead in their tracks: the doors they had so carefully locked earlier stood ajar, and there was no doubt that it was the Fiat's horn bleating at full blast.

Toby held up a warning hand. "Possibly some blighter trying to pinch the car," he whispered. "The noise probably has scared him off, but we'd better not take any chances. Do you recall where the light switch is?"

"By the back door," she whispered back.

"Damnation! Then you'd better stand back, I'm going to throw open this half of the door. The light from the street will show us if he's still *here*." With a sudden jerk he threw it back, and they peered in, but other than the wailing car there was nothing to be seen.

"A short circuit?" she suggested.

"That doesn't explain the door," Toby said, edging carefully along the wall towards the driver's seat. "Anyway, there is no one here now." He tried the door, but it did not yield. "That's odd!" He fumbled in his pockets for the keys as she edged past him and made for the light switch by the back door.

Just as she reached for it Toby opened the car door and the interior light went on. She heard him gasp and swung around: there was someone in the driver's seat. She froze, but the figure gave no sign of movement. Toby turned a shocked face to her. "Is that door locked?"

She tried it. "Yes, but who, what . . . ?"

He drew himself up with a quivering sigh. "You'd better come and see for yourself. It's incredible! I don't believe this can be happening. . . ."

She scurried around the car and her eyes widened in shock

and disbelief. Giovanni Lippi was slumped in the driver's seat, his swarthy forehead pressed to the steering wheel, activating the horn. At first she thought he was drunk, then she saw—buried to the hilt between his shoulder blades was a large, black-handled knife.

Toby felt frantically at the neck for a pulse. He shook his head, then, wrenching open the hood of the car, he pulled some wires and disconnected the horn.

In the heavy silence that followed, they stood looking at each other in the dim light. Unheeding, the traffic of the Antica flowed past in a steady stream. "Well, it is murder for sure," Toby said in a flat voice. "You'd better go and call the police, while I close up the scene of the crime. I hope we haven't messed it up too much. Here we go again. . . ."

Chapter 3

"The Roman paparazzi certainly don't waste any time, I see—
they must have a permanent tail on the police," Penny said,
gulping coffee and looking dazedly at the headlines of *Il
Populo* that announced with lurid inaccuracy FAMOUS ENGLISH
DETECTIVE PAIR BRING MURDER TO THE APPIA ANTICA. Accompanying the news item were two grainy pictures of Toby and
herself, evidently culled from the files of some earlier newsworthy case, as well as a picture of the fatal garage—or at
least its closed doors. "We'll have to barricade ourselves in for
a while."

Toby, gulping down his own coffee, grunted. They were
both red-eyed from lack of sleep, for it had been three o'clock
in the morning before the last of their many statements had
been taken and they were at last able to tumble into their beds.
"Well, it looks as if our part in it is already over," he said. His
voice was hoarse, for he had borne the brunt of the questioning by a series of policemen, gradually ascending in rank to
the plainclothes Inspector Cicco of the Murder Squad, and all
of whom, discovering Toby's fluency in Italian, had rapidly
switched from their own tortured English and had, by and
large, ignored the less fluent Penny. "Cicco seemed to think it

would be a simple matter of tracking down which cuckolded husband in the area had got up enough courage to stick a knife in Lippi. The late Giovanni was pretty well known and notorious, it appears."

The garage and its environs had yielded the grim, if simple, facts of the murder. Whoever had murdered Giovanni had evidently waited in a dark patch by the garage—there were footprints in the dust and ground-in cigarette butts. As Giovanni had opened the garage door, the murderer had struck, missing the heart but hitting his right lung. The wounded man had left a sinister blood spoor indicating he had staggered to the car and locked himself in to escape his attacker. There he had collapsed and died. There had been no fingerprints on the knife or car door other than Toby's and the murdered man's, so the attacker had not pursued his prey.

Further light had been thrown on Giovanni's frequent nocturnal ramblings by the discovery of a small yellow motorcycle parked in a shed at the *Albergo del Sole,* which a kitchen helper there had professed to be Giovanni's, who had slipped him a few lire on the side for parking privileges. This explained something that had slightly mystified Penny, for the Appia was well away from the nearest source of public transport and she had wondered how Giovanni had managed to roam so far and free. Further, Giovanni's favorite haunts were already well known to the police, for he had favored the bars of a notorious slum area situated on the Via Ardeatina, that ran parallel to the august Appia Antica and which, in the amazing fashion of capital cities, nestled almost up to the backs of some of the rich villas on the Appia. It was a tenement area noted for its violence and its Communist or terrorist-leaning inhabitants and in which the police went about in twos. It was there the police had picked him up on several occasions during communal bar fights, but he had always been released with a caution, since he was employed and at a good address, whereas most of the combatants were not. "Thought himself a cut above them, he did," one *carabinieri* had volunteered. "Always boasting about being a Florentine—and he certainly knew how to handle the women!"

"It will be a simple case, you will see," Inspector Cicco had comforted them, and with a touch of arrogance had continued: "A peasant murder of revenge, I'd say. We find the owner of the knife, we find the wronged husband—and that will be that. I regret infinitely that you have seen this darker side of our wonderful city and that your holiday has been upset. I do not think we will have to bother you further. It is fortunate for his wife that she was away, otherwise I would certainly have suspected her. If anyone has cause to murder him, it was she, poor woman!"

This was what was currently worrying Penny. "I do wish Rosa would call," she fretted. "Although I dread breaking this awful news to her. What a fool I was not to get her address in Naples!" There had been no call from Rosa the previous night and, though the morning was well advanced, there was still no word. She finished her coffee and sighed. "Well, I suppose it's no use waiting any longer. I had better call Angela and tell her the bad news." But she made no move to get up. "At least we can be thankful that there wasn't a break-in." The police had gone through the villa with them and had checked everything, but there was not a sign that the murderer had entered. Giovanni's keys were all accounted for. They had been found on the floor of the car where they had slipped from his dead hand.

Toby looked at her over the rim of his coffee cup. "It has put rather a damper on things, hasn't it? What do you want to do, pack it in and go home?"

She wriggled uncomfortably. "I feel I ought to stick around for Rosa. She'll need somebody to see her through this miserable time, but if you want to go I quite understand. I'm just sorry I dragged you into this, Toby."

"It is not *your* fault," he growled. "And no, I'm not going to leave you in the lurch. It has been fine up to now, and if we lie low for a couple of days the press will get tired of it, and then we can go on as we were. I don't suppose the Redditchs will want to come rushing back—after all, there is nothing for them to do."

"Anyway, I'd better find out what they *do* want done." This time she stood up with decision and made for the phone.

"How *terribly* inconvenient!—for you." There was a fractional pause in the statement as Angela's voice echoed tinnily over the phone. As an epitaph for the late Giovanni it left a lot to be desired, Penny reflected, as Angela spoke. "Er, I do hope that doesn't mean you and Sir Tobias are thinking of leaving. It means so much to Henry and me having you there. Our minds were quite at rest—and now this! I am *so* sorry."

"I thought at least we would stay until Rosa gets back and we have seen her through the worst of it here. You don't happen to know her aunt's address in Naples, do you? She hasn't been in touch yet, you see."

"I didn't even know she had an aunt in Naples—*too* trying for you. But fortunate in a way. I mean if she *had* been there, I'm sure the police would have suspected her!"

"Has Giovanni always been this bad?" Penny queried. "The drinking, other women and so on?"

Again there was a pause. "He seems to have been much worse of late." Angela's voice was thoughtful. "Though God knows where he was getting the money from—gambling, I suppose. You see we *never* gave him any money, we just gave it all to Rosa, and she always kept him on a pretty tight rein. Maybe he *was* getting it out of her, after all—you'll have to ask her. Oh dear, I do hope she won't want to leave us now—she's *such* a treasure. Would you tell her when you talk to her that we are *devastated* by the news and if there is anything she needs, money for the funeral or whatever, we'll be *only* too happy to pay? And she is *not* to worry about anything, we'll see she's all right. Oh, do please try and encourage her to stay!"

Penny sighed inwardly. "What do you want me to do about the garden? She won't be able to cope with that."

"Have you seen Diane yet?" Penny confessed she hadn't. "Then perhaps if you *would* call her? The embassy has an agency they use, and I'm sure she can find someone to do the garden and keep up the pool on a temporary basis until we get back. I'd be terribly obliged. We're hot on the track of a very nice house in Esher and are very tied up, as you can imagine." Angela's voice was shrill with anxiety.

"Very well, I'll do what I can and will let you know in due course," Penny said resignedly and hung up.

Making her way back to the dining room, where Toby was taking time over more coffee, she was electrified to hear the sound of a key in the front door. She froze in her tracks, as the noise brought Toby, coffee cup in hand, to the dining room door. The door swung slowly open to reveal Rosa and a woman of similar height and build, swathed in black, on the threshold. They were both clutching suitcases and were red-faced with anger. Rosa came in slowly, dark eyes flashing, and waved a hand at the black-clad woman. "My aunt," she hissed. "Nothing wrong! Giovanni lie—she no telephone, she no want me! He want to get rid of me. Where is he? We have this out, right now! This time I kill him, I think, that no-good, lying son of a bitch. . . !"

Penny opened her mouth, but Toby forestalled her, "You'd better let me do it," and launched into a spate of Italian. As he spoke, the anger in their faces turned to disbelief, then consternation. Rosa's ruddy color ebbed and she staggered, her eyes opening so widely that the whites were visible all around the dark irises.

"Quickly, Toby!" Penny charged. "Tell her aunt to get her

into the kitchen and give her something to drink. She's going to pass out on us."

The older woman already had a stout arm around Rosa's shoulder and was muttering away at her. One of Rosa's hands fluttered to her mouth and a strange mewing sound came from behind it, as her aunt urged her in the direction of Toby's pointing finger. As the kitchen door closed behind them, an eerie wail arose.

Penny and Toby were left looking at each other. "That rather tears it, doesn't it?" he said quietly.

"It most certainly does," she gasped. "He *deliberately* got her out of the way. And that means he either *knew* something was going to happen or was expecting *somebody* here he did not want her to know about. Either way it puts a whole new complexion on things! What do you think we should do about it?"

Toby pondered. "Obviously Cicco has to be told, and preferably by her." He looked towards the kitchen where the macabre wailing had ceased abruptly. "I could call him and have him come out again, if she hasn't calmed down, but better still, I have to go in to pick up a new rental car and could take her and her aunt along. Cicco has been very decent about that. He just impounded the Fiat for further photos and forensic tests and said he'd explain and see it got back to the rental agency—minus the floor mat, which will be needed as evidence. He'll pick up another for us. I'm to collect it from him."

An uneasy thought had come to Penny. "I suppose she did *go* to Naples? We've only her word for all of this, come to think of it: the call, the rush to be off, no sign of Giovanni and now this sudden return. What if this is some kind of set-up? What if she ducked back to Rome, lurked about for him to return and did him in? As indeed everyone, including the police, seemed to suspect."

"Oh, come off it!" Toby protested mildly. "We saw her off ourselves, and that was a Naples express she was on—no stops. I suppose she *could* have caught the next train back, but what about the aunt? She looks the genuine article to me. And if that was an act Rosa put on when she came in, well, she's the greatest actress since Eleanora Duse! No, it's just too devious."

"People can be devious when the need is great," she murmured. "But I suppose you're right. It was just a thought. Shall I check to see how she is?" He nodded and she cautiously opened the kitchen door on to a serene domestic scene that would have rejoiced the heart of a Vermeer.

A shaft of golden sunlight framed the two women seated at the white formica-topped table, their faces calm and absorbed as they bent over large bowls of *caffelatte* and munched quietly on bread and cheese. Rosa looked up as Penny came in and her eyes were dry and steady. "Signora?" she queried huskily.

"Sir Tobias thinks, if you feel up to it, that it would be wise if you went with him to the police and tell them about Giovanni's trick on you. It may be important," Penny spoke very slowly. "Your aunt should come with you to support you and your story."

Rosa's shoulders rose in a resigned shrug. "As you wish, Signora. When we finish, we come."

"Good. Then Sir Tobias will call a cab and you can all drive down together. No hurry," Penny said and returned to Toby to report success.

"You coming?" he asked.

She dithered for a second, then said, "No, I don't think so. There's no need for it and I'd better try and get hold of Diane Grant at the embassy and arrange for a gardener and handyman. In this weather everything grows like crazy and it may take a few days for them to locate someone. You can fill me in later."

Some twenty minutes later she let them cautiously out of the front gate to board the waiting taxi and was surprised to find no lurking pressmen—apparently the murder of Giovanni was not as newsworthy as the morning's headlines had led them to suppose. Relieved, she locked the gate behind them and returned to the house to make her call. Just as she reached the phone it rang, causing her to jump. Gingerly she picked it up and said in her best Italian, "*Pronto. Casa Redditch.*"

"Is that Dr. Spring?" It was a male voice, American.

"Er—yes," she agreed cautiously.

"This is Andrew Dale. Do you remember me, by any chance?"

The name prodded at her memory and was followed by a flash of vivid, tortured blue eyes in a young face. "Why, yes!" she gasped. "Pergama, wasn't it?"

"Yes, that's right." His voice was eager. "I was astounded and delighted to see in the paper that you and Sir Tobias were here. I wonder if I might come and see you right away? It is rather urgent and important."

"It's not about the murder, is it?" She was suddenly suspicious. "We are not really involved in that, you know."

"No, nothing like that," he assured her. "It's to do with a movie I'm making here in Rome. I need some help."

"Oh?" She was relieved but a little puzzled. "Well, yes, I suppose I could see you now. But where are you? This place is not the easiest to find, so I'll have to give you directions."

A chuckle came over the phone. "I know where you are. I'm right next door. I can be there in four minutes."

"At the *Albergo del Sole?*" her suspicions revived.

"No, in the Scorsi villa beyond the *Albergo;* its garden actually adjoins yours behind the inn, you see."

"You mean we're neighbors?" She was incredulous.

"No, I'm not living here—look, I don't want to explain over the phone, it's rather complicated, but I'd be so relieved if you would see me now. May I come over?"

Now she was intrigued. "All right. Come to the main door and knock, then I'll have to let you in because, for the moment, we've barricaded ourselves in against the press."

"How well I know that feeling!" he said with fervor. "Then I'll be right along. Make it three minutes."

Diane Grant and the gardener would just have to wait, she decided, as she walked slowly back to the gate. She was racking her brains to call to mind the name of the girl Andrew had married after the unfortunate Pergama affair—what *was* it? Marlo? Cara? No—Carla, *that* was it!"

When the knock came and she unlocked the door upon the tall, slim figure, she found that, but for the eyes which were still the same vivid blue, she would not have recognized him at all. Though she had recalled him as a baby-faced blond youth, he had matured and aged, his face now thin, almost gaunt, and partially shrouded by a neat, dark-blond beard. Also his hair had darkened to the same shade and, as they gravely shook hands, she was quietly shocked to see it sprinkled with gray at the temples. Surely it wasn't *that* long ago?

"May we talk in private?" he said.

"I'm all alone here at the moment. But why don't we sit on the patio?" She waved a hand at it. "Unless I can get you a drink or something?"

"No, thank you. I'm fine." He was scanning the garden with alert eyes. "Yes, the patio will be fine."

"And how is Carla?" she asked.

He gave her a sideways glance. "Oh, er, I'm afraid our marriage didn't last very long. Two years actually. I've been married again since then and that too broke up." He sighed. "I'm alone again now."

"Oh, I'm so sorry," she muttered, waving him to a deck chair and sitting down beside him. "So what can I do for you?"

The blue eyes searched her mild hazel ones. "I have come

36

to ask a favor—a great favor," he said uneasily. "I need some help and I have good reason to remember how kind and how concerned with people you are."

"Toby and I are here on a much needed vacation," she said bluntly. "What kind of help?"

"You've heard of Margo Demerest?" he queried. She nodded. "Well, I am here directing a picture starring her: a spy thriller. Two-thirds of it is in the can, but this last portion is set in Italy so we are filming at Cinecitta. Been here a month and we've still got about a month of shooting left. Most of us are staying out near the studios, but Margo is very keen on her star image, so she insisted on having a villa on the Appia. You've probably heard that she has been hailed as the Elizabeth Taylor of the nineties? Well, she was all set on having the one Liz had when she was doing *Cleopatra* but we couldn't get it. Margo settled for the next best thing—Villa Scorsi next door. It's actually more opulent than the one Liz had, so that pleased her. . . ."

"Well?" Penny prodded. He did not seem to be getting anywhere.

"Everything was going fine for the first couple of weeks, and then she started acting 'nervy'—she's very temperamental." He grimaced. "I tried to find out what was troubling her but she wouldn't say. That's unusual because she is normally only too willing to share her problems. Then three or four days ago she actually broke down on the set—a real bout of hysterics—and I got a little out of her then. It seems she has taken a dislike to the villa—says odd things have been happening there; noises in the night, lights in the garden—that sort of thing. She claimed she hadn't said anything before because, well, she has a reputation for dramatizing herself and, earlier in her career, pulled some stunts for the sake of publicity that have made her a bit suspect ever since. She says she did not want all that to get started again and that she *isn't* making all this up. But she *is* frightened, and this murder,

right next door, was the last straw. She called me in an absolute frenzy this morning and we'll have to shoot around her
today because she's in no fit state to act. So would you help
me?"

"To do what?" Penny said waspishly. "I have no idea what
you want of me!"

"I've already sent for her latest ex to come and stay with
her," Andrew went on. "She still relies on him quite a lot, but
he won't be able to get here for a week and I can't afford to
hold up production for that long. I'd gladly pay any fee you
care to name if you'd only come and talk to her. Would you?"

"About what?" Penny almost yelled.

"Well, just to calm her down and set her mind at rest. You
see, she's convinced now there is evil here. That something
strange is going on and she is being threatened by it." He
looked at the impatient Penny with troubled eyes. "In short,
she thinks the place is haunted and that she is in danger. Can
you help us?"

Chapter 4

Against her better judgment Penny had been talked into meeting with Margo Demerest. Andrew had been at his most winning and most persuasive, so she had agreed—albeit reluctantly—to go with him to meet the afflicted star as soon as he was through with shooting. "I'll pick you up on my way back from Cinecitta. We'll have a couple of drinks at the villa and then I'll take you both out to dinner at the Casa d'Oro. Then you can really get the feel of the situation."

"I don't know about the dinner part," she said doubtfully. "After all that's happened here I feel I should be in the house to give Rosa some support. And then there's Toby . . ."

"Bring him along too! Margo *loves* anyone with a title," Andrew said, striking precisely the wrong note.

Nettled, she would not commit herself beyond the drinks and he took a reluctant departure, leaving her to mull over how she was to explain this new development to her irascible partner. She should have known better than to predict the reactions of the ever-unpredictable Toby. Instead of the sarcastic tirade she had expected about "getting herself involved," he listened to her tale with the gravest attention and at its conclusion said, "It sounds most interesting, I'd be delighted to go along. I've been wanting to see the garden next door—maybe get some idea about the entrance to the catacomb, you know?—and it's not every day one gets to see a private Roman villa of that vintage. If the woman proves too impossible, I'll just slip on out and have a good snoop around and leave the histrionic Ms. Demerest to you."

"Well, thanks a lot!" Penny said, but she was more than a little relieved.

Part of his unusual amiability was due to the fact that Inspector Cicco had provided a new rental car in a subdued silver-gray far more to Toby's taste than the original red abomination. Another part stemmed from the inspector's having provided him with both a large sample from an obscure Frascati vineyard, hitherto unknown to Toby, which produced a delectable white wine at what, to him, was an absurdly low price. He was already making plans for a future visit and a large purchase for shipment to England.

"Er, how did it go with Rosa and the police?" Penny enquired.

"Oh, very well. She appears to have calmed right down—almost cheerful, in fact—and they've found that she and the aunt did indeed catch the morning train, so she seems completely in the clear. Cicco thinks the late unlamented Giovanni may have wanted the coast clear for an amorous rendezvous here. He surmises the husband or boyfriend of the intended got word of it and showed up instead with blood in his eye. The police have so much else on their minds just now that I don't think this homicide will be exactly their highest priority. Cicco was very insistent we just forget all about it and get on with our holiday."

"Well, that's good," Penny said absently. "But it's a bit odd all the same. All these lights and noises that reportedly have got Margo Demerest so worked up, apparently only date from the time just before we got here."

Toby snorted. "Probably a thoroughly neurotic type anyway. *You* know what actresses are like after all the hoopla we went through in Pergama with them! This murder right on her own doorstep has given her a heaven-sent opportunity to emote, and she's emoting on cue. Just a lot of moonshine, you'll see!"

But it was not quite like that, Penny decided later, as she sat submerged in a blond leather couch of surpassing softness in the elegant cream and gold drawing room of the Villa Scorsi. She was watching her hostess closely, as the beautiful face of the star turned first to the still amiable Toby, then to Andrew, as they chatted casually over their drinks: behind the larger-than-life persona and the striking good looks lurked a truly frightened woman, she surmised. Margo's violet eyes were—appropriately and tritely enough—haunted. Her whole lush figure gave the impression of being so tightly strung on a wire framework and under such tension that the whole framework would come irreparably apart if a single wire should give way. And on the famous photogenic face there were lines of strain that even the most elaborate makeup could not hide.

The impression that here indeed was a woman with something eating at her and who was longing to unburden herself was augmented by the fact that, despite Andrew's earlier protestations, Margo had been quite taken aback at the sight of Toby, whom she evidently had not expected. She had grasped Penny's hand almost desperately as they had been introduced, and the gorgeous eyes flashed an urgent panic-stricken appeal that had been unmistakable. There was nothing Penny could do until Toby made his move, so she just sipped her drink and continued to collect her impressions.

Toby, having finished his second brandy and soda, diffidently proposed exploring the grounds, to which Margo responded with an almost patent relief and alacrity. She sprang up from her own easy chair, forcing thereby the men to rise from theirs, and cried, "Why, of course, Sir Tobias, Andrew would be *delighted* to give you the grand tour both of the villa and the grounds, he knows *all* about it." She managed to get out one of her famous husky laughs. "I'm afraid I'm a total ignoramus on such things, so I'd be no good to you at all. I'll just stay here and have a nice chat with Dr. Spring while you're gone." So obviously dismissed, Toby slid a blandly ironic glance at Penny and followed Andrew out the door.

Margo, moving with noiseless feline grace, was across the room in a flash. She sank onto the couch beside Penny and said, in a voice totally unlike the melodious "social" voice she had been using on the men and which now held some of the shrill flat harshness of her Manhattan origins, "Oh, I am so thankful you came. I'm desperate—did Andrew tell you that? I need help. Will you help me? Can you? You've had *so* much experience." Her voice soared on the edge of hysteria.

Penny was soothing. "Well, of course I'll help if I can, but I didn't really gather from Andrew what the real problem was, so why don't you tell me from the beginning?"

Instead of answering her directly Margo looked around the room, shivered, and hugged herself, her fingers biting into creamy arms on which Penny could see goosebumps starting to rise. "Don't you feel something here? Something threatening, something cold and vicious and evil?"

"The Italians use so much marble in these places that they *are* cold," Penny said practically. "And it's still only springtime here. And no, I don't feel anything and I don't think this is the way to start either, if I am to help you. I need facts." She groped in her tote-bag and brought out a notepad and a ballpoint pen to underline her stolid and mundane approach. "For instance, who else lives in this house?"

Margo let out a little gasp and collected herself with an effort; she settled back into the couch and threw back her shining mane of honey-blonde hair. "Only Carmella. The maid."

"The girl who let us in?" Penny asked. The girl had been very young, very pretty in a rustic Italian fashion, and suspiciously red-eyed.

"Yes, she came with the house," Margo said shortly. "Part of the deal. Count Scorsi said if I wanted extra staff, like a cook or something, *I'd* have to see to it. I couldn't be bothered. I like to be alone. I don't want a lot of servants snooping around me anyway."

Penny cocked an appraising eye at her. "And you did not bring anyone with you from America?—a secretary? a dresser?"

Margo hesitated for a fraction of a second, then with another toss of her hair, said, "No. My last secretary just quit on me to get married. Damned inconvenient too. I didn't feel like going through the hassle of finding another one until I was back home and through with this movie. I do have a dresser in Hollywood, but she doesn't travel with me—we make do with locals on location." And then she added obscurely, "Things aren't what they used to be."

"How about the grounds? Who looks after them?" Penny persisted.

"Oh, two gardeners—again from Scorsi—come in twice a week to keep the pool up and the grass cut. They never come in the house."

"And how do they get in?"

This elicited an impatient sigh from Margo, who got up and freshened her drink before replying. Slumping back on the couch, she took a hefty swig before she said, a slight edge in her voice, "There's a telecom box at the gate that buzzes in the kitchen. They press the buzzer and talk to Carmella, who goes down the drive and lets them in. They don't seem to have heard of electric gates in Italy." She sniffed and took another swig. "Then when they're through they let her know and she lets them out."

Poor Carmella must spend an inordinate amount of her time trekking up and down that long driveway, Penny reflected as she noted that down. "So only you and she have keys to the gate and the house?"

"Oh, so *that's* what you were after. Why didn't you say so? Yes—well, I *did* have an extra made for Andrew on the quiet. Scorsi was so fussy about the keys. He's fussy about everything." Again she sighed.

After a mental note to have a quiet word with Carmella, Penny abandoned her nuts-and-bolts approach. "Now, why don't you tell me what things have been happening, and when, in sequence?" she urged.

Margo visibly brightened and at once launched into an animated narrative. She was not, however, a good storyteller; she rambled, was vague about dates and times, and kept interlarding her tale with her own premonitions of danger and convictions that something was "going on." Penny listened patiently, jotting down the few salient facts that emerged from the ramblings. Boiled down, it amounted to this: nothing untoward had happened in the first two weeks after Margo had arrived at the villa. The only thing she had ever experienced in the house itself was the sound of doors opening and closing in the small hours of the night, sounds she had been too frightened to investigate. Outside was a different story, and Penny's interest quickened when she realized these more recent events had started up just after she and Toby had taken up residence next door. Again Margo was vague as to dates, but on several occasions she had awakened to see lights reflected on her bedroom ceiling, and on getting out of bed and switching on her light, she had looked out but seen nothing moving in the garden below. She also averred that she had heard "voices" muttering—although she could not tell how many, or whether the voices were male or female. On one occasion she had been brave enough not to put on her own light, and that time she swore she saw a beam, either from a lantern or a large flashlight, moving towards the back of the house. "I was *terrified*," she gulped, looking at Penny, her violet eyes wide in appeal.

"So what did you *do?*" Penny prompted.

"I—I called Count Scorsi," Margo muttered. "It was three in the morning and he was furious."

Penny was astounded. "Why didn't you call Andrew?"

A faint flush appeared on the high cheekbones and Margo looked away. "I didn't think that would be a good idea," she said in a faint voice, but she did not elaborate.

The only thing Penny thought at all significant was an incident that had occurred five nights earlier. "It was such a warm evening that I thought I'd take a dip in the pool to cool off before going to bed," Margo said. "It was filled two weeks ago but it hasn't really been all that warm and so that was the first time I had tried it out. I went down and put the floodlights on and was actually *in* the pool when suddenly I got the feeling that I was being watched. I was certain of it—you know how you get that feeling sometimes?" She shivered and again Penny saw the goosebumps come up on her shapely bare arms. "I swam to the steps and got out. I think I called out 'Is anyone there?' I thought maybe one of those damned paparazzi had managed to get in somehow and was taking 'candid' pictures . . ."

"Did you hear anything?" Penny interrupted.

But again Margo retreated into vagueness and muttered about "noises in the shrubbery." Instead of investigating she had fled back to the house, leaving the lights ablaze around the pool all night.

A possible explanation of both lights and voices had occurred to Penny. "Maybe you could show me your bedroom and then the pool, and I think I may be able to put your fears at rest," she said briskly, heaving herself out of the couch's downy depths.

Margo uncoiled gracefully and looked at her in utter astonishment. "Really?" And she added with amazement, "Yes, well, Andrew should have Sir Tobias in the garden by now, so the coast is clear," and led the way up the white marble, shallow-treaded staircase to a wide, red-carpeted corridor and thence to a large and light-filled corner room, luxuriously appointed in delightful shades of cream and rose. It was situated at the extreme left of the villa facing towards the Appia Antica, and once she had got herself oriented, Penny's neat theory came crashing to the ground.

"Well?" Margo demanded, hopefully.

To cover her dismay, Penny peered out of the long windows and saw the swimming pool to her left and the high wall, embellished with the same horrendous-looking spikes as their own, masking all sight of the Antica, directly ahead. "Yes, well, I *did* think you might be picking up some of the noises and the lights from the Albergo del Sole and its parking lot next door, but now I see that you are too far removed for that to be the case," she confessed.

Margo looked at her scornfully. "It is why I *chose* this room. It's the quietest in the house. Listen!" Even with the windows standing wide, all that could be heard of the Antica traffic was a muted murmur, almost submerged by the light wind rustling in the trees and the calls of nesting birds.

"However," Penny went on, in a desperate attempt to regain some edge, "I think it perfectly possible that the lights you observed could be reflected from the traffic on the road."

"How?" Margo demanded. "What would they reflect from? There isn't a house with windows next door. It's a part of the grounds of the catacomb of St. Sebastian."

"Oh, the refraction of light is a very funny business," Penny stated, with far more confidence than she felt. "It could be refracted from the leaves of those trees surrounding the swimming pool, reflected onto the surface of the water and then back onto your bedroom ceiling."

"Oh!" Margo said in a small voice, visibly impressed.

Feeling a complete fraud, Penny said hastily, "Perhaps we should go down to the pool and you could show me where you heard the noises?" And on their way down and out of the house, she said, "I'd like to have a word with Carmella before I leave, if that's all right with you?"

"I'm sorry but it's not," Margo said in a harsh voice. "This murder of yours has upset her as much as it has me. She's been in tears ever since she heard about it. I can't afford to have her further upset. She may quit and I don't want that. Things are difficult enough with Scorsi as it is, and I can't stand any more rows."

Penny's eyebrows shot up, but she held her peace. "Well, perhaps when she has calmed down," she murmured, but her mind was already busy with another theory that she had no intention of disclosing to her nervous escort. They gained the edge of the pool, which was enclosed on three sides by wattle fencing and, while larger, was of a much older vintage than their own. It was lined with rather ornate maroon and white tiles, many of which were mottled with age, some even cracked. "So where did you hear the noises?" Penny prompted.

Margo waved a vague hand towards the shrubbery beyond the wattle fence on the Appia Antica side. "Let's take a look—there may be footprints or something," Penny said, and they ducked into and through the bushes. The search yielded nothing, but they emerged on a path that apparently led to a gardener's hut on the extreme left wall of the property. Penny had noted one very odd fact. Whereas the grounds on the whole were not kept in an impeccable condition, the earth under the shrubbery had recently been very carefully raked. She forbore to point this out to her increasingly restive companion, who had turned back towards the house.

"So what do you think?" Margo asked flatly.

Penny took a quick look at her set face. "I understand that your husband—or rather your ex-husband—will shortly be here," she said carefully. "Then you will have someone you can depend on *in* the house, and that is what I think you badly need. Until he does arrive, since you are obviously upset by all this, my best advice would be to move into a hotel. You need people around you. Murder, even at some remove, is always an upsetting business. You need to get away."

Margo looked at her, a curious light in the amazing eyes. "I can't do that," she said softly. "I wish I could but I just can't. You see . . ." But her disclosure was cut short by a hail as they converged onto the main driveway, and Andrew and Toby came striding towards them. "Seen all the sights?" Andrew demanded with an almost jarring cheerfulness. "Everybody ready to eat now? I sure am."

Margo's face closed up and she looked coldly at Penny. "Oh, are you both joining us?"

Penny took a quick look at Toby, who gave an infinitesimal shake of his knoblike head. "Well, no, but thank you anyway. We must get back. The dead man's wife is still very upset, you understand? We should be there for her." It seemed to her that both Margo and Andrew were quietly relieved, and to her further amazement, as they escorted them back down the drive and saw them out of the formidably high iron gates, they chatted casually to each other about the shooting schedule for the morrow.

Once outside Toby lengthened his stride and as she scurried to keep up with him Penny said, "Whoa there! What's the sudden rush?"

He turned a preoccupied round blue eye on her. "Something I have to check on right away," he murmured. "I found a door in the garden of the Scorsi villa which must go through into ours, and yet I'm blessed if I've noticed it on our side."

"So?" she demanded.

"It's a door that, by its condition, has not been used in years," he mused. "And yet the lock and the hinges have been recently and thoroughly oiled. I think that bears looking into, don't you?"

Chapter 5

"I'm sorry, but for me it just does not add up. Tempting as your theory may be there are too many discrepancies, too many things that do not go together." Toby's tone was fretful, as he and Penny gazed at each other across the dining table like boxers coming out of their corners for the final round after a long and exhausting bout. The polished surface of the table was littered with scraps of paper on which they had been scribbling their thoughts and passing them to each other ever since the now shrouded-in-black, but apparently cheerful, Rosa had cleared away the dinner things. As soon as they had heard her television set switched on at high volume, murder or no murder, he and Penny had got down to work on the late Giovanni.

"Well to *me* it makes a whole heap of sense," Penny snapped. "Here we have a pretty young servant girl—who, I might add, is probably a dead ringer for our Rosa at the same age—and a lech like Giovanni right next door. She would have been a natural target for him, and the very fact she is so upset by the murder seems to bear this out. If he had been romancing her, all the odd happenings at the Villa Scorsi could be explained—even his strange behavior in getting Rosa out of the way. As I see it, first off, he was visiting Carmella *in* the house—hence the doors opening and shutting, the lights in the garden, the voices, even the incident by the pool. He was *just* the type to snoop on the gorgeous Margo in a swimsuit. Then Carmella tells him her mistress is getting upset, and he decides to shift operations here by sneaking Carmella in through that door you found. . . ."

Toby was shaking his silver head vigorously. "No! That's where for me the whole thing breaks down. You have evidently 'bought' Margo Demerest's entire story—which surprises me more than a little for reasons already stated—and I'd be more *inclined* to your theory if her tale could be discounted entirely. Think about it! If Giovanni was responsible for oiling and opening that door, there would have been absolutely *no* reason for him to have been on the side of the house where Margo Demerest's bedroom is, still less to be hanging around the swimming pool in the front of the house. That door lets into their garden right at the back of the villa, because it stands so much further back from the road than ours. He would have had a straight shot at the kitchen quarters and a quiet rendezvous up the back stairway, so why go tramping around the outside of the house and talking? And another thing: in my exploration next door I saw a dog run—empty, but there were turds in it that did not look that old to me, and I would think a guard dog would be a natural thing to have there. Come to think of it, we *heard* a dog barking on that side of the wall when we first moved in. So where is it? Did la Demerest mention a dog to you?"

Penny shook her head and interrupted him heatedly. "Maybe some of Margo's story is embroidered, but I'm certain she is genuinely upset about something and if she *was* making it all up she'd have come up with a more startling and convincing tale. And the fact that the shrubbery *had* been so carefully raked indicates that somebody was very anxious to obliterate any footprints in that dry earth—you could actually see the deep tine marks of the rake." She cogitated for a moment. "What if one of Scorsi's gardeners is involved also? That would make a lot of sense—a pretty young thing like that cooped up by herself alone in that big place most of the time. They come in twice a week, remember, and apart from the odd delivery man are probably the only people she sees on a regular basis. So maybe she had chatted them up and had something going with one of them, and then he got wind of Giovanni's interest, got jealous, started snooping around at night spying on them, and that would explain the lights and so on—maybe even the murder."

"How did he get in?" Toby demanded promptly. "They don't have keys. You said so yourself."

"Not so far as we *know*," she hedged. "I'll obviously have to zero in on Carmella as soon as I can. I'm sure she can tell us a lot."

"Well, I hardly think it is worth passing any of this on to Inspector Cicco," Toby muttered. "Except perhaps about the door."

"Oh, I quite agree," Penny said hastily. "Certainly not before I've had a talk with Carmella. If she quits, Margo will throw a fit."

From behind the closed door came the faint tolling of the front doorbell. They looked at each other in surprise. "Who could that be at this time of night? It's after eleven," Toby growled, and got up. The door opened and Rosa came in looking disgruntled. Penny guiltily gathered up all the papers on the table and assembled them into a neat pile. "There's a young man wants to see you," Rosa said in Italian. "A Signor Dale."

"Well then show him in!" Toby rasped back, turning a stony blue eye on her. She wilted and scuttled out to be replaced by Andrew who came in with some hesitation and smiled tentatively at them. "Sorry to barge in on you this late, but I've only just got through seeing Margo safely tucked away, and I was sort of anxious to hear, er, what you thought about it all. . . ." Aware of Toby's frosty glare, he looked in appeal to Penny.

"We were just about to turn in," Toby announced.

"Yes, well, I won't stay long—but, please! It is rather important."

Penny eyed him thoughtfully and waved him to a chair. "Margo has obviously taken a dislike to the villa and is in a very nervous state. I don't think I can tell you anything more than I already told her. Until her ex shows up I think she'd be better off in a hotel. I'm surprised you hadn't thought of that yourself, it seems an obvious solution."

Andrew sighed. "I'm afraid it's not *that* simple. You see, I'm only the director; the producers of the movie—like so many these days—are a sort of conglomerate of independent backers and they have a keen eye on the balance sheet. There was one hell of a fight with them to get the villa for her in the first place—they just did not want to fork out for it. Now, if they hear she has up and left it, they'll be furious. Neither she nor I want that."

"Then why tell them?" Penny demanded. "Since it is only for a week anyway, surely she can pay for the hotel herself and they'd be none the wiser."

Andrew gave a mirthless laugh. "You evidently do not know what the paparazzi are like in Rome. They'd be swarming around her hotel like bees around a honey pot and in no time flat. They are a very special breed; if they can reduce a veteran trooper like Katy Hepburn to tears you can imagine what a job they'd do on Margo. Publicity is fine, but not the sort *that* would engender. And actually I had some good news for her tonight. Paul Warner, her ex, will be here in three days. So she has decided to stick it out. She wanted me to thank you, by the way: her chat with you calmed her down a lot, and she said she doesn't want you to bother about what she told you; just forget about it and get on with your vacation."

"In other words, she does *not* want me to talk to the maid?" Penny said and glanced over at Toby, who had resumed his seat and was stonily puffing away on his pipe.

"Er, yes." Andrew was again uncomfortable. He fell silent for a second, then said hesitantly, "Did you believe what she told you?"

Penny stared at him. "I thought there were some things in it that warranted further investigation. Why? Don't you?"

He threw up his hands in a sudden gesture of despair. "I don't know, I just don't know." Taking a deep breath, he went on, "I feel I should be quite honest with you. You see, although Margo has a big reputation, well, she is thirty-six years old, and that—in Hollywood—is getting up there. Also her last two pictures did not have the impact or the success of her former ones: only did so-so at the box office and not even a hint of an Oscar nomination. She has won one and been nominated several times, and in this volatile business just the hint of slippage is often enough to turn it into a landslide." As he paused, Toby gave a quiet snort and nodded in satisfaction.

"I'm not sure I understand what you're getting at," Penny said.

"The thing is," Andrew continued with a rueful grimace, "that when Margo was still clawing her way up the ladder she was notorious for some of the stunts she pulled to get herself in the public eye. Just to give you one 'for instance', she 'disappeared' in the middle of one movie and was 'found' a few days later sitting at the feet of some guru—in Nepal of all places. She said she had been 'called' by him because the part she was playing was of such great significance to mankind and he had to inspire her to do it right! That, by the way, was the movie she won the Oscar for: it was a smash hit."

"So you think she may have seen the writing on the wall and is reverting to her old tricks?" Penny demanded.

"It *could* be that . . . ," he shook his head in bafflement, "I just don't know. I thought maybe you could tell if she was faking it."

"I can only repeat what I've said." Penny was irked. "I would say that she is genuinely upset and afraid, but then on the strength of one short encounter I could be quite wrong. And if she does not want me to talk to the maid or investigate further—well, I don't see what more I can do. I take it she is going back to work tomorrow and that's the main thing you had in mind, wasn't it?"

Andrew stood up. "Yes," he sighed. "I suppose so, there is that. And thank you for being so patient. Thank you both very much." Disconsolately, he took his leave.

"What did I tell you?" Toby said, getting up. "Moonshine, sheer moonshine. Not even he bought it. So, for heaven's sake, let's forget this whole business and get on with our holiday! The police have said as much, you've had your walking papers from the movie people, so what more do you want?"

"I suppose so," Penny said reluctantly, getting up in turn. "But I can't help feeling that something very strange is going on here—and I feel so sorry for them."

"Who?" Toby said blankly.

"Rosa, Margo, Carmella: all of them. Andrew too."

"I notice you never feel sorry for *me*," Toby snorted, and stamped off to bed.

But as she went around turning off the lights and trying the catches on the long windows, her mind was still full of unanswered questions. Was there something more between Andrew and Margo than the usual director-star relationship? Why, if Margo's story had any validity at all, had she not turned to him immediately in her terror? Why, when truly scared, had she called *Scorsi* of all people and not Andrew? Was she afraid to encourage him, or was she just plain afraid of him, and why? Frustrated, Penny also stamped off to bed.

At breakfast Toby took what he fondly imagined was firm

control of the situation. "For today I propose . . ." he stated, peering myopically at two poached eggs on toast that appeared to be staring back, ". . . that we take a run out to Praeneste and visit the Temple of the Goddess Fortuna—Rome's Destiny— and then swing back by Frascati, where I intend to visit a very promising vineyard and where we could have lunch. Does that suit you?"

Penny roused herself with a start. "Oh, yes, fine, just fine," she agreed absently.

But Destiny decreed otherwise. Its decree arrived in the shape of a visibly impressed Rosa, proffering with excitement an envelope on a silver salver. "Hand delivered by a man in livery," she muttered in awe. "I thought it might be important." It was addressed to Toby in an elegant script, and the heavy ivory-vellum envelope, embossed with an elaborate crest, warranted the deference she accorded it. Toby's silver eyebrows rose as he opened it, and scanning it quickly he handed it over to Penny. "It appears we have been summoned," he murmured.

She read the note: "Count Scorsi requests Sir Tobias Glendower and his companion to wait upon him at the Palazzo Scorsi in the Via Corso at their earliest convenience and on a matter of extreme urgency. Kindly be here by ten AM." The signature was a florid and illegible squiggle. Since this was far more to her taste than trekking around yet another temple in Toby's learned wake, she said quickly, "It sounds important. I think we should go, don't you?"

Toby eyed her sardonically. "Not to mention imperative and autocratic! I'd like to know who the hell this count thinks he is. Mind you, I spotted a case of bric-a-brac next door that was a twin of the one in your room, so it must have been a 'one for me and one for you' type of tomb looting. I'd like to quiz him about that." He looked at his watch. "We'll let him wait for us though. Let's go at ten-thirty."

"Let's," she agreed with enthusiasm.

But they had forgotten about the difficulties of parking in central Rome and so, by the time they had found a place for the Fiat and hurried back along the via Corso, it was almost eleven when they arrived at the forbidding face of the Palazzo Scorsi, whose outward aspect at least had changed little since it was erected in the fifteenth century. A poker-faced major-domo was lurking in wait for them as they entered through the wicket gate of the massive wooden doors and Toby announced their identity and purpose. "You are an hour late," he announced. "I shall have to ascertain whether the count can see you now." And he led them to a small, gloomy antechamber sparsely furnished with massive antique furniture that looked as if it had been there from the very beginning.

"Scarcely the red-carpet treatment," Toby murmured, settling into a high-backed, carved, black oak chair and lighting up his pipe. "I wonder what the count has on his mind."

Penny looked up with distaste at the narrow mullioned windows set high in the stone walls. "This is more like a fortress—or a prison—than a home. If it's all like this, can you imagine *living* here? In the words of Bette Davis, 'what a dump'!"

"It probably was a fortress when it was built. I must check up on the Scorsi history," Toby said, sucking contentedly on his battered briar. "I seem to recall that they were even bigger thugs than most of the big names back then; very palsy-walsy with some of the more notorious—like Alexander Borgia."

"Really?" Penny continued to peer at everything in the room, but soon exhausted its possibilities and went over to the door and opened it.

"Hey!" Toby said in sudden alarm. "Where are you off to?"

"May as well do some exploring." She gave him an impish grin. "If I run into any servants I can always ask for the ladies, and if they're the chatty sort I'll ask them about the gardeners at the villa."

"Oh, well, don't get lost," he mumbled, settling down to

read the overseas edition of the London *Times* he had brought with him.

A gray marble staircase soared up into dusky gloom from the tapestried hall which, apart from some suits of armor and a formidable array of medieval weapons, was as void of furniture as of life. Penny hesitated at the bottom of the staircase, looking around at the closed doors that led off the hall and behind which she could detect no sound of life. At the sound of footsteps hollowly echoing from on high she looked up hopefully. But it was no servant who eventually emerged from the gloom: the woman was small, slim, honey-blonde, and beautifully dressed in a sage-green suit that Penny recognized as the latest in Italian *haute couture.* As she came nearer, a startled look on her thin, high-cheekboned face, Penny saw she was expensively bejeweled; a diamond brooch gleamed in the vee of her blouse and several diamond rings sparkled on the long thin fingers that clasped a Gucci handbag in soft suede—it matched her costume exactly. "Er, am I addressing la Contessa Scorsi?" she ventured in her best Italian. "My name is Penelope Spring, and Sir Tobias Glendower and I are waiting to see Count Scorsi. I wonder if you would kindly direct me to the ladies' powder room?"

The woman's dark eyes narrowed. "*La contessa non habita qui*—the countess does not live here. I am Gabriella Vanni. Come!" she commanded in a shrill high voice. She crossed to one of the doors and opened it to reveal a narrow corridor again lined with doors; at the second door she paused and pointed. "*Ecco il gabinetto,*" but made no move to get out of Penny's way. Instead she said in slow, careful English, "Why do you come here?"

"Because the count asked us to do so," Penny said equally slowly. "He did not give a reason. Perhaps you could tell me?"

The dark-brown, almond-shaped eyes probed Penny's mild hazel ones. "I know nothing." With a brisk movement she flung open the door to reveal an old-fashioned lavatory with a wooden seat and pull chain. "Goodbye. I must go now," she declared, and clicked away down the passage on her three-inch heels.

Penny waited until she was safely out of sight, closed the door and followed after her down the corridor. She peered out into the hallway, again empty, and crossed over to their waiting room. Toby was no longer there. "Damn!" she muttered. "Now what do I do?"

The answer came at once in the clatter of footsteps on the staircase and the majordomo hurried towards her, disapproval writ large on his heavy, sallow face. "Sir Tobias is already with the count," he announced. "Please follow me, Signor Vanni would like to see you."

Puzzled, she followed him up two long flights of the grand stairway and then through double doors that led into a more modern section of the palazzo which had evidently been refurbished about the time of the Risorgimento and which, while less gloomy than the lower reaches, was heavily Victorian in its appointments: stuffed glazed-eyed animal heads sprouted from the walls, and the furniture was a mixture of ornate plush-covered couches with elaborately carved woodwork and chairs of dark maroon leather, many of them much the worse for wear. All in all it was a sad contrast to the comfortable elegance of the Villa Scorsi. Behind one of the closed doors Penny heard Toby's deep rumble interspersed with a lighter, higher voice, both very loud. She started towards it, but was checked by the majordomo's hand on her arm. "No, Signora, in here *per favore*," and he opened a door upon a small study dominated by a large cluttered desk behind which sat a young, dark-haired man.

One look at him and Penny hastily revised her theory that she was about to meet the husband of the glamorous Gabriella: despite the difference in hair color, the faces were strikingly alike, although his almond-shaped dark eyes were set so close beside the very thin-bridged nose that it gave him a walleyed shifty look. He got up and said in excellent, almost unaccented English, "Ah, Signora Spring! So glad to meet you. I am Pietro Vanni. Kindly be seated." His smile was ingratiating, revealing strong white teeth.

Penny plopped into the indicated seat. "And you must be Gabriella's brother," she observed.

He looked momentarily disconcerted. "Why, yes. I also manage the count's real estate affairs. And in light of what has just occurred I need to ask you some questions."

Penny's quick eyes had noticed the open copy of *Il Populo* on his desk. They widened slightly as she realized she was looking at a photo of Toby and herself exiting from the gates of the Villa Scorsi. She had a knack of reading upside down and so quickly read the accompanying headline: ENGLISH DE-TECTIVE DUO QUESTION FAMOUS FILM STAR IN APPIA ANTICA. Her eyebrows rose and her heart sank. She decided to play dumb. "What about?"

But his answer surprised her. He leaned forward and said earnestly, "I need to know exactly what Margo Demerest told you about the recent happenings at the Villa Scorsi. The count is very upset about this."

"What happenings?" She looked at him wide-eyed. "I think you must be laboring under some mistaken impression, Signor Vanni."

His face tightened. "Oh, come now!" He took up the paper and handed it to her. "How do you explain this? You know Margo Demerest. If you do not read Italian I will translate for you."

She took it. "I read it well enough," she said, and she hastily scanned the article. "What a load of rubbish!" She handed it back to him and chuckled. "Really, Signor Vanni, if the count is upset by this I can assure you he has no cause. I'm surprised he believes the ravings of some paparazzi! The picture was taken yesterday evening after we had had drinks with

Margo Demerest and her director Andrew Dale, who is an old friend of ours and had heard that we were on vacation and staying at a friend's villa next door. It is the first time we had met Miss Demerest, who is a delightful person, and it was purely a social occasion."

His dark eyes bored into hers. "She did not consult you about anything? She did not ask about the murder of Giovanni Lippi?"

"Well, naturally, we all agreed it was a terrible thing to have happened on our very doorstep—but no, it was not discussed. It is nothing to do with us." Penny stood up decidedly. "So, I'm afraid I have nothing to tell you and must ask that you take me to join Sir Tobias. We have another engagement and are already running late."

He looked at a loss, but stood up. "Very well," he muttered and ushered her out. The door to the next room also opened and Toby stalked out. One look at him and she could tell he was in a towering rage; his round blue eyes behind the round glasses were steely, and the tip of his little button nose a shiny red. A small, slight, gray-haired man was close on his heels; he also was looking far from amiable.

Toby came to an abrupt halt at the sight of her. "Count Scorsi, may I present my distinguished colleague Dr. Penelope Spring," he said in Italian, and to her in English, as the count bowed stiffly in her direction, "We're leaving."

"Will you see them off the premises, Pietro?" the count said, and went back in, slamming the door behind him.

Toby did not say a word until they were once more outside the gate and on the thronged narrow sidewalk of the Corso. Then he burst out, "Of all the insufferable, arrogant pipsqueaks! There's a dyed-in-the-wool Fascist if ever I saw one!" He turned an outraged blue glare on her. "You're right, absolutely right. There *is* something going on, and I'm damned well going to find out what."

Chapter 6

They retreated to a nearby bar on the Corso to compare notes on what had transpired at the Palazzo, but it took Toby two stiff drinks to calm down enough to give a coherent account of his heated confrontation with Count Carlo Scorsi; and in the retelling he grew indignant all over again. "The idiot tried to *bully* me. Imagine, *me!*" he gobbled.

Penny was secretly amused. It had been a long time—a very long time—since Toby, secure in his wealth, his mighty reputation and his honors, had been faced with anything remotely approaching this, and his astonished and outraged reaction was highly predictable. The count, she thought, must indeed be something of an idiot if he had thought to get anywhere with Toby by that approach.

The article in *Il Populo* had, of course, been the spark that had lit this bonfire, but she was interested that the count's reaction was vastly different from Pietro Vanni's: he had said nothing of the "happenings" at the Villa Scorsi, but had laid into Toby about getting his tenant upset by involving her in "that drunken peasant's murder" and about bringing unwanted publicity and notoriety to the sacred name of Scorsi. He had ranted on about how neurotic she was and how he wished he had followed Pietro's advice and never rented it to her in the first place, but that the money offered had been tempting and the lease short, so, as a good business man, he had allowed it. "But it has upset my entire household," the count had fumed. "And now all this on top of it!"

Up to that point Toby had remained cool and had dealt with him firmly but calmly; it was the next bit that had really enraged him. To change the subject he had brought up the question of the catacomb artifacts he had seen in the villa which matched those in the Redditch villa and had asked where and when they had been found, and at that the count had blown up. "I might have know it!" he had raged. "I know all about you and your treasure hunting and your tomb-robbing publicity seeking. I warn you—if you so much as try *any* of that here, I'll have you run out of Italy. We have laws here, strict laws, and those catacombs that lie beneath the villas are sacred ground and sacrosanct and will remain so."

Toby's face was livid with shock as he recounted this. "Imagine! Tomb *robbing,* treasure *hunting,* publicity *seeking*—*me,* of all people!" he stuttered, then visibly took himself in hand and continued. "It became very evident to me at that point that there was something very strange going on and that somehow it is linked to the catacomb—I mean no one would be *that* hysterical over a simple archaeological question. What can be in the catacomb that is so important I have no idea, but I jolly well intend to find out. First I'll try the British School of Archaeology here and then I'll have them get me into the Vatican Library. I'm sure I'll find some answers there. What will you do?"

Penny was quietly delighted; all this being far more to her taste than an ongoing endless round of temple visiting. "Oh, I've got all sorts of things in mind. For one thing I'd like to get a line on the missing Contessa Scorsi, who apparently doesn't live with her count. Then there's the glamorous

Gabriella. Other than Pietro's sister, who is she, what is she? She is a *dish* and a very expensive one at that, by the looks of her. I think my best bet is to start with Diane Grant at the British Embassy. I have to arrange for a gardener for the Redditches anyway and she may be able to point me in the right direction."

"Try and find out more about Scorsi too," Toby interjected. "I'll do the same, but I noticed a photograph in his study of a man who might be his father—he's too young of course— with Mussolini. I am willing to bet the Scorsis were heavily into Fascism. Oh, and one thing more, if you get back to the villa before I do, would you ask Rosa about keys? I'd like to see any key she *can't* identify. If Giovanni was responsible for the oiling of that door, there has to be a key for it somewhere, and, if there is anything in your theory, he may even have had one to the gates of the Villa Scorsi."

"Right!" Penny was hastily scribbling some notes to herself. "So we'll rendezvous at the villa for dinner?" He nodded. "I'm not sure that today's the day for Rosa," she continued. "The police are releasing Giovanni's body today and the funeral is set for tomorrow morning—we must go to that. She will probably be in a furor of preparation, although I can't imagine—Giovanni being what he was—who is going to turn up for it."

"The aunt still here?" Toby asked. He was not at his best on matters domestic.

"Of course she is! Although I believe she is heading back for Naples after the funeral. I asked Rosa if she wanted to go back with her for a little vacation but she said no. By the way, you can take the car. I don't fancy driving in downtown traffic, but you can drop me off at the British Embassy. I believe it's on the via Conte Rosso—wherever that is."

"I know it," Toby grunted. "Little street behind St. John Lateran."

"That out of your way?" she demanded.

"Frankly, yes. My first stop, the Villa Julia, is in the opposite direction and on the far side of the Borghese Gardens."

"Right, then I'll get a cab, it'll be quicker than hiking all the way back to the car anyway," she retaliated. "There's a cab stand just down the road." And on that brisk note they parted.

In the cab on the way over Penny cudgelled her brains to bring to mind what she remembered of Diane Grant, which was not a great deal. She recalled that she had been quiet, serious minded, and a dogged rather than a gifted student, but that she had been a good listener. Her appearance had suited her character, dark, gray-eyed and with a rather heavy jawline that had given her face a solemn, pugnacious look. Penny wondered how the years between had treated her and how best to approach her about their strange quest.

Later, seated in Diane's small office in the inner recesses of the embassy, she found that she had not changed much: the jawline had thinned down from the puppy-fat lines of her student days but it still overwhelmed her other features and gave her a determined, almost belligerent, look. She was duly impressed, however, when Diane, the initial greetings done with, crisply dealt with the matter of a gardener for the Redditches and had arranged it all inside of fifteen minutes. She may not have been much of a student, but she certainly turned into a good administrator, Penny reflected, and launched into her second matter of business.

"I meant to be in touch with you before this, but the past few days have been rather hectic," she explained, and expanded on the murder. This did not seem to elicit much interest from the attentive Diane, but when she mentioned their meeting with Margo Demerest, Diane's gray eyes positively lit up and she demanded breathlessly, "You actually met her? Oh, she is my favorite actress—how *thrilling!* What is she like in person?"

Encouraged, Penny went into a carefully edited account of Margo's problems at the villa and the perplexingly hostile behavior of her landlord, Count Carlo Scorsi. "Sir Tobias and I find his reaction to all this so strange that I wondered if you could possibly help us with any information on him, his family or the villa," she ventured. "We'd greatly appreciate it."

Diane had been listening with avid attention but her face clouded. "I could probably dig out the history of the Scorsis . . . ," she waved a vague hand at a line of reference books in a bookcase, ". . . but that's not what you want, is it?" The gray eyes narrowed suddenly. "Wait! I don't know, but there's somebody in the embassy who would—Cordelia Forrest. She's been here for *ages* and knows everything about everybody." She jumped up. "We'll go and see if she's in."

"Who is she and what does she do?" Penny asked en route.

"I'm not quite sure," Diane confessed. "She functions as a sort of social secretary and I believe our Intelligence people use her quite a lot. She's one of a kind!"

She opened the door of a tiny cubby hole of an office in which floor-to-ceiling bookcases were stacked with files to such an extent that there was scarcely room for the desk, from behind which its occupant looked up enquiringly as they crowded in. "Cordelia, are you very busy? We need your help," Diane said and introduced Penny.

Cordelia Forrest was a tiny woman with a brown, seamed walnut of a face that could have been any age between fifty and a hundred, but out of which twinkled two very bright dark eyes, alive with intelligence. She offered a tiny clawlike hand to Penny and asked, "How can I help you?" Diane breathlessly explained their mission. Penny took an immediate liking to her as Cordelia nodded and said briskly, "Yes, I think I can. Sit down, Dr. Spring," and waved a claw at the plain wooden chair that stood by the desk. "I'm afraid there's no room for you, Diane."

"Thanks so much for your help," Penny called to Diane's retreating back and looked over at Cordelia, who was grinning at her like an amiable crocodile. "So you'd like all the dirt on the Scorsis, eh? Nasty lot!" And, seemingly without looking, grabbed a large file off a shelf and dumped it on her desk. "Current or past?"

"Current," Penny said, warming to her. "Maybe I'd better tell you why."

"Maybe you had," Cordelia agreed, and listened attentively as Penny gave her a greatly expanded account of what she had told Diane.

"Hmm, interesting, very," Cordelia commented, her black eyes shrewd, and then let out a shrill cackle of laughter. "Unless he's changed a lot, I bet Toby Glendower was fit to be tied."

"You know him?" Penny asked in astonishment.

"Haven't seen him in twenty years, but yes," Cordelia grinned. "Does he still drink like a fish?" She flipped open the folder and started scanning it. "Yes, well, vital statistics. The Scorsis are Papal counts—what is known as the 'Black' aristocracy, which is quite apart from the main-line aristocracy like the Sforzas and so on. Have kept a big 'in' with the Vatican, but have come down in the world in the past four generations, who all seem to have had an amazing knack for backing the wrong side. Carlo's father was a great pal of Il Duce and an ardent Fascist, which did not win him any plaudits in post-war Italy, and Carlo's a chip off the old block, a strong neo-Fascist and reputedly a pal of many of the German neo-Nazis we harbor in our bosoms here—a lot up in the Lake Garda area, you know, and there's one particular one near here . . ." she paused and flipped through the file. "Herman Krantz he calls himself, though *I* think he's an escaped war criminal. He lives in the Alban Hills near Albano, supposedly a retired business man." She snorted her disbelief. "Carlo got in deep three years ago with the latest Vatican banking scandal—the second they've had in the past ten years—I don't know the details but he had to repay one hell of a lot of money. That's when Lucia split; she'd had enough of him by then."

"Lucia?" Penny was almost overwhelmed by this spate of information. "Who's she?"

"The Contessa Scorsi." Cordelia screwed up her eyes. "Let me see now, her maiden name wasn't Barberini, but I know she's connected with them somehow. They had two children, a boy and a girl. The boy's an officer in the Alpini regiment, the girl . . ." Again she consulted the file. "Married a Milan business man a couple of years ago. Both of them went off when their mother did. No divorce, of course—Papal aristocracy, you see." She looked up. "If you're interested at all in the banking thing, Lucia could tell you. Has an apartment in EUR, 16 Montagne Rocciose. She's pretty bitter so would probably open up, if I called to pave the way. Speaks good English too."

Penny gulped. "Yes, I'd like that. Er, where do the Vannis fit in?"

"Ah!" Cordelia again did her trick of extracting a much slimmer file without looking and consulted it. "The Vannis, by Italian standards, are Johnny-come-latelys. They only emerge after the Risorgimento where Pietro Vanni made a fortune out of the War of Independence—arms, I think. Like most 'new' money it didn't stick and so the current lot are broke, if pretentious. Gabriella has been Carlo's mistress, oh, must be six or seven years now—she started young. Very expensive tastes, which hasn't helped Carlo's financial position. He used to keep her out in the Villa Scorsi, even after Lucia had moved out, and her brother Pietro has been his assistant ever since he finished his military service—reputedly he pimped Gabriella to the count. There was another brother . . . ." again she dipped into the file, her brow wrinkling, "I *think* his name is Paulo, but I don't seem to have anything on him. Hmm, strange." The spate dried up and she looked up at Penny. "Any of this of any use?"

"Why, yes, it's all fascinating," Penny stuttered. "Er, you don't happen to have anything on the St. Crescentia catacomb, do you?"

"A *catacomb!*" Cordelia looked at her in blank amazement. "No, not my bag. People are my bag."

"Mine too," Penny murmured. "Anyway, I'd certainly like to meet the contessa if it could be arranged, although I don't quite know how to approach her about all this. Also I'd like that German's address, and if you could give me a little more on how the count stands financially?"

"Carlo's far from penniless," Cordelia resumed. "But I'd say he's hurting, and hurting pretty badly. Most of his real estate holdings have gone, except for the Palazzo—which is a complete white elephant—the villa on the Antica and an estate somewhere in Campania. He also hung on to some business interests, although a lot of them did go down the tubes in the aftermath of the banking scandal."

"Has he anything in the antiquities line?" Penny thought this a possible explanation for his violent reaction to Toby's innocent question.

"Not that I know of. More in the commodities line—Libyan oil and that kind of thing. Lucia would know more about that. And, speaking of her, I shouldn't worry too much about just showing up on her doorstep. She's all alone now with both the children gone, and there is not much of a place in Italian society for a separated woman." Cordelia grimaced. "Unfair I know, but that's the way it is. She leads a very lonely life nowadays, and if you let her tell you her troubles you'll probably make a friend for life. Want me to call her and set up an appointment? This afternoon?"

Penny nodded, "Yes, that would be fine." But there was no answer at the contessa's and after some reflection Cordelia commented, "Probably out playing bridge. I'll try again later and let you know. Will tomorrow morning do?"

"No, I'm afraid I'll be at Giovanni's funeral, and his wife will probably need me around afterwards. Tomorrow afternoon should be all right though." She noted down her phone number and address, while Cordelia scribbled on the other side of the desk. "This is Krantz's address—I think he has an unlisted number." They exchanged the bits of paper and smiled at each other as Penny got up. "I've kept you from your work long enough, but my most grateful thanks for all this. You've been extremely helpful. I don't know how you do it—you're a very remarkable woman, if I may say so."

Cordelia got up and grinned her crocodile grin. "So I've been told." And Penny saw with a pang she suffered from a marked scoliosis, her back humped into such a curve that made her tiny frame almost that of a midget. "Give my regards to Toby, and I'll be in touch," Cordelia said. And following Penny out she scuttled purposefully off down the corridor in the opposite direction.

Penny treated herself to a late and lengthy lunch at a nearby trattoria and from there got a cab back to the villa. A peek into the kitchen revealed Rosa and her aunt in a frenzy of baking, so she decided to postpone her enquiry about the keys and instead put in a call to Angela Redditch to inform her about the gardener and to get formal permission for Rosa's funeral feast.

"Oh, *super!* So you met Diane then, *so* efficient," Angela gushed. "And yes, poor Rosa, the *least* we can do for her!" But rather marred the effect by adding, "If it's a nice day, have her put up the tables outside, then there'll be less of a mess in the house. Caught the murderer yet, you clever things?"

"No. The police have the matter well in hand. It's really none of our business," Penny said shortly.

"Oh, but how can you *resist* it?—a murder on your very doorstep!"

Penny firmly changed the subject. "Diane introduced me to

someone today at the embassy. Cordelia Forrest? I did not gather exactly what her function was though. Do you know?"

"Oh, Cordelia—*most* peculiar, isn't she? I haven't the faintest idea. She's not exactly mainstream, you know," Angela shrilled.

"I suppose not, but I found her fascinating," Penny said icily, and rang off.

Toby arrived back much before she had anticipated, but appeared preoccupied and uncommunicative, so she launched into her own litany of news to which he gave due attention. "Diane Grant was a veritable mine of information, I see," he remarked, getting up to fix himself a drink.

"Oh not Diane! Cordelia Forrest—an amazing woman. She sends you her regards, by the way." He was behind her at the drinks table, so she was unaware of the sudden sharp glance he shot at her as he tensed up. "Good Lord! Is *she* still around," he said casually, sitting down again. "I thought she had long since gone to her reward. She must be nearly in the Methuselah category by now. She dates back to my father's time—knew him quite well." Unconsciously taking a leaf out of Cordelia's book, he went on. "The third Lord Forrest's daughter—adopted, so they say. Touch of color in her, of course; Indian probably or possibly Iranian. Er, did you tell her anything about what's been going on?"

"Why yes! She seemed so 'with it' that I thought honesty was the best policy. Any reason I shouldn't have?" she demanded, bristling slightly.

"Oh, no. The way things are shaping up, it is probably just as well," he murmured, but did not elaborate.

"So how did you get on?" she asked.

"It took a while to get the wheels turning, but now that I have the clearance to all sections of the Vatican Library it should go quicker. I'll go back tomorrow after the funeral." He sighed heavily. "One thing I have already established is that there has never been an *official* investigation of the catacomb. And I could not find a damn thing about where the entrance might be." He rose and stretched. "I think I'll take a turn in the garden and see if inspiration strikes."

The phone started to ring as he ambled off, and when Penny answered, it was Cordelia. "I just got hold of Lucia, and you are all set for two o'clock tomorrow afternoon. She's eager to see you. Apparently she has something very much on her mind, but she didn't tell me what. . . ."

Chapter 7

The attendance at the funeral was as sparse as Penny had feared, and mostly female in composition: not relicts of Giovanni's amours but the wives of local shopkeepers, whose spouses were presumably home minding the store, and who were acquaintances, maybe even friends, of the bereaved widow. Rosa had her moment of glory as, supported by her aunt, she wept and wailed loudly when the coffin was lowered into the grave. Once Giovanni was safely out of sight, however, she cheered up rapidly and was soon chatting animatedly with the gathered females. There was a small crowd of curiosity seekers at some remove from the burial party, and Penny kept a keen eye on it, hoping above all to see the face of Carmella, or indeed any observer that did not fit in with the gaggle of gawkers, but she looked in vain. Giovanni's murder was apparently of so little interest that there was not even a member of the press or a single paparazzi on hand.

After the cortege had returned to the villa for the funeral feast, she and Toby put in the obligatory twenty minutes, during which they sampled the fruits of Rosa's vast efforts of the day before, praised everything in sight and, to the vast relief of all parties, slipped away about their own business.

"Well I'm off," Toby declared, busily stuffing papers into a briefcase. "What time do you think all this will be over?"

"By the level of noise, I'd say not for quite a while. Anyway I told Rosa that we'd eat out tonight, so no need to rush back."

"You can have the car if you like," Toby said graciously. "Today *I'll* get a taxi." Then spoiled the effect by adding, "It's so damned difficult parking around St. Peter's, it'll be much quicker by cab."

"Oh, all right," she said doubtfully. "They say EUR is a quiet suburb so I shouldn't have too much trouble, and if Lucia Scorsi comes up with anything I might take a spin out to Albano and scout out Herman Krantz's hideout."

She left early for her appointment, not trusting the vagaries of Roman traffic, but having successfully negotiated the great artery of Cristoforo Columbo that spewed southward into the lesser veins of the exclusive garden city which had grown up around Mussolini's vainglorious *Expositione Universale di Roma*—the world's fair that had never taken place because of the war—she found she still had plenty of time to spare, so drove slowly around, taking in some of the more incredible buildings Il Duce's dreams had spawned.

There was an enormous long-stemmed concrete mushroom which sprouted a restaurant at the top; a slablike building that looked like a huge Swiss cheese; the glass and concrete ultra-modern facade of the NATO Defense College with all the flags of the allies bravely flying in front of it; two enormous piles that looked as if they had been inspired by the Baths of Caracalla but which housed, she noted, the Folklore Museum of Italy and the Museum of Roman Civilization, and an even more enormous auditorium, again with a row of flagpoles before it, currently unflagged, but on whose facade she noted workmen busily putting up gargantuan swags of red, white and green bunting—the national colors. There were fountains and pools galore, surrounded by massive statuary that leaned towards plunging horses and blank-faced nudes of both sexes, and multitudinous carefully planted flowerbeds and well-tended municipal lawns.

Compared to the gloomy Palazzo Scorsi it was not at all a bad place to go into exile, she mused, as she cruised past secluded villas behind their ornate iron railings, but when she eventually turned off the viale Africa and onto via Montagne Rocciose, she revised her opinion to a degree. There was no such thing as a "wrong side of the tracks" in EUR, but this was evidently a much humbler neighborhood than the others she had seen. The small apartment buildings were uniform and mostly faceless in design, and she could see, as she parked before number sixteen, that the via Laurentina at the other end of the road was lined with small and undistinguished stores. Maybe, after all, the contessa had cause to be bitter: it was a far cry from a palazzo on the via Corso and an even farther cry from the elegant luxuries of the Villa Scorsi.

She was still a little on the early side, so after locking the car she dawdled on the sidewalk looking around her, but was duly startled when an unseen voice called to her, "Dr. Spring? I'm up here, third floor to your left. There's no elevator. I'm afraid." And she looked up to see a woman with improbable red hair peering anxiously over a beflowered balcony. "I'll open the entrance door for you," she said and disappeared from sight.

Penny made for the modest glass door in time for the harsh buzzer that signaled the release of the lock and pushed her way into a small entrance hall, walled and floored with the usual grayish-white Roman marble and empty, save for a line of glass-fronted mailboxes along one wall and the iron-railed white marble staircase. She puffed on up to the third floor where one half of the light oak double doors to her left stood open. There she hesitated: should she knock, ring or go right in? She was spared the trouble of deciding by the appearance of the contessa on the threshold. "Please come in, it is so nice that you visit me," and stepped aside waving a hand into the interior. She ushered her guest through the entrance lobby into a pleasant living room that looked out on to the balcony facing the street: it was crowded with furniture, some of the antique pieces being of such magnitude that they overwhelmed the sizable room.

The contessa waved Penny to a loveseat covered in rose-colored plush and asked, "May I get you something? Punt a Mes, Sambucca, Cinzano?" And she made with determination for an array of bottles ranged on a heavy silver tray whose handles were enormous bees and which sprouted more bees on the crest of its engraved surface. Penny, who had absorbed a great deal from Toby's learned tours, deduced from this that Lucia indeed was a Barberini.

"Er, just a little Cinzano, thank you," she said, although she would have much preferred a cup of coffee. As the contessa fussed about with the crystal goblets, Penny took stock of her hostess, who was as short and dumpy of figure as herself, but with exquisite legs and shapely ankles and delicate, tiny feet and hands. The red hair was undoubtedly straight out of a bottle, but then Penny—having seen the dark-haired Pietro—suspected Gabriella's honey-blonde hair came from the same source. The red hair sat ill on the sallow, dark-eyed face that turned towards her and deep lines grooved downwards from the contessa's tiny rosebud mouth, giving her a despondent look, augmented by a permanent pucker above the bridge of her aquiline nose.

The contessa, having charged her own glass with a hefty slug of Sambucca and three obligatory coffee beans, sat down in a gilt-framed easy chair upholstered in pale blue plush, took a long gulp of the liqueur, and waved a hand at her surroundings. "So, you see what sad straits I am reduced to—and after twenty-eight years of marriage." She sighed woefully. "But the sacrifice had to be made. I could stand the shame of it no longer. I owed it to my own family and to my children."

"Yes, I'm so sorry. Cordelia did tell me a little, and I do so sympathize with you," Penny said.

"You, too, have had trouble with him?" the contessa demanded.

"Yes, but nothing compared to yours, I'm sure," Penny cooed. "It is just that his hostility has so puzzled us that I thought perhaps you could help us understand it."

It was enough to open the floodgates and Lucia Scorsi's tale of woe spewed forth. At times she wept, at times she raged, as she relived her traumas. As she listened quietly, Penny reflected on how many times and in how many places—mud huts, thatched huts, felt tents, semi-detached houses, even palaces—she had heard this same sad tale: the hopeful beginnings, the arrival of children, the increasing indifference of a busy husband, the amours—casual and overlooked at first, but then culminating in the grand amour of a middle-aged man with a young woman, an amour that the middle-aged wife no longer had the weapons to combat. "It is all *her* fault, I know it," Lucia shrilled. "All this endless extravagance, nothing was too good for her—she drove him to all this . . . this wrongdoing. Before, he had his weaknesses as any other man has, but they were understandable in a man of his rank and position." She looked challengingly at her listener. "After all, many of us—although Mussolini was a brutish peasant in many ways—do not think that all of Fascism is so very wrong. He did many good things for Italy, and just see what has happened here since his death—Communists, terrorists, strikes all the time! Our world is being *destroyed!* No, I do not blame him for his rightist views, but when it comes to dealings with all those nasty foreigners—Arabs, Germans, even blacks! Well, he was denying everything he stood for. I blame Pietro Vanni for much of it. He got Carlo's ear and he and that whore have poisoned his mind." She finished her Sambucca with a defiant gulp and glared at her guest.

Penny decided it was time to give the contessa a jolt. "You mean Pietro Vanni was responsible for the count's involvement in the banking scandal, not Herman Krantz?"

Lucia flinched visibly. "Oh, that horrible man!" She gave a little shiver. "I am sure they are *all* responsible—pressuring Carlo into it, mixing him up so he didn't know what he was really doing with those funds. An official from the Ministry of the Interior came right into the palazzo and accused him to his face of being a traitor to Italy, of diverting funds to subversive groups—imagine that! Accusing a *Scorsi* of using Papal money for such things!"

But when pressed as to details she was woefully vague as to the precise nature of Carlo's wrongdoing, of what groups were involved, or even to what extent restitution had been made. The only thing that quickened Penny's interest was a remark about Krantz. "He wormed his way into Carlo's good graces by showing off his knowledge of antiques, that I am sure of. He made one or two very good sales for him."

"Krantz was in that business before he retired?" Penny queried.

"So far as I know, he *is* in that business," Lucia returned, and helped herself to another Sambucca.

Penny felt she had pumped all there was to be pumped on Carlo's financial woes from his contessa, so decided to pursue the antiquities line. "Sir Tobias Glendower and I appear to have fallen into the count's bad graces because of a visit we made to his tenant, the film actress Margo Demerest, at the villa, and an enquiry Sir Tobias made about some antiquities he saw there," she explained. "I expect you have seen the unfortunate article in the paper that caused his annoyance."

Lucia favored her with a blank stare. "I never read the papers," she declared. "Much too depressing."

Penny struggled on. "Well, it was just a social visit, but Margo did mention some strange happenings at the villa and I just wondered if, perhaps, the count was responsible for them—hoping that she would break the lease and move out and he could get the villa back again for some reason."

"Why should he do that?" the contessa demanded, wide-eyed. "I understand it is a very short lease anyway and very profitable to him." So she must have an inside pipeline of information to the palazzo to know that, Penny thought, and wondered who it could be. "And what has that to do with the antiquities?" Lucia continued.

"Well, I don't know. It was just a caseful of Early Christian artifacts from a catacomb Sir Tobias asked about and it was to this the count reacted so violently. Could he be selling them to Krantz, do you think?"

Lucia shrugged her plump shoulders, "I do not think so, but then I know little of such things. The articles Krantz sold from the palazzo were all pieces of old furniture. If things have been happening to this Margo Demerest then it is more likely those wretched Vannis are behind it. Carlo did over the whole villa for that whore—a fortune it cost!—while we lived with nothing but old things at the palazzo. She is there now in my place at the palazzo and I fancy that would not be to her taste at all. Maybe she wants her precious villa back. . . ." Her grievances welled up again and Penny let her rant on for a while, before breaking in when the spate showed signs of drying up. "Well, Contessa, it has been a pleasure and an honor to meet you, and I thank you for talking to me so frankly, I do appreciate that." She stood up.

"For me too it has been a pleasure," Lucia said, the desolate look back on her face. "It is good to talk to someone who understands so sympathetically what I have been through." She sighed. "I hope we may meet again. Give my regards to Cordelia. She also understands much."

As her hostess walked her to the door, Penny had one final thought. "Do you know anything about Carmella, the maid at the villa, and also which of the Scorsi gardeners work on its grounds?" she asked.

But apparently Carmella postdated Lucia's flight from the domestic hearth, so she knew nothing of her. On the gardeners, however, Penny was in for a pleasant surprise. "Carlo has no gardeners," Lucia said. "The palazzo has no garden, so he hires the gardeners for the villa on a part-time basis from an agency . . ." and named the same agency Diane Grant had used.

Quietly delighted, Penny thanked her again and scurried back to the car hellbent on finding a pay phone. As she unlocked it, she looked up to see the contessa peering sadly down at her and waved an energetic goodbye to the lonely woman. She found the phone in a nearby coffee bar and, fortified by a much needed cup of coffee, put in a call to Diane Grant, who immediately went into a state of quiet alarm. "Oh, don't tell me the gardener they sent to the Redditches is hopeless!" she exclaimed.

"No, it's not that at all. I just want to know about the Villa Scorsi gardeners: who they are, where they live, if possible, married or unmarried, that sort of thing," Penny said hastily. "It is just some ground clearing on the Scorsi business."

"Oh!" Diane sounded at a loss. "Well, I'll see what I can do and get back to you later." She hung up.

The Cinzano had given Penny a terrible thirst, so she had another cappucino and sipped its frothy creaminess slowly, as she consulted her road map and her watch. She decided to have a crack at finding the hideout of the shady Herr Krantz. The map told her the shortest route was by the Appia Antica itself, so she fumbled her way back to it from EUR and then turned south on its arrowlike straightness.

As she drove slowly down it, she was struck afresh by the cavalier treatment the Italians gave their ancient heritage, for around the crumbling remnants of the aristocratic tombs that lined the road were piles of plastic garbage bags, old tires and all the modern detritus of urban blight. Beyond the ancient Casal Rotonda which was still being lived in amidst the garbage, the monuments and the garbage thinned out, and the only visible evidence of Rome's former might were the broken arches of gray marble aqueducts that still marched proudly across cultivated fields towards the Seven Hills of Rome. At Albano she turned east and steeply upward towards the old volcanic crater in which the Lake of Albano nestled: if her map was correct, the little road on which Krantz's villa was situated should run along its rim. She found to her relief that the villas that lined the rim road had numbers, either carved in their stone gateposts or on little blue-and-white enamel plaques. Locating Krantz's number, she drove on by, spotted a tourist lookout just beyond it, parked and pondered her next move: the only thing that distinguished Krantz's villa from its neighbors was that both walls and gates were appreciably higher.

"Why not?" she asked herself, and getting out walked back along the road and peered through the heavy grillwork of the double gate. There was a narrow driveway, thickly lined with rhododendron bushes, that curved away to the left. There was no sign of life. She tried the iron handle of the gate and to her surprise it yielded. Another idea burgeoned and she stepped inside, closing it behind her and started with determination up the driveway. She had almost reached the curve when she was transfixed by a deep-throated growl from her right and, looking up, saw one of the biggest Dobermans she had ever seen peering at her from a small side path in the bushes: its teeth were bared and it looked anything but friendly. "If you value your skin you should not move," a softly guttural voice said in English from her left, and a man with a shotgun stepped out in front of her. "Who are you and what do you want here?"

"I . . . I was looking for Herman Krantz," Penny gulped and

took an involuntary step backwards, whereupon the growl deepened and the dog padded silently towards her.

"Franz can tear your throat out. I told you not to move," the man said. "*Setzen*, Franz, *achtung!*" The dog sat, its baleful glare fixed upon her. "Now I ask again, who are you and what do you want?"

She was so terrified that her temper flared. "Really there is no need for this ridiculous show of violence! I was in Albano and wished to consult Herr Krantz about some antiquities. He was recommended to me. Not that it is any of your business!"

"Oh, but it very much *is* my business when someone trespasses on my property without warning," the man said softly.

"*You* are Herman Krantz?" Penny stuttered and took stock of her captor. His head was bald save for a fringe of white hair, and his large pink face was accentuated by the total lack of eyebrows over his pale blue eyes; eyes that had no trace of warmth. His figure was trim and taut and it was only the liver spots on the bald pate and on the steady hands that held the gun on her that betrayed the fact he was an old man. "Well, I'm sorry, Herr Krantz, but I am not a trespasser—your gate was open, so naturally I came in. Kindly call off your dog and put down that ridiculous gun, and let us talk in a civilized manner. I came here to consult with you."

He did neither. "Who are you?" he repeated. "What antiquities? The name of your friend?"

Penny dithered and almost gave him a false name, but decided against it. "My name is Penelope Spring. It is about some Early Christian artifacts from a catacomb on the Antica, and it was the Contessa Scorsi who suggested you."

The blue eyes narrowed and searched hers. "Indeed?" he murmured. "The contessa is not a well-informed woman. In the first place, I am no longer active in the business of antiques; in the second, I know nothing of Christian artifacts. So you see I cannot help you. So, if you will turn around very slowly and walk back to the gate, I will see you out. The gate was open because I am expecting an *invited* visitor, but Franz here can always tell when someone enters."

There was nothing for it but to do as he said. Penny turned around slowly and marched back to the gate, acutely aware of the hot breath of the Doberman on her heels. Krantz opened the gate and bowed stiffly, a mocking light in his pale eyes. "Good day to you, Dr. Spring. I do recognize you, you have been much in the news of late." And he shut the gate behind her with a resounding clang.

Weak at the knees with relief, Penny walked back to her car with as much dignity as she could muster, aware that Krantz was watching her. "Well, two can play at that game," she muttered crossly as she climbed into the driver's seat and found she was still trembling. She turned the car around, but did not drive away. She sat watching the gate, where she could still make out the man and the dog. A battered, gray panel truck drove past her car and she caught a glimpse of the driver before Krantz had swung the gates open and the van pulled in sharply and stopped. She started the car and drove past in time to see the driver emerge and pat the dog on the head. He was as bald as Krantz, but his fringe of hair was dark and he had a black beard: his profile seemed vaguely familiar, but she could not place him.

Still shaken, she drove slowly back down the Antica and with great relief gained the sanctuary of the Redditch villa. She went in to find her partner ensconced in the dining room, drink in hand, and the whole of the table littered with papers. Toby looked up as she came in, contemplated her in silence, then demanded, "What's the matter? You look terrible!"

She took the drink out of his hand and took a large gulp. "I feel awful! How would you feel if you had almost been eaten by a huge dog? It was Krantz's dog. That man's a bloody sadist."

Chapter 8

Penny was awakened from a nightmare in which she was being pursued by a pack of blue-eyed Dobermans through the Palazzo Scorsi, by the opening of her bedroom door. Toby's tall figure slipped noiselessly through the crack, an expectantly hopeful look on his round face, and he padded silently over to the case containing the catacomb relics and began to try key after tiny key from a bunch dangling from a rusty iron ring. She watched him through slitted eyes; she had had a restless night full of vivid dreams about storm troopers and savage dogs and was not about to be roused at what the bedside clock told her was the ungodly hour of six-thirty.

There was a tiny click and Toby straightened up with a satisfied sigh and gingerly raised the glass cover. He proceeded to take out the artifacts one by one and examine them minutely with a magnifying glass. Suddenly he gave a little grunt of satisfaction and went over to the window, a small Roman pottery oil lamp in his hand, and held it up at different angles to the light. Her curiosity got the better of her tiredness. "Don't mind me," she mumbled. "But what the hell are you up to?"

Startled, he swung around, his eyes sparkling. "Oh, sorry!

Didn't mean to wake you, but Rosa found the keys for me and I wanted to see if I could get confirmation for something before I go to Florence on the seven-thirty train. And, by Jove, I've found what I was looking for!"

"Florence?" She struggled up groggily on one elbow, her mouse-colored hair sticking up in wild spikes around her pixie face. "What on earth for?"

"Fittipaldi," he said, as if that explained everything. "I should have thought of him before. He's the man I need. If anyone knows he will."

"Oh, good," she subsided again with a wide yawn. "You can tell me all about it when you get back. Don't slam the door."

He pocketed the lamp and carefully locked the case again. "I may not get back until tomorrow," he informed her, and padded out again.

She slipped easily back into her dreams, this time of a gentler nature. Now she and Cordelia Forrest were children and were playing hide-and-seek in what appeared to be a catacomb; somewhere down a dusky corridor she could hear Rosa's voice scolding them for getting their clothes dirty, as they scampered giggling away from her. When she finally awoke it was ten o'clock and, after a hasty shower, she dressed and went, rather guiltily, in search of Rosa and breakfast.

She found her slumped at the kitchen table, hands limp in her lap, gazing sightlessly out into the sun-struck garden, a sad expression on her high-colored face. "Sorry to be so late," Penny apologized, "but could you just make me some coffee and perhaps some toast?"

Rosa roused with a start. "Oh, *si*, signora, *prontissimo!*" She sprang up and hurried to the stove, as if thankful for an interruption of her thoughts, "Your aunt has gone?" Penny asked, as the widow bustled around getting out butter, jam and bread from their various hiding places. "*Si,* signora. Signor

Tobias took her to the Termini with him this morning. Would the signora like her breakfast in the dining room?"

"If you'd put it on a tray, I think I'll take it out to the pool—it's such a nice day." Penny looked at her sad face. "You know, Rosa, you can still change your mind and go away for a few days if you like. We can manage."

"No, it is best I stay here." Rosa looked at her with a faint, apologetic smile. "I will get used to it soon. It is better for me to work, I think. It is all that I know. But you are very kind to think of it."

Penny collected the tray and ambled out to the enclosure by the pool. She still felt tired and drained of energy. "You're simply not as young as you used to be, letting a little thing like a damn dog upset you," she chided herself. "You've got to pull yourself together and get on with things." The problem was what to get on with—at least until Toby returned from his mysterious mission. By her third cup of coffee she had mapped out her strategy for the day: first some telephone calls and then a visit to some of the catacombs in the neighborhood. Not that she could see the remotest connection between the murder, what had happened next door or the doings of the Scorsi/Vanni clan and this elusive catacomb, but Toby was evidently following a strong hunch, and his hunches were so often right that the least she could do was be well informed on the subject.

Her first phone call to Diane Grant left her more at sea than ever. Diane had found the names and addresses of the gardeners right enough, also the fact they were both married, but their respective ages of sixty and sixty-five made her own theory of one of them as a possible lover of the comely Carmella highly unlikely. "Really, I'm getting absolutely nowhere," she muttered crossly. "Maybe Toby is right and this whole business of Margo's is moonshine."

Her second phone call was long distance to London University and was, she knew, a very long shot indeed. "Is Professor Oppenheim there?" she asked. "Tell him it's Penny Spring of Oxford calling from Rome. A matter of some urgency." And, in a matter of seconds: "Lou? Penny here. Look, I know you've been involved in some of the Nazi war-criminal hunts and have access to the records, and I wonder if you could possibly check on someone for me. . . ?" She went on to give a description of Krantz and the few meager facts she had on him and on the neo-Nazis around Lake Garda. "He's supposedly very knowledgeable about Italian antiques," she added. "I know it's not very much for you to. go on, but someone I have a very high opinion of seems to think he *is* a war criminal, so anything you can dig up will be much appreciated. I'd say he was around seventy-five now, so that would make him about twenty-five at war's end."

"Will do," Lou Oppenheim said briskly. "Where can I reach you?"

She gave him the telephone number and her thanks and hung up. She collected a book on the catacombs from Toby's bedside and skimmed through it, trying to decide on her first target. They had already "done" St. Callisto as part of their initial sightseeing. She discarded St. Sebastiano, in spite of its proximity, on the grounds it was too big: what she needed, bearing in mind Toby's strictures, was one of the smaller ones. She decided on St. Domitilla's as being the nearest and the most suited to her needs, and, getting out the car, drove the short distance down the via della Sette Chiese to the entrance of the catacomb just beyond the Fosse Ardeatina, with its giant sculpture of World War II Italian martyrs, who had been executed by the Germans on this very spot.

Inside the catacomb she struck lucky, for it was evidently an "off" day for tourists and she was the only customer. The Dominican monk on hand as guide pounced upon her with enthusiasm and proceeded to escort her around; since he turned out to be Irish there was no language problem. Like most enthusiasts he was something of a fanatic on his subject and ranted on at great length about the mistaken notions about the Christian martyrs of Rome: ". . . there were far, far more in the Roman provinces and relatively few here," he trumpeted. "Many of these catacombs were started merely as cemeteries *above* ground for aristocratic families and their dependents and only subsequently were deeded over to the Christians. This one is a case in point. It was the burying ground of the Flavian family. St. Domitilla and her martyred brother St. Clemens were Flavians who just happened to fall foul of the Emperor Domitian, and subsequently their cemetery above was dug into to provide the catacomb."

Penny listened intently as he led her through the narrow, slightly claustrophobic red-earth corridors with the quiet tombs carved out of the soft tufa in tiers on either side. They reminded her somewhat of the Pullman sleeping cars of her early youth; each one snugly interred in his own little bunk along the narrow gangways, so that she half expected an angelic conductor to appear—St. Gabriel—calling, "Everybody up! Next stop the Pearly Gates." With an effort she brought her roving attention back to her earnest guide, who had now shepherded her into a tiny chapel carved into the rock and she gazed dutifully upon the shrines dedicated to St. Petronella, supposedly St. Peter's daughter, and the martyrs Nereus and Achilleus.

"We are in the deepest level now," he informed her. "This is fourth century. Good thing to remember about the catacombs: the deeper you go, the later it gets. The earliest tombs are up above." They climbed up more narrow flights of stairs until they emerged into a larger room where a marble table was surrounded by seats of red tufa carved out of the living rock.

"Is this where they hid out during the persecutions?" she asked.

He snorted derisively. "Another great misconception! No, highly unlikely. For one thing there isn't enough room for a large number of people, for another, there's no water in any of the catacombs, so they would have had to go outside for it and it would not have taken the Roman soldiers long to spot something like that! No, this place was used for their 'love feasts,' the agape, where they'd get together to celebrate their Christian brotherhood. Not the eucharist, you understand; that would have been held in the chapels. The agape was just a meal—like a modern church supper. It was garbled versions of what went on at the agape that gave rise to the violent anti-Christian feelings of most Roman citizens towards them—rumors of cannibalism, ritual sacrifice of babies, et cetera, et cetera. . . ."

"Do you happen to know anything about the catacomb of St. Crescentia?" Penny demanded, stopping him in full spate.

He looked confounded. "Never heard of it," he spluttered. "It can't be one under Papal jurisdiction or I would know of it."

"It's over on the Antica near St. Sebastiano—supposedly under the Villa Scorsi and the one next door to it."

"Must be very small and unimportant then," he stated firmly. "It must be on land held by one of the Papal aristocrats, otherwise it would be looked after and kept up by us."

"Hmm, so I've gathered," she murmured, and after thanking him profusely, took her leave and returned to the villa feeling slightly overstuffed with information. When she got back she found an elderly man diligently mowing the lawn—Diane's gardener had finally arrived—and they nodded affably at each other. She thought about questioning him about his fellow gardeners from the agency, but decided against it. Instead she went for a wander around the garden herself trying to locate Toby's door from this side. It took some finding, and when she did come upon it she saw how they had missed it on their first exploration. It was masked from the front by a gardener's hut almost identical to the one she had seen next door, and from the villa side was almost completely hidden by a flowering vine that clung to the wall beside it. She tried its ring handle, which moved easily but did not yield, and went off in search of Rosa to ask about the key.

"Signor Tobias also ask that," Rosa said, diligently laying out two places at the kitchen table—evidently she and the gardener were lunching tête-à-tête. "And I give him all the keys I have, but he no find it."

"I see." A bright idea struck Penny and she scurried back to the gardener's shed, which she proceeded to search inch by inch. Dusty, cobwebby and discouraged, she finally gave up: either Giovanni had carried the key's hiding place to his grave or it was in the hands of someone else entirely—who or why she hadn't the remotest notion. Again she wished fervently she could have a heart-to-heart talk with Carmella and looked longingly at the high wall dividing them, but no bright idea as to how to bring this about came to her.

She lunched in solitary state in the dining room, and when Rosa brought it in Penny said tentatively, "The new gardener is lunching with you?" Rosa slid her a sidelong glance and nodded. "I wonder if you would ask him if he knows anything about the gardeners who work next door? I believe they work for the same firm." Rosa's gaze sharpened and she stared at Penny, who hurried on, "It's of no great importance, but I would be interested in anything he has to say."

"I will ask him," Rosa said, her tone noncommittal, but when she returned to clear off the dishes she said flatly, "He know nothing about the villa next door. He is new here."

Penny had had two glasses of red wine with the excellent spaghetti marinara Rosa had provided and was beginning to feel drowsy again. "One call and then a nap," she told herself, and went to the phone to tell Cordelia Forrest of her adventure with Krantz.

Cordelia did not take at all kindly to her news. "I don't

think it was very wise to show your interest like that," she said tartly. "If Krantz *is* in anything shady, you've alerted him now."

Nonplussed by this negative reaction, Penny omitted to mention her call to Lou Oppenheim; instead she shifted to a more social vein. "I so enjoyed meeting you the other day, I was wondering if we could get together for lunch sometime this week? You choose the place."

Again Cordelia was negative. "I'm sorry but you've caught me at a bad time. We'll be up to our ears in it until the conference is over—what with the Prime Minister expected here and everything."

"Conference?" Penny echoed blankly, "what conference?"

For the first time Cordelia appeared to thaw. She let out a cackle of laughter. "My, you and Toby *must* be living in a world apart! It is *the* conference for all the heads of European countries to set up the Federation of Europe. It is scheduled to open next week: one of the biggest things that has happened here in decades. Every European embassy is flat out, preparing for it."

"Oh, I see—is that what they were getting ready for at that huge place in EUR?"

"That's where the general assembly will be held, but all the in-fighting will take place elsewhere," Cordelia said airily. "And there will be plenty of that, I warrant."

"Well, I won't keep you if you're busy. Maybe we can get together after it, if I am still around, although our children will be here visiting us shortly."

Again Cordelia cackled, "Oh, yes, I've read all about *them*. Life is full of surprises, isn't it? Let's play it by ear then," and she rang off.

Penny was too sleepy to contemplate any further activity, so tottered off to bed and slipped quickly into a mercifully dreamless sleep. She slept long and when she finally woke up just lay in a soggy daze, contemplating the fading sunlight and the lengthening shadows. There came a light tapping at the door and Rosa peered in cautiously. "Telephone for you, signora. Signor Dale. I tell him you take siesta, but he say he must talk so he wait."

Penny came out of her daze instantly. "I'll be right there. Tell him to hang on." She scrambled out of bed, slipped into her sandals and scurried in Rosa's wake. "Andrew? Has something happened?" she demanded, all of a tingle.

"No, all is very well. I'm sorry if I disturbed or alarmed you, but Margo is all keyed up about this and wanted to make sure you and Sir Tobias were on hand for the big bash at the villa tomorrow night."

"Big bash?" she echoed stupidly.

"Yes, well, Paul Warner is coming in tomorrow and she's hellbent on throwing this big party for him—informal though, so no need to dress up unless you want to. Kicks off at seven-thirty—it'll be mostly cast and crew of the movie, but she's set on you being there, so I hope you can make it. Please come!"

Penny was not about to turn down this heaven-sent opportunity to talk to Carmella. "I'd love to," she said quickly. "But I can't answer for Toby—he's in Florence and I've no idea when he'll be back. If he is back he'll probably be delighted to come also. How do we get in though? Won't there be guards and things?"

"If you can make it by seven-thirty, I could probably pick you up and take you in with me. If not, I'll be at the gate vetting the initial crowd of people, but the two security guards we've hired to keep out gatecrashers will have a list of the invitees to the party, so even if you show up later there'll be no problem."

"Is Scorsi coming?" she asked with rising expectations.

There was a momentary silence, then Andrew said, "Margo did think it would be a nice gesture, so he was asked but he said no. His estate manager is coming though—probably wants to make sure we don't break the place up—and he's bringing his sister."

Better and better! she thought in high glee. "How's Margo doing?" she asked. "Any further alarms?"

"Not that she has confided to me." Andrew's tone was dry. "That particular storm in a teacup seems to be over. Things have been going just great on the set the past two days—if I can only keep the roll going we may be able to wrap it in a couple of weeks. You didn't see Margo at her best, but she should be in top form tomorrow—she adores parties. And I think you'll like Paul Warner—he's something of a has-been, but basically a very nice guy. I'll give you a call then tomorrow about seven to see how things are shaping, shall I?"

"Yes, do!" she agreed with enthusiasm and went off to make a little list of things she had to ask Carmella about. It read, "Dog? Door? Lights? Giovanni?" After some thought she crossed off the last item. "Not yet. Not until I see how the wind blows," she told herself.

Chapter 9

"A party? I *hate* cocktail parties," Toby said on a rising note.

"Yes, but I want to talk to Carmella and with all the prowling around you've been doing in this garden, I should think you'd be delighted with the chance to have another go at next door's. For heaven's sake! We're not likely to get another chance like this, you know." Penny was edgy, for it was already past seven o'clock, Toby having arrived back but a few minutes earlier.

"I am tired, hot and very hungry," he said peevishly.

"There'll be things to eat there, and we don't have to stay very long once we've done our thing. Go grab a shower and change into something decent and *hurry*, for Pete's sake! Andrew will be here shortly."

"You said it was informal. Won't this do?" He looked down at his baggy tweed jacket and khaki pants that had seen much better days.

"For God's sake! You look like a superannuated ragman. Put on a suit!"

"Umm—actually it *would* be useful to get another look at the garden on that side," he murmured, absently extracting the pottery lamp from a bulging pocket and gazing at it. "If my theory is correct . . ."

"Later, later!" she cried. "Just *go* and get changed."

"Oh, very well!" he said huffily, and went out, slamming the door.

When he reappeared some twenty minutes later he was looking relatively neat in a dark suit, white shirt and Old Wykehamist tie, but there was a huge bulge on one side of the suit. "What on earth?" she yelped. "Are you carrying a gun or what? You look positively misshapen!"

He traded her glare for glare. "It's a torch. I'll need it in the garden. It'll be dark soon."

"Oh, honestly!" she fumed, and fumbled in her tote bag for her own smaller flashlight. "Here, take this instead—you can't turn up looking like Quasimodo."

"Hmph!" he snorted, making the exchange, but any further sparring was cut short by the front doorbell, quickly followed by Rosa ushering in Andrew, who was dressed in a sports shirt and designer jeans. Toby cast a reproachful glance at his partner, as Andrew said brightly, "Oh, great! Both of you here. All ready for the fray?"

Lights blazed from every window of the villa as they drove up to it and Andrew parked by the steps that swept up gracefully to its Palladian facade. "I'll just take you in and get you started and then I'll have to buzz down to the gate again. The parking is going to be a nightmare—only the VIPs allowed in here—I've bribed the Albergo del Sole next door to let the also-rans park there. Since they are doing the food catering, they couldn't very well say no."

Toby's very gloomy expression moderated to one of semi-gloom at the sound of food, and as they went up the steps Penny noted colored lanterns strung among the trees and the pool shimmering under its floodlights. Andrew ushered them into the large cream-and-gold drawing room, where the furniture had been pushed back against the walls, and where

Margo, clinging to the arm of a dark-haired man who matched her in height, was chatting with a couple of early arrivals.

At the sight of them, her face lit up with a radiant smile and she waved a crystal goblet in her left hand as she tugged at the man's arm with her right. "Darling, look who's here with Andrew! Our wonderful and *very* distinguished neighbors—this is *Doctor* Penelope Spring and *Sir* Tobias Glendower—both from Oxford University, no less! Aren't you impressed? Darlings, this is my wonderful ex, Paul Warner, *all* the way from New York to be with me."

Since both his hands were fully occupied, Paul Warner could only smile and nod at them in greeting, revealing a perfect set of teeth in his tanned face; a tan so uniform that Penny suspected it owed nothing to the sun but much to a tanning salon. His black curly hair had retreated a little, giving extra height to the unmarred forehead, but there were deep lines at the corner of his dark eyes and slight pouches beneath them. Under makeup the even-featured face would still be very handsome, but the signs of aging were unmistakably there. To Penny's quiet relief he, too, was clad in a dark suit.

"And this is Harry Daws, the man who makes me tolerable to look at on the screen . . ." Margo gushed on, indicating a man in a lavender suede suit and a purple silk shirt from which multitudinous gold chains glittered, ". . . and his friend Arthur." Arthur was a well-muscled young black in white sweatshirt and blue jeans. "Oh, darlings, we are going to have *such* fun—I can feel it!" She flashed a wide, violet-eyed look at Penny. "This is what this old place needed - people, lots and lots of people. Can't you just feel the change?"

She was looking utterly ravishing in a formal chiffon gown that shaded from the deepest purple on the bodice to the palest lilac at its hem and was cut and swathed Grecian-style to leave one creamy shoulder exposed. Penny glanced at Toby to see what effect such spectacular beauty was having on him, only to find he was gazing in pop-eyed disapproval at the lavender-clad makeup man. Luckily, a batch of new arrivals erupted into the room and Andrew ushered them out of the way. "I'll just point you at the dining room—the buffet is set out there—and then I'll have to get back to the gate. I'll be back later. . . ." He gave a rueful grimace, "I hope you won't be bored, but if you do get a chance to talk to Paul I think you'll find him a cut above the average."

"Oh, we'll be fine," Penny assured him as he led them into the green and gold dining room, where a lavish buffet was displayed on two long tables and a bar with several bartenders behind it stood along the third wall. She looked at him curiously. "Isn't this sort of thing a bit above and beyond a director's usual line of duty?"

Above the beard his fair face flushed and he gave an uneasy laugh. "A director's duty is to get the best out of his actors, and now that I've got Margo back to normal I mean to keep her there, so I don't want anything to go wrong tonight, and as I don't think too much of our PR people I would rather see to it myself."

"I see," Penny murmured, thinking that she did. He waved and was gone.

"One more 'darling' and I'd have vomited back there," Toby stated, making with determination for the food. "The *things* you get me into!"

Only the sight of all that tempting food restrained Penny from clobbering him. For a while they sampled diligently: smoked salmon, pâté, porchetta cooked with truffles, caviar . . . the Albergo del Sole's chef had surpassed himself. In spite of his declared hunger, Toby had deserted the food table for the bar long before Penny finished sampling the many delights. He wandered back to her, a glass of red wine in each hand and held one out to her. "Here, you'll need this to wash that down. I don't know where you put it all."

"It's all so delicious," she mumbled through a mouthful of miniature vol-au-vent stuffed with crabmeat.

"The wine's not bad either," he observed. "A couple more of these and I'll go about my business. We don't have to be *social* do we?"

"Not at the moment, no. But when you're ready to go, don't forget to come back for me, and we'll have to say goodbye and thanks to our hosts."

"Naturally! I trust I am not a complete boor," he snorted.

"Have you spotted Carmella yet? I've been keeping an eagle eye out, but I can't see her anywhere," Penny fretted.

"I probably wouldn't recognize her if I did—she's your department," Toby said smugly and went back to the bar.

Replete at last, and bereft of companionship, she began her search. The drawing room was now a solid mass of people and the dining room almost equally crowded, but as she threaded her way through the chattering groups she could see no sign of her quarry. She even ventured outside to the pool, where tables had also been set up and where a few hardy souls were already splashing about under the floodlights, but again with no success. As she returned to the house she saw a white Lamborghini draw up and park by the steps and Gabriella and Pietro Vanni emerge. They were both dressed formally, Gabriella in a fabulous evening suit of bright vermilion red crushed silk, her honey-blonde hair upswept in an elaborate coiffure. She, too, looked utterly ravishing. I wonder how that will sit with Margo, Penny thought, hanging back. Not too well, I imagine—for one thing their color schemes will clash. She waited until they were safely out of sight before going back in herself and making for the kitchen quarters. Here she had her first break, for she spotted the waiter who had served them on several occasions at the Albergo and was a singularly amiable youth who spoke excellent English. "Mario, a word with you," she called.

He came towards her bearing a laden drinks tray. "Yes, signora, what can I do for you?"

"Do you happen to know where Carmella, the maid who

works here, is serving tonight? I need to see her."

He shrugged expressively. "I have seen no maid. I come early to help set things up and there was no one here in the kitchen, no one at all. We bring everything, you see. Maybe she have the night off? I'm sorry, signora."

"Maybe so," Penny said, her heart sinking; she had not even considered that possibility. There was only one way to find out—she'd have to ask Margo. "Well, thanks anyway." And followed him back to the salon, where she was glad to see Margo was no longer clinging to Paul Warner, who had disappeared, but was standing a little apart, talking to an older dark-haired woman: neither looked too happy.

She edged her way through the crowd and, with an apologetic smile to the older woman, said, "Margo, could I just have a quick word with you?" The woman slipped away, a look of relief on her face, and Margo turned to Penny, her eyes a little unfocused, and it struck Penny that she was already a little drunk. "Yes, of course. What is it?"

Penny decided on an oblique approach. "I was just wondering, in light of what you told me the other day, what happened to the dog? There was one here and a guard dog would make a lot of sense in your circumstances."

Margo looked at her in astonishment. "Dog? Oh, that! I can't stand dogs. They don't like me. And that one was *always* barking, so I told Carmella it had to go."

"What happened to it?"

"I haven't the faintest idea." Margo was curt.

"Perhaps Carmella would know. Is she around?" Penny said hopefully.

"Oh, she's gone too." Margo's eyes were roving absently over her guests.

"You mean she left—or did you fire her?" Penny asked in dismay.

"*I* didn't fire her, though a fat lot of use she has been since the murder. No, she up and left, bag and baggage, and without a word! Must have slipped off last night, because she wasn't here when I got up this morning. Probably couldn't stand the thought of an extra person to do for in the house after the easy time she's had of it here. A damn nuisance!" Margo paused, and took a vicious swig of her drink.

A trickle of unease went up Penny's spine. "Have you asked Scorsi about this?"

"No, not yet. I must have a word with the Vannis about it before they leave." Margo directed a glare to where the Vannis stood on the opposite side of the room, looking a little lost and considerably overdressed in this motley throng that ran heavily to jeans and floral shirts. "If they want this place kept clean, it's up to them, not to me. Not that they will probably be any more helpful than that s.o.b. Scorsi!" As if aware they were being talked about, the Vannis were now staring fixedly in their direction. "Where's your sidekick?" Margo said abruptly. "Abandoned you, has he?"

"Oh, Toby was very taken with the statues in your garden—he has gone to have another look at them."

"How very naughty of him! Paul so much wanted to talk with him—though God knows where *he's* got to. . . ." Margo gave a mirthless laugh. "Can't trust them for a minute, can we? I think I'll go find your Toby and tell him he's just an old party pooper." With a slight lurch she turned away and started to weave through the crowd.

"Where's Margo off to in such a hurry? I was just coming to tell her everyone's here and accounted for," a voice said in Penny's ear, and she turned with relief to find Andrew standing behind her.

"Not everyone," she blurted out in her new anxiety. "Did you know Carmella has gone?"

"How do you mean—gone?" he queried.

"Left without a word. Vanished. And with all her things. Last night, according to Margo. I don't like it."

"Neither do I. Margo said nothing of this to me." Andrew's

face was anxious. "Well, thank God Paul is here. I'll have a word with him about it."

"Good luck! He seems to have disappeared also, and Margo wasn't any too thrilled about that either."

"Oh God!" he groaned. "Is that where she was off to in such a rush—hunting for him?"

"No, she was after Toby, who also is amongst the missing," Penny said drily. "That should stir him up a bit."

Andrew took her arm. "Then let's look for them together. But first I need a drink—a very strong drink. You also?"

"Yes indeed," she agreed and they headed for the bar.

Toby was happy. "Eureka!—you just don't fit in, old boy," he breathed as he gazed upon the weather-worn features of the god Janus, who was nestled snugly in an angle between the back wall of the garden and a small greenhouse backed up to it. "It's all beginning to come together—now, where could it be. . . ?" He tried the door of the greenhouse, but it was locked. Peering in through the grimy windows he could make out nothing but dusty shelves and empty flowerpots. He sighed and turned back to contemplate the pedestal on which Janus sat; the moonlight was so bright there was scarcely any need for the flashlight, so he pocketed it and got out a small, black, leather-covered notebook and started to pace off carefully the distance between the statue and the wall dividing the two villas. He entered the figures in the book and walked back along the line of statues ranked against the wall, peering carefully at each one. Back at Janus he turned around and paced off once more to check his figures, muttering to himself. He had reached the wall again and was leaning up against it, filling his pipe and cogitating, when a vision detached itself from the shadows of the shrub-edged path and floated towards him.

"Naughty, naughty!" the vision said archly. "Sneaking away from my lovely party like this. What *are* you doing out here all by yourself in the moonlight?" Margo Demerest surged up to him, looked mistily up into his face and put her arms around his neck. "You've hurt my feelings, darling. Don't you like my party?"

Toby was simply petrified, for she had him cornered in all senses of the word. "Er, not at all, Miss Demerest!" he spluttered. "Lovely party, lovely. I just—er—was here checking on something."

"What, darling?" she murmured, nestling closer.

"Er . . . catacomb. Looking for entrance. Undiscovered. St. Crescentia. Under here somewhere. Very interesting," he choked out in his panic, trying to sidestep away from her along the wall.

"Ooh! You mean secret passages, hidden treasure? Here? What fun!" she squealed. "Where is it?" She stepped back and looked dizzily around. "*I* don't see anything."

Free of her embrace, he sprang away from the wall like a scalded cat and tried to pull himself together. "Well, I'm afraid I was mistaken. Nothing here at all," he said quickly. "It must be in our garden next door. My apologies for absenting myself. Let's go back to the party, shall we?"

"Anything you say, darling," she murmured, taking his arm. "Let's go find Paul—he's naughty too, leaving me *all* alone. . . ." With as much dignity as he could muster Toby stalked back to the villa.

In the drawing room it was reunion time, for Paul Warner was there talking to Penny and, nearby, Andrew was in consultation with the Vannis. Margo dropped Toby's arm like a hot potato and grabbed at her husband, "Oh, there you are, darling!" she shrilled. "Look who I've found for you. You'll never guess what this naughty man was doing - looking for catacombs in *our* garden. Imagine!"

That's torn it! Penny thought, seeing Pietro Vanni snap to attention. She looked at Toby's stricken face and decided it was time to develop a diplomatic headache. "I hate to be a party pooper," she said, as Andrew joined them looking perplexed. "But I think that last drink with Andrew was one too many for me—my head is splitting. So, Toby, if you don't mind, I think you'd better take me home."

"Oh, you can't go yet—have one for the road," Margo urged, her own good temper restored as she again clung to her ex-consort. And, in spite of their protestations, the drinks were supplied while Toby made stilted archaeological conversation with his host, and Penny managed to whisper to Andrew, "Anything on Carmella?" He shook his head slightly, his eyes fixed on Margo with an unfathomable look.

Relief arrived in the shape of a small crowd of guests clamoring for music for dancing, and she seized the chance to say a hasty thank you and goodbye, steering Toby to the door. Once outside he let out an explosive sigh. "What a God-awful mess! My fault I'm afraid. I lost my head. Come on, there's a lot I have to tell you," and he scooted away down the drive.

Later, they faced each other across the dining room table scattered with the fruit of Toby's Florentine labors, and he said, "So, what do you think?"

"To be honest, although it's all very interesting, I don't think we have a single thing that matches up," Penny said bluntly. "I mean, all right, you think you've found the key to find the catacomb—although I must admit I'm too muzzy to follow all this 'intra' and 'infra Januculi' business you've been throwing at me. But so what? I can't believe Carlo is into the tomb-robbing business. It *certainly* isn't Krantz's field, and would there be *that* much money in Early Christian artifacts?"

"I asked Fittipaldi that—since this is not really my field," Toby said slowly. "And no, he didn't think there was a very active or profitable market. But suppose there is something else down there—something valuable."

"What?"

"Until I find the way in, I don't know, do I?" He was testy.

"Even if there is, why *now?* The Scorsis have had centuries to do something about it."

"Maybe they haven't needed it until now," he retaliated.

"But you can't tell me that in the short—what is it, two months lease on the villa?—they *have* to have it. All they have to do is wait. It makes no sense to me. Well, sufficient unto the day, et cetera . . . I've had it," she said as she headed for the door.

"Where are you off to?" he demanded.

"Bed. Now I really *do* have a headache with all this information to chew on. Maybe it'll all seem clearer in the morning," she declared and left him gloomily contemplating his notes.

Sleep came swiftly and she roused unwillingly from its comfortable depths to the awareness that something was demanding her attention. The moon had set and it was pitch dark, the illuminated hands of the clock showed five o'clock: from the hall came the steady pealing of the telephone. She closed her eyes and willed it to stop, but the clamor just went on and on. "Oh, hell!" she groaned and groped her way out of bed and out into the darkened hallway. She could see the light go on in Toby's room as she picked up the receiver. "*Pronto, Casa Redditch,*" she said automatically.

"Is that you, Dr. Spring?" Paul Warner's voice came muzzily through the wire. "I'm sorry to bother you, but is Margo there by any chance?"

Toby shambled out to join her, struggling into his robe and blinking like a blind owl without his glasses. "What on earth would she be doing here at this time of the morning?" Penny growled. "Do you know what time it is?"

"I don't know what to do," Paul Warner mumbled, and it was evident he was very drunk. "I've looked everywhere for her, inside and out. She's gone, disappeared . . . I need help."

Chapter 10

Andrew had been summoned from his bed, they had descended on the villa and, while he and Toby—both equally ill-tempered—searched the house and grounds, Penny concentrated on the far from easy task of sobering up Paul Warner. He was indeed a sorry sight; the faint pouches now prominent bags beneath his heavily bloodshot eyes, the tanned face mottled to a greenish khaki against which the blue stubble of his unshaven chin stood out. His tale, when he was coherent enough to tell it, was an even sorrier one, showing up as it did the tarnished reality that lay behind the tinsel glamour of the "beautiful people" of the entertainment world.

The party, according to him, had been a wild success, but in spite of that Margo had become increasingly tense as the evening progressed. The caterers had folded their tents at midnight and stolen away, but the diehards had kept going until two, when the last of them had wobbled off home and the security guards had locked up and left. Alone at last, Margo and he had had a final nightcap, during which they had started to bicker, and the bickering had flared up into a full-scale battle. "It was always the same," he said wearily. "All the old accusations, the old insecurities—we just couldn't help turning on each other, saying things we didn't really mean, we just couldn't help hurting one another. It was why we split up in the first place." He sighed and passed a shaky hand over his bleary eyes. "Anyway, I'd had enough of it. I grabbed a bottle and staggered off to bed and locked myself in my room. She followed me up. Kept banging and kicking the door and calling to me. By that time she'd changed mood again and was wanting to make up. Wanted me to go to bed with her." He grimaced. "I was too drunk, and I couldn't face another fiasco, so I just flopped onto the bed and passed out. . . ."

He paused and looked longingly at a half-empty bottle of champagne that stood forlornly on the marble mantlepiece. Penny firmly poured him another cup of coffee and pushed it into his hand. He took a reluctant gulp and shuddered. "When I woke up it was after four o'clock, the lights still on of course, my head splitting—I got up and was sick in the bathroom. It made me feel a bit better, so I thought to myself—hell, I'll be staying here for a while so I'd best make my peace with Margo. So I went to her room—the door was open, lights all on, but the bed not slept in and no sign of her. Got a bit frantic then. Went all over the house calling and looking. Nothing. Then went out to the pool, looked everywhere—not a sign. I was feeling awful again by then, so I called you. . . ." His face crumpled. "Where can she be? Where could she have gone?"

Toby and Andrew had reappeared for the final part of his tale, both of them grim-faced. Penny cocked an enquiring eyebrow at Toby, who shook his head, looked around with distaste at the debris from the party and, settling in one of the oversized easy chairs, began to fill his pipe.

"She is certainly not anywhere in the house or grounds," the ashen-faced Andrew reported. "And since there is no sign of her evening dress, she must still be wearing it. I can't be sure if anything else has gone—she has so much stuff, it's hard to tell. Damn it, Paul, didn't she say anything? Threaten anything? Think, man! God damn it, I brought you over expressly to *avoid* this sort of thing—why the hell couldn't you have kept your goddamn mouth shut?"

Paul gave him a hangdog look. "I'm sorry, I really am," he muttered. "But no—not a thing that I can remember."

"I think it would be a good idea if you took some aspirin, went back to bed and got some sleep," Penny broke in firmly. "Maybe when you've slept it off something will come back to you."

"But shouldn't we do something about finding Margo?" Paul protested.

"We could call the police," Toby put in. "That, I imagine, would be the correct procedure."

"*No!*" Andrew exploded. "That's the *last* thing I want at this stage. It would be all over the papers by this evening. She's probably holed up with another member of the cast or crew. I'll check with all of them first and then the hotels. I do *not* want the police in on this." He was quivering with tension. "I can shoot around her today. And yes, the best thing you can do, Paul, is to get over your hangover and we'll go over all this again when you're sober."

Like a chastised obedient child, Paul got up shakily, and Toby rose with him. "Here, let me give you a hand, old chap," he said, giving Penny a hard stare, and he shepherded the stricken actor away.

As soon as they were out of earshot, Penny said quietly to Andrew, "You know Toby is right about calling the police. We are not dealing with one disappearance here but two—unless the Vannis had some ready explanation about Carmella's vanishing act?"

He stared distractedly at her. "They were as surprised as you were—knew nothing about it. Said they'd send a replacement eventually, but were going to send over a professional cleaning crew to clear up after the party. They seemed very set on that."

"Do you know how long they stayed at the party?"

"They left just a little after you did. I didn't stay too much later myself—Margo seemed to be fine." His face was wretched. "Well, I'd better start making those calls, I suppose." He looked at his watch. "Some of the crew should be stirring by now. Because of the party we were going to start late today anyway, so I'll leave the cast until later."

She looked at him searchingly. "What will happen if she doesn't turn up today?"

He looked away from her. "I can shoot around her for a couple of days and use her stand-in for back shots for a couple more. I really must get on with it. . . ." And he hurried out.

Toby shortly rejoined her. "He's safely bedded. Poor chap, I know just how he feels," he reported. "I must say I find young Andrew's conduct very strange. What do you make of it?"

"Well, in the first place, I fear Andrew is repeating a pattern we've seen once before," she said. "Unless I'm very much mistaken he is in love with his leading lady—and Andrew seems singularly unlucky in love. In the second place, I think that *he* thinks this disappearance is a phony: that it's something he's been half expecting and dreading all along. She has rather an unfortunate reputation for this kind of thing."

"Good Lord, really?" Toby exclaimed. "And do *you* think it is?"

"I'm not sure," she confessed. "If it were not for Carmella's disappearance I'd be a lot more certain, but that does disturb me. However, Margo is an actress and a damn good one at that, and if this was all part of a carefully orchestrated plan on her part to do one of her disappearing/reappearing acts, getting Carmella out of the way may well have been part of it. After all, we have only *her* version to go by. She may have sent the girl off somewhere deliberately."

"Extraordinary people!" Toby snorted. "Doesn't seem a lot

more we can do here then, does it? I'd just like to have another look at the Janus statue and then let's get on back."

"Oh, very well, if you must." Penny was not feeling any too frisky herself. "But after breakfast I'm heading back for bed and some more shut-eye. Shouldn't we say goodbye to Andrew?"

"He knows where to find us if he wants us. My impression is that he'd be glad to be rid of us," Toby rumbled and led the way out.

Penny watched while Toby fiddled with and pushed at the statue of Janus: nothing happened. Again he tried the door of the greenhouse to no avail. Baffled, he explored the statues lying beyond it, and she leaned against the wall, drowsy from the sun and her early morning rising. Her eyelids drooping, she was looking dazedly at the lower branches of the shrubs lining the path from the house when an incongruity struck her eye. As she focused on it her eyes widened and she stood up. "Toby," she called urgently. "Come back here! I've found something."

He came hurrying back as she went over to the bush and peered down at her find: hanging from a dark-green sprout was a scrap of lilac-colored chiffon. "What do you think?" she demanded as he joined her. "Should we take it or leave it there?"

"It certainly matches the dress she was wearing," he agreed. "But then, it *could* have been torn off when she launched her assault on me, I suppose. She did come down that path. Better take it anyway." He sighed heavily. "My idea does not seem to be working out too well, although there is a very worn statue further along that could be another Janus. I think I'll just take the measurement from it to the wall and then get on back to my notes. Maybe I'm missing something." He started to pace away from the wall as she scrabbled in her tote bag, came up with an old envelope and dropped the scrap of chiffon into it.

They walked back through the garden and he pointed out the door that led into their garden and tried it once more; it was still locked. "You do see what I mean about the oil though?" he said, indicating the dark hinges and dark patches on the lock. "The other day you could actually feel some of the oil on it." And as they passed the empty dog run she remarked, "Margo was responsible for getting rid of the dog. To me that is yet another indication that she was up to something, although I suppose I should check with Andrew to see if she really disliked dogs as much as she made out." He grunted assent as they made their way out.

At breakfast Rosa was all anxious smiles and hung around trying to anticipate their every whim. Penny put this down to a curiosity about why they had been abroad so early in the day, but was not about to satisfy Rosa's curiosity at this juncture. Toby, as usual, was finished first and took himself and his notes off to the study. She finished her coffee as Rosa came bustling in again, stood up and stretched and said, "I'm going back to bed. We had a disturbed night so I need some sleep. If anyone calls, take their name and number and tell them I'll call them back later. Don't wake me up."

"*Si,* signora, I understand," Rosa said with a nervous smile.

As she crawled thankfully into bed, something nagged at Penny's mind; something had been different in the house when they got back from the party, something unusual. Just as she was slipping into sleep she remembered what it was, Rosa's television had not been on. "Maybe she took the night off and went out," she thought drowsily, "I'll have to ask her . . . ."

She was roused by a hand shaking her arm urgently and opened her eyes to see Toby bending over her, his face rosy with excitement, his eyes dancing. "I've found it!" he boomed. "I've found the entrance to the catacomb—want to investigate it with me? I haven't entered it yet."

"Done it again, eh? What a stubborn old thing you are.

Congratulations!" she said, struggling up with a yawn. "Yes. Just let me dash some cold water on my face and I'll be right with you."

"I'll get the flashlights," he said and dashed off like an eager schoolboy.

"Think we should send Rosa off somewhere while we do this?" she asked upon his return as they went out into the garden through the French windows in the study.

"I think she's out," he said. "Leastways she is invisible, and she isn't likely to disturb us." They ducked into the vegetable garden masked by its privet hedge and hurried towards the back wall.

"Very ingenious," Toby declared. "It wasn't Janus after all, although he was part of it. Watch!" He went over to a small ornamental cistern that had once been a fountain, set against the back wall. The spout of the fountain, set into the wall, was a lion's head with a ring in its mouth. The lion's head in turn was set into a bronze plaque inscribed around its outer edge with the twelve signs of the zodiac. "See the notch on the ring?" said Toby, and with some effort turned the notch, first to Aries on one side of the plaque and then to Libra on the other. He returned the ring to its central position, gave a mighty heave, and the whole base of the cistern fell away into blackness. He shined the flashlight, revealing a very narrow set of steps leading downward. "I'm willing to wager this was not the main entrance but a sort of emergency exit," he went on enthusiastically. "But once down there we should be able to spot where the main entrance was. I'd better go first in case the steps have crumbled."

"For God's sake be careful!" she fussed. "You don't want to break another leg." But she could feel her own heart beginning to pound with anticipation. "Here, give me a hand—my legs aren't long enough to reach that first step." He helped her over the edge of the cistern and down, then turned the flashlight into the darkness below and edged gingerly step by step downwards. Some twelve feet below the surface he stopped and looked back at her. "Here's the passageway," and he disappeared from view. The air was dank and musty and she found herself breathing hard as she hustled after him, her skin creeping with incipient claustrophobia. As in St. Domitilla's, their lights revealed the same bunklike tombs ranged along the walls flanking the narrow passage. Toby was shining his flashlight downward at the red earth. "Well, no sign of footprints here," he muttered, sounding faintly disappointed. He continued along the passage, his light revealing some of the tombs gaping blackly, others still sealed with thin marble slabs. "I'll investigate the contents later. I only want to get the general layout of the place now. We must be just about under the dividing wall of the two villas according to my figures." They went on another twenty yards and he stopped so abruptly that she cannoned into him. "Well, I'll be damned!" His light showed a solid wall beyond him against which stood a simple marble monument. "It's like a Tropaion!"

"A *what?*" she said, peering around him and gazing at two marble columns supporting a slab of white marble about six feet off the ground; the columns, in turn, standing on another marble slab that ran under a carved slab of marble set into the wall. On top of the upper one was a pedestal but no statue graced it.

"This is a poor man's version of the Tropaion erected above the tomb of St. Peter in the deep levels below the crypt of the present St. Peter's basilica. The exact significance is not known," he pontificated. "However . . . I think in this case it may have been used as an altar by Early Christians for the celebration of Mass and that pedestal probably had a crucifix set on it."

"Surely it's much too high?" she protested. "It's way over my head."

"Yes, but that was a subterfuge often used by the Christians in case they got raided," Toby went on. "The priest would have stood on a box or a footstool to celebrate mass and they usually had a fake tomb nearby decorated with pagan symbols into which they could shovel the crucifix and the altar vessels."

"If this is all there is to the catacomb, it's very tiny, isn't it? Compared to the other catacombs?"

"Yes, very," he agreed absently, his light directed at the base of the marble pedestal, against which lay a ridge of loose earth and pebbles. "But there are probably other levels. We'll have to retrace our steps and look for another staircase." He squeezed past her and led the way back and, as predicted, another narrow flight of stairs was revealed just beyond the first flight leading downward in a counter-direction. Another ten feet brought them to the second level and here the unmarked red dust was thick beneath their feet, the tombs all sealed and intact, but, as she followed him, it was evident even to Penny's untrained eye that this passage was much longer than the one above and ended in a wall of solid earth. Toby was quietly counting paces to himself. "It's longer, isn't it?" she asked.

"Yes, thirty yards at least," he muttered. "Curious. I saw another staircase leading down from this back there. Let's check that."

They went through the same process, although this third flight was shorter and the roof of the passageway lower, so that Toby's head was almost touching the roof. Some of the tombs here also gaped open. "These would be the later ones— fourth century?" she said, showing off her recently acquired knowledge.

"Probably," he grunted, still counting paces.

The dust rose beneath their feet in clouds and that, coupled with the knowledge she was at least thirty feet below the surface, began to suffocate her. "I'm sorry, but this place is getting to me," she gasped out. "I can't get my breath. I'm going to leave you to it."

"Look!" he commanded, and again his flashlight showed up a solid plain wall ahead of them, a carved tomb standing against it. "This passage is the same length as the first one. Now that is *damned* strange."

"Well, you figure it out, I'm going." She was getting panicky. "That opening above will still *be* open, I trust? No handy automatic shutoff or anything like that?"

"No, you go on up—it's open. I'll take a look at some of the tomb contents while I'm here," he muttered.

"Don't stay too long," she called back over her shoulder as she scuttled away. "If you're not back in an hour, I'll come looking for you."

"Oh, I'll be all right," he said testily. "Just don't *touch* anything when you get to the surface. I'll see to it."

She was so relieved to see daylight that she positively vaulted out of the cistern and on to solid ground. She stood breathing in the warm air open-mouthed, and waited until her heart stopped pounding, brushing the red dust off herself as best she could before going back to the house. She went in again by the study window, then quietly out into the hallway where she saw Rosa with her back to her by the phone. The maid swung around with a little scream then gasped, "Oh, *scusi,* signora—you startled me. I thought you were out."

"Just in the garden," Penny said. "Any calls?"

"*Si,* signora." Rosa's cheeks were flushed. "Two. One just after you went to bed. A man. Long distance I think. He say he call back."

"Was the name Oppenheim?" Penny said quickly.

Rosa shook her head. "No, he say his name is . . ." her face wrinkled in concentration, "Alessandro or something like that. The line not good."

"That must have been my son, Alexander Spring. He and his wife will be here in a couple of days, you know," Penny informed her.

"*Si,* signora, you tell me that. And the other call just came.

113

See, I write it down—Diane Grant. You call her very soon, she said. You want lunch now?"

"In about an hour will be fine. Sir Tobias will be here also," Penny said, making for the phone and dialing the embassy. Rosa nodded and went back to the kitchen, firmly closing the door behind her.

Diane was breathless when she answered. "Oh, I'm so thankful you called. A rather bothersome thing, I'm afraid. The owner of the Redditch villa called this morning, very upset. He's had a complaint about Sir Tobias digging for a catacomb? He wants to put a stop to it right away. I told him, when the call was transferred to me, that I thought it very unlikely, but he insisted I call you immediately. Have you any idea what this is about?"

Penny thought quickly: obviously Pietro had wasted no time in reporting Margo's gaffe and Scorsi had reacted promptly. "The owner—what is his name, ah, Signor Umberto?—has been misinformed," she said with some asperity and literal truth. "I can assure you Sir Tobias has not put spade to earth in the villa and has no intention of doing so. I have a good idea by whom the complaint was made and why, but you can assure the owner that Sir Tobias is not *digging* for any catacomb, and that if he wishes to check on this himself, he is welcome to do so whenever he likes. In fact, we would welcome it, to put a stop to the harassment from the owner of the adjacent villa, Count Scorsi."

"I see. What a relief!" Diane breathed. "I'll get back to him and tell him right away, and I'm sure that will settle the matter. He lives up in Pisa so I doubt that he'll bother, though if he wants to send someone to check I'll have him call you first, shall I?"

"Do that," Penny said, grinning to herself as she hung up.

She had just settled down in the living room with Toby's catacomb book when the phone rang again and she hurried to answer it, thinking it might be Andrew with some news. Instead it was her son's rich voice on the line. "Surprise, Ma! I thought I'd better call ahead and see if it's okay if we descend on you early. We decided to drive down from Vienna through Switzerland, but it rained solidly there so we didn't stop over and headed for sunny Italy. We're in Bologna. If we drive on we could be in Rome by this evening—we're both dying to see you, but if it's not convenient we could make an overnight stop in Florence."

Penny gulped, then collected herself. "No, of course it's all right. We're dying to see you too—come right along. Will you be in for dinner?"

"No, we'll eat on the way and should be in around eleven tonight. That okay?"

"Oh fine, just fine! See you then," she said as the time-up beeps of a pay phone exploded in her ear.

She headed for the garden to alert Toby to this new development and saw him coming across the lawn, dusting himself off, a perplexed look on his face. "Alex just called," she announced. "He and Sonya will be in tonight. They are driving down. Come in and I'll tell you all about it, but one thing I think is paramount—we say *nothing* of what's been going on here. After all, they are on their honeymoon and we don't want them mixed up in any of this, do we? We've done all we can for now. Let's just forget about all this and enjoy their visit."

"Oh, I agree completely," he rumbled. "Mum's the word! Besides, my theory seems shot to pieces. There's nothing down there of any but historical value. Apparently I was quite wrong."

She opened her mouth to tell him about Scorsi's latest move, then shut it again. "Mum's the word," she agreed.

Chapter 11

For forty-eight hours Penny and Toby lived in a fool's paradise and kept to their excellent intention of silence, although both had a tendency to dash for the phone every time it rang and to sneak a hasty peek at the papers in the rare moments when they were not paying proud attention to the recitation of their children's honeymoon saga or squiring them around the sights of Rome.

"How well they are both looking," they told each other. "How happy they are. In spite of its weird beginning it does appear to be the most suitable of matches. What a joy it is to have them here, we certainly have been fortunate." Only occasionally did Penny intercept a preoccupied look on Toby's round face, as he gazed towards the study and his accumulated notes, and, as Sonya and Alex chattered gaily on about their busy lives and plans, she found herself wondering what was going on next door and whether she should risk a call to the still silent Andrew.

It was Alex who burst their rosy bubble on the second night of the visit. He had insisted on taking them out to the famous Domus Aurea restaurant, with its romantic view of the floodlit Colosseum and the Roman Forum. The dinner had been superb and they were at the coffee and brandy stage, replete and lulled into a state of euphoria, when he dropped his bomb-shell. He leaned back in his chair, looked with mild disap-proval at his father-in-law who was lighting up an after-dinner cigar, and said, "So what's all this I hear about you two being mixed up in another murder?"

Toby promptly choked on his cigar and Penny said weakly, "What on earth gave you that idea?"

"It appears to be one of the topics of the moment at the American Embassy," her son said drily. "I had occasion to pop in there today—our Intelligence boys like to keep tabs on us while we're abroad, because they remain convinced the Russians might try to snatch Sonya back to the ranks of the Ballet and Mother Russia. Anyway, they asked about the mur-der and wondered if there was more to it than met the eye. Since neither of you have breathed a word about it, I conclude there must be. So, how about filling us in?"

"It was pure happenstance,"—"Nothing to do with us," they said simultaneously.

Sonya fixed an icy-blue stare on her father. "You say noth-ing of this to me, nothing at all!" she reproached. "Am I a child then to be kept in the dark? Me, I know much of murder, as you well know!"

Toby wilted. "But it really *is* nothing to do with us. The police have it in hand, Sonya. We just happened to find the man's body in our garage. He was the gardener at the villa, the husband of the maid who is still here: a thoroughly unsavory type—a drunk, a womanizer. The police think he was stabbed by an outraged husband or some such. Nothing to do with us . . ." he repeated.

"In that case why do you both jump like startled fauns ev-ery time the phone rings?" Alex demanded, looking quizzi-cally at his mother. "I know you both too well to believe you've stayed out of it. So what's the rest of the story?"

Penny sighed and looked over at her partner. "We may as

well tell them what's been going on and get it over with. You'll see for yourselves it is nothing to bother our heads about, and then maybe we can get on with just enjoying your visit. But let's get on home. It'll take some time to tell it all."

They got on home. The reassuring sound of Rosa's television on at full blast told them she was safely out of the way, so they settled in the living room and broke out a choice bottle of Armagnac the honeymooners had picked up in their travels. Alex and Sonya settled on the couch. She tucked up her long dancer's legs and leaned her head on his shoulder, as he put his arm around her and cuddled her up to him, kissing her dark silky hair, thereby earning a stare of disapproval from his father-in-law. "Shoot!" Sonya commanded, snuggling down.

They took it in turns to relate the sequence of events, eliciting varied responses from their children. At the mention of Margo Demerest, Alex sat up and took notice. "Wow!" he exclaimed. "You have been flying high! Is she as gorgeous off-screen as on?"

"This Margo Demerest, who is she?" Sonya asked suspiciously.

"A famous American movie star, my little Russian ignoramus," her husband informed her.

"Oh, an *actress*," Sonya sniffed, and settled down again.

At the mention of the catacomb it was her turn to sit up and take notice. She swung her legs off the couch and leaned forward, two spots of color on her high cheekbones. "A catacomb—under here?" she exclaimed excitedly. "How thrilling! Maybe we can find it?"

"I *have* found it," her father said, preening a little. "One of my better bits of research, if I do say so myself."

"Tell me about it," she commanded. "This is most exciting!"

"It's rather complicated and may take quite a while," he dithered.

"Yes, go on, Toby, tell us how clever you've been," Penny

put in. "I must confess I didn't quite follow when you tried to explain some of it to me."

"For you to understand it properly I shall have to start at the very beginning," Toby said. Alex shot a resigned look at his mother and settled back, as Toby continued. "The name of St. Crescentia threw me at first, because there was nothing to speak of in the Vatican archives about her. Then I found out she was a Scipioni—a famous Roman family whose main tomb lies beyond the chapel of Quo Vadis, just down the road from here, but for whom I found a reference to a *later* Scipioni burying ground *in vicino catacumbas St. Sebastiano*—in other words on this side of the Antica—and found the catacomb had undergone a name change over the centuries. Originally it was St. Demus and St. Crescentia—both of them Scipionis and both martyred by Diocletian at the same time."

"So she eventually got top billing like St. Domitilla got over St. Clemens," Penny said, determined to get in her two cents' worth.

"Precisely," he approved. "Once I had got on to St. Demus, a folio I had found among the *Scorsi* papers in the Vatican began to make some sense. Apparently this particular tract of land was given to the Scorsis by the pope of the time early in the sixteenth century. This villa was already here, but sometime in the early eighteenth century the then Count Scorsi put up the villa next door, and I suspect that during the building stumbled across the entrance to the ancient catacomb. This is when, I imagine, the cases of artifacts we have here and next door were removed from the tombs, the catacomb was explored and its entrances found. That Count Scorsi was evidently something of an antiquarian for he left this cryptic document written in dog Latin concerning a catacomb." He looked over at Penny. "This is where Fittipaldi was of such great help, having had so much experience in this kind of thing . . . . There was a reference to 'St. D' and the phrase *intra and infra Janiculi*. I thought this referred to something on the Janiculum—the hill on which St. Peter's is built—but Fittipaldi pointed out that in dog Latin that could mean 'between and under the *Januses.*' I had already spotted a Janus statue in this garden and there turned out to be another in the Villa Scorsi, possibly even a third. Now these proved to be not a clue to the entrance but merely a general indicator as to where the catacomb was. When I went back to the document I found a further clue—'in the lion's mouth a balance between the ram and the scales'—and so I found *an* entrance but not the main one," he concluded abruptly.

By this time Alex's eyes were glazed with boredom, but Sonya was agog. "You will show me?" she demanded. "Tomorrow, first thing, eh? We find what you look for together, father."

"Well, yes, but we have to be a bit cautious," Toby hedged. "It appears to be a dead end. There may be more information in my notes. I haven't had an opportunity to check them again."

"A very clever bit of work," Alex said tactfully. "But I don't see the faintest connection between it and all the rest of what you've been telling us. You said yourself you didn't find anything to link it with Scorsi, the *supposed* goings-on next door—which may be just a publicity stunt—or the murder."

His mother sighed. "Nor do we. But I am convinced there was a connection between Giovanni and Carmella, the maid next door—and *her* disappearance has me disturbed. But I agree that none of it makes much sense, so that's why I think we should just forget about it and enjoy ourselves."

"But no!" Sonya protested, looking at Toby. "Don't you see? There must be more to the catacomb—you say yourself the measurements do not fit. We must go look next door. And you must translate the Scorsi paper for me. I am good at puzzles."

"Easier said than done!" her father snorted. "We've been warned off by Scorsi and until Margo Demerest turns up again

I don't think the movie people will be in the mood to help us. But we'll see."

"One thing did strike me, Toby," Penny said thoughtfully. "If St. Domitilla's is anything to go by, we didn't find anything here like the meeting room for the agape or, for that matter, any chapels. Isn't that a bit odd?"

He shrugged. "Catacombs differ. Although, you're right, most of them do have one or the other and some have both. I'll just have to do some more research."

Alex got up and stretched and grinned down at his wife. "Well, I for one have other ideas about how to enjoy *la dolce vita* of Rome. Can I interest you in my ideas? In bed?"

She smiled up at him. "Philistine! Capitalist bourgeois beloved pig, lead on! But tomorrow I see the catacomb—so there!"

And on the morrow, after breakfast, that is precisely what this unlikely father and daughter team did, after ascertaining Rosa was embarked on her morning round of marketing. "Aren't you going with them?" Penny asked her son, for she was itching to make a phone call to Cinecitta.

"No, the underworld is definitely not my bag. In fact the very thought of it gives me claustrophobia."

"Oh! You too? How interesting, I thought maybe I was losing my marbles," his mother said brightly. "I had a regular panic attack when I was down there."

Alex looked knowingly at her. "You are also evidently dying to get on with something, so why don't you? I'll take the car and gas it up in case Sonya feels like a spin this afternoon, and I'll hunt for a New York *Times* while I'm about it. Anything I can get for you while I'm out?"

"You're sure you don't mind?" She felt guilty. "And no, not a thing."

As soon as he was out of the door she put in her call, only to be told that Andrew was already on the set and could not be disturbed. "Then is Miss Demerest available?" she demanded, hoping to jerk loose some information. "Miss Demerest is not available," the icy voice told her, leaving her none the wiser. "When may I speak with her then?" she asked, but the line went dead. She tried the villa, hoping for better luck with Paul Warner, but the phone just rang and rang. Baffled, she sat by the phone wondering what to do next, so that when it rang in her ear it startled her and she grabbed at it: it was Lou Oppenheim on the line.

"I think I've turned up something," he announced. "Or a distinct possibility at least: someone who fits in with the few facts you were able to give me. There was a Heinrich Herman Kreitzer from a prominent Prussian family, all of them ardent Nazis. His mother's name, incidentally, was Krantz. He was a lieutenant in the S.S. stationed in Rome after the German takeover there, and one of his jobs was shipping Italian art treasures back to Germany. The other was shipping Italian Jews and dissidents off to labor camps—which is why he's in our files, but too small a fry to have been the object of any intensive search. However . . ." he paused, "his commanding officer and friend was a Major Otto Limbeck, whom we *were* after. When the Allies started their advance on Rome, Limbeck and Kreitzer shifted their operations to Northern Italy, and when the Axis crumbled, took off for Switzerland. There their trail disappeared, but it is thought they went from there to the Middle East, taking with them the proceeds of what art treasures they managed to unload in Switzerland. Then they disappeared completely. But some eight years ago a man called Schwartz, whom we think *was* Limbeck, surfaced in the Lake Garda area and became very active in the neo-Nazi group there. It is known that he had contacts with extremist groups in both Libya and Iran and was very well fixed for money. He is also believed to have had a partner in the Middle East. Before we could get after him Schwartz/Limbeck died, so that was that. However, all that we have on Krantz *as*

Krantz is that he, too, was part of the same group and showed up in it shortly before Schwartz died. He moved to the Rome area about three years ago. If you can establish at your end any kind of link between Krantz and Schwartz, it would seem highly likely that Krantz *is* Kreitzer. Is this of any use to you?"

"Well, yes, I think so," Penny muttered. "Though how I'm not quite sure. Have you anything else?"

"Kreitzer's whole family—parents, brothers, I believe there was even a wife—were all wiped out by the Russians when they occupied Prussia so, rather understandably, he was reputedly rabidly anti-Russian. Oh, and just one other thing. If Krantz is Kreitzer he *should* have a long knife-scar on his right arm—an infuriated Italian tried to stab him to death but didn't quite make it." Lou's voice deepened. "You know, Penny, if you're proposing to tangle with Krantz in any way, be damn careful. These rightist terrorist groups play for keeps, and the ones with ties to the Arabs are the *worst*."

"Oh, I hope it won't come to that," she said uneasily. "And I can't thank you enough, Lou. You've been a great help. I owe you one. We'll get together as soon as I get back."

"Just don't take any chances. If you get anything take it straight to the Italian authorities and let them handle it," he said and rang off.

How to find out about a link between Krantz and Schwartz? And even if she did, where would that get her? Penny's thoughts were in a whirl—*nothing* seemed to match up. She reached for the phone again and got Lucia Scorsi. "I was wondering if you could help me on a couple of questions, Contessa. Do you happen to know if Krantz had a partner in his antique business?" Lucia didn't. "Did he have any ties with the Middle East?" On this Lucia was vociferous: yes, it was he who had introduced those awful Arabs to Carlo. But on being pressed for details she could not supply names or dates or even countries of origin. "One last thing," Penny said desperately. "Has Krantz a long scar on his right arm?" Lucia informed her stiffly that, no, she did not know since she had never seen Krantz without a jacket, and she failed to see what all this was about. "Nothing important. I'm sorry to have bothered you, but thanks anyway," Penny said, and hanging up on the contessa dialed Cordelia Forrest's extension.

Cordelia was snappish when she picked up the phone and listened in an uncompromising silence as Penny gave a precis of Oppenheim's information and then asked the same questions she had put to Lucia. Instead of answering her, Cordelia said in a very decided voice, "Penny, would you get hold of Toby and both of you come to the embassy right away? This is important."

"Our children are here, so I don't know . . ." Penny began. But Cordelia interrupted, "No, I really must insist. Please come as soon as you can. I'll explain when you get here. There have been some developments."

Mystified, Penny went in search of Toby and Sonya, whom she had heard reenter the house during her phone call to Lucia and who were now in the study. She poked her head in to see them on opposite sides of the desk, their heads almost touching as they pored over his notebooks. "Toby, a word with you," she said. "Cordelia Forrest wants us both at the British Embassy right away—something is up."

"Oh?" he looked enquiringly at her. "What?"

"She didn't say, but it sounded urgent."

"You coming?" he asked Sonya, who shook her head. "No, I stay here—this is more interesting, I think." She gave him a dazzling smile. "By the time you get back I will have everything solved."

On their way out they met Alex coming in, and on learning their destination and intent he said, "I'm parked just outside. I dropped in to see if Sonya was through and wanted to go for a jaunt, but if she's busy I can run you down and you won't have to bother getting out your car."

Once more Penny related Oppenheim's findings to them while Alex drove down the congested Antica, through the Aurelian Walls and, at Toby's direction, through the maze of narrow streets beyond to the embassy. "Shall I wait for you or what?" Alex asked, as he drew up before it.

"There's something you could do for us," Penny said. "Why don't you go over to the American Embassy on the via Veneto. You said you knew the Intelligence people there—ask *them* if they know anything of Herman Krantz and his doings, and then meet us back here later."

"Will do," he said cheerfully. "This is getting more cloak and daggery by the minute." And he drove off.

They were not ushered up to Cordelia's office but instead were shown into a small and empty conference room. "Miss Forrest will be with you shortly," their escort informed them and left them alone. They settled into saddle-backed leather chairs around the dark mahogany table and looked at each other uneasily. "I wonder what this can be about," Penny muttered. "Not more about your digging, I hope. I thought I had scotched that once and for all."

The door opened on the tiny stooped figure of Cordelia and, behind her, a tall heavy-set man with a beefy lugubrious face. "Sir Tobias, Dr. Spring, may I introduce Reginald Jackson, a colleague," she said formally, and as they all shook hands she and Toby eyed each other warily.

Once they were resettled around the table, she said, "I wonder if you would mind telling us again everything that has happened since you arrived at the Redditch villa, the whole sequence of events."

"You mean since we came in contact with Count Scorsi?" Penny asked.

"No, from the time you first encountered Giovanni Lippi," Cordelia said to their surprise. "Everything and anything that struck you as being a little out of the ordinary."

"You be spokesman, Toby," Penny said promptly; after her

many recitations of the morning she was feeling a little worn. "If you leave anything out I'll chip in." And as he launched into a meticulous recital of events, she sat back and watched Cordelia and the unexplained Reginald Jackson and tried to gauge something from their reactions. As the recital went on, his long face became even more lugubrious but Cordelia's betrayed nothing. Toby got to the party at the Villa Scorsi and she tensed slightly, wishing they had had time to confer, but relaxed again when he said nothing of the night of Margo's disappearance. Instead, he cut adroitly to Scorsi's most recent accusation of his "digging" activities, repeating the rebuttal that she had already given Diane, and then went on to the new information about Krantz.

But they were not out of the woods: Cordelia broke silence and leaned forward. "So when, exactly, did you last see Margo Demerest?"

"When we said goodbye to her at the party," Toby said haughtily.

"And you had no further contact with her?"

"None," he said with literal truth.

"But you have continued to look for the catacomb?" Jackson asked; his voice was reedy for such a big man. "Have you found it?"

Toby hesitated and Penny's heart sank, for he hated to lie and was very bad at it. "I have been doing some research," he admitted. "To the point where I believe I know where it is."

She thought it was high time to take a hand. "I believe I told you, Cordelia," she broke in, ". . . that our children are now here on vacation and naturally we are very anxious to spend as much time with them as possible. Not that we object to being summoned here in this rather peremptory fashion if it is of some value to you, but I do think we should be given some explanation of this sudden avid interest in us and our activities."

Cordelia and Jackson exchanged glances, then she said quietly, "Yes, well, there has been a startling development—one which no doubt will be splashed across the papers by day's end, so there is no point in keeping it from you. At dawn this morning the body of Margo Demerest was found floating in the Tiber. She had been dead for several days. The preliminary police autopsy revealed she was full of barbiturates and alcohol so, as of now, they are treating it as a suicide. But in light of what you have told us, I think there may be more to it than that. I believe she was murdered. And, for reasons I *cannot* tell you, we simply must know. Will you help us?"

As Penny sat in horror-stricken silence, Toby cleared his throat and said, his voice husky, "Do I take it that this is an official request from Barham Young, Cordelia?"

"He will phone you himself here to confirm, if you wish it," she said evenly.

"In that case we will do what we can," Toby said, and it penetrated Penny's shocked mind where she had heard that name before and what it signified.

Chapter 12

Sonya looked up from her father's notes, her blue eyes slitted in thought, giving to her Slavic features an almost Oriental look as she pondered. She got up and started to pace around the room, her mobile face quickening with a growing inner excitement. She made another dart at the desk, checked a notebook and scribbled a lengthy note to herself in Russian. She read it through and nodded her round head rapidly, "Yes, that is it, I am sure of it." She heard the front door open and rushed out, still gripping the note, but it was only Rosa returning with the morning's shopping and laden down with groceries.

"Can I help you with those?" Sonya said in Italian. As she had already informed her father, she did not approve of being waited upon by servants; it, she had opined, was a thoroughly outdated capitalist idea. Her present gesture she thought was practicing what she preached.

Rosa looked at her with positive alarm. "Oh, no, signora, I can manage very well." And scuttled past her to the kitchen, blocking the kitchen door with her stocky body until she had it open and her bags inside. Then she turned back to Sonya and smiled. "But thank you for the thought, signora, you are *multo simpatica, multo gentile.*" And she firmly closed the door behind her.

Sonya wandered through the house, searching for her husband, but finding no trace of him inside wandered out into the garden. There was no sign of Alex there either, but while she was out there she located the masked door behind the gardener's shed and fretfully tried its handle: she *had* to get into the Villa Scorsi. Frustrated, she looked up at the dividing wall and her quick ears caught the sound of voices on the other side: so there were people in the villa! Maybe she could bluff her way in there—for nobody had warned *her* off. Afire with new purpose, she hurried back to the house and collected her purse, then tapped on the kitchen door. There was no immediate answer, but some hasty scuffling from inside, and then Rosa opened the door a crack, her face flushed. "What is it, signora?"

"I need a screwdriver and a pair of pliers," Sonya announced. "You have those?"

"I think so. You wait here and I see," Rosa muttered and disappeared. She was back within seconds with the required tools and thrust them at the tall girl. "I am going out now for a while," Sonya announced, a little disconcerted by Rosa's evident disapproval. "You will tell my husband to wait for me when he gets back?" Rosa nodded and again closed the door on her. Sonya collected a flashlight from the study and let herself out.

Once outside in the busy, sidewalkless Antica some of her initial elation died, as she edged cautiously along by the wall of the villa while cars hurtled past her. She was struggling to think up a likely excuse to gain entrance to the villa beyond and had reached the Albergo del Sole without coming up with any bright solution, when her interest quickened as she saw a battered gray panel truck draw up before the gates of the villa and then pull into its driveway.

If only she could slip in before those gates were locked

again! She quickened her pace, but by the time she got up to them the truck was out of sight and the gates shut. She tried them anyway and to her delight they yielded. No one was in sight within so she quickly slipped through, closed the gates behind her and ducked into the bushes edging the drive, quietly cursing herself for not having changed out of her high-heeled pumps into flats. She wormed her way with silent grace through the shrubbery until she was in sight of the house, which looked deserted, with most of its windows shuttered and no sign of the panel truck in the front driveway. It must have gone round to the back by the smaller drive that swung to the right of the house, she decided, so, as an added precaution she kept to the left. Skipping from bush to bush she spotted some of the landmarks her father had mentioned— the empty dog run, the locked door in the wall—and kept on going until the rear wall of the garden with its ranked statues appeared before her. Peering out of the bushes she located the Janus statue nestled by the greenhouse. Getting out the screwdriver she broke cover and was at the greenhouse door in a few lithe bounds.

Before beginning operations with the screwdriver she tried the handle, and to her surprise the grimy-paned door opened. She slipped inside and shut it, her heart pounding, then crouched down out of sight as she inspected the interior. It was just as she suspected and had hoped for. "Camouflage!" she breathed, as her eyes took in the narrow wooden shelves that ran around three sides of the small glass enclosure, leaving a wide space in the middle of the greenhouse. She got out her note and studied it, then looked down at the earth-covered floor and scuffed at it with her shoe—the earth was only about an inch deep and beneath it lay a stone slab. On the side of the greenhouse by the Janus statue a pile of burlap bags lay underneath the bench and she edged over to them and pushed them aside; the edge of the large slab was revealed and embedded in it were two iron rings.

With a quick glance outside, she stood up and did a quick flamenco flourish with her high heels on the slab, evoking a hollow echo from beneath. "I've found it!" Delighted, she knelt down and started to tug with all of her strength on the two rings. She was so intent that she failed to notice the flicker of a shadow that passed above her or the silent opening of the door—and by the time she did so it was too late. . . .

With Cordelia's revelation, the conference had been prolonged, as Toby and Penny had gone on to relate the whole story of Margo's disappearance and of the discovery and exploration of the catacomb. "So you think the disappearance of Margo Demerest may just have been a publicity stunt? And you found no trace of any recent usage of the catacomb?" Jackson exclaimed, his voice squeaky with disappointment.

"We kept silent because that is what her director so evidently thought and that is what he wished. But I had doubts even then because of the disappearance of Scorsi's maid, Carmella. We never got to talk to her at all, but if Margo was right all along about the happenings at the villa, I am sure Carmella must have known something of them and that is why *she* had to be got out of the way," Penny said grimly.

During this little speech Toby was evidently having a mental struggle with himself, and as soon as she finished, he said, "It is true I found no *solid* evidence of recent investigation of the catacomb, but there is one thing I did observe that warrants further investigation. The dust on the floor of the second and third levels is thick and has evidently not been disturbed in at least a couple of centuries: there was no such dust in the first level."

Penny let out a little exclamation as Jackson said, "I don't quite follow you. What would that signify?"

"I think," Toby went on, "that the first level has recently been *swept* carefully to erase footprints. I noticed this morning, when Sonya and I investigated, that on the first level you could not even see where Penny and I had walked the other day, whereas down below our footprints were clearly visible." He stood up with determination. "I must get back and take another look. It is possible there is a masked entrance on that level that leads to an extension of the catacomb under the Villa Scorsi."

"And I had better get in touch at once with Andrew Dale and Paul Warner, Margo's ex-husband. I suppose they have been notified?" Penny said, getting up with him.

"That we don't know," Cordelia said. "Our information came from our own contact within the police force, but he did not mention that."

"Then how was she identified so quickly?"

"She's a very famous person. Even the *carabinieri* who dragged her out of the river recognized her immediately."

"After several days in the water!" Penny exclaimed.

"That's just it. If she *had* been in the polluted waters of the Tiber that long she would have been bloated beyond recognition, but the body had scarcely *started* to decompose. That is why I'm convinced it is murder," Cordelia declared. "She must have been dumped in the water very recently—possibly as late as last night. So, obviously, she did not jump in herself, and it seems unlikely—even for movie people—to sit around with a suicide on their hands for several days without doing something about it. I imagine, though, the police will be quizzing the ex-husband pretty thoroughly."

"He couldn't have had anything to do with it," Penny stated firmly. "We would testify to that. Drunk as he was, he was anxious to raise the alarm the very night she disappeared." She fell silent as the uneasy thought struck her that Andrew's actions in the light of all this could be construed in a much more sinister fashion.

"Let's go, shall we?" Toby said impatiently, and glared at · Cordelia. "You'll keep us informed of any new developments I trust?"

"And you likewise," the tiny woman snapped.

They found Alex waiting for them in the reception area of the embassy, a concerned look on his handsome face. "I was just about to give up on you and go on home," he said as they came up to him. "Was it about this terrorist business, by any chance?"

They looked at him blankly. "No, it wasn't. What terrorist business?"

"I'll tell you on the way. Your info on Krantz really has our Intelligence boys in an almighty flap," he said, and they piled back into the car and sped off. "Of course they are not directly involved in this big conference about the Federation of Europe that is shortly upcoming, but with all the pro-American heads of state in Europe in town naturally they are concerned. Krantz is known to them as rabidly anti-American as well as anti-Communist, and with all the terrorist activity that's been going on in Italy over the past few years—the kidnappings and the killings—they are terrified that something along those lines will happen at the conference. The Antica has a very bad reputation in that regard. Did you realize that it is one of the first places the Italian police look when anything like that goes down nowadays? The embassy did not insist on it but they hinted pretty strongly that I should take Sonya elsewhere until the conference is over."

Penny and Toby looked grimly at each other. "It might not be such a bad idea at that," Toby said. "The British Embassy called us in about Margo Demerest. She's dead—probably murdered. Since we were already involved, they want your mother and me to help out. Maybe it would be best if you took Sonya touring in the South for a few days—Pompeii, Amalfi, Capri and so on—until we get this sorted out. I'll be glad to foot the bill. And no need to worry Sonya about any of this."

"Good God, there's no need for that, and you damn well know it!" Alex exploded. "I am quite capable of taking care of

Sonya in all senses of the word."

To stop them getting into one of their inevitable shouting matches, Penny hastily intervened. "I think a trip south would be an excellent idea, and I am sure Sonya will see the sense of it, but there is *no* sense in keeping this from her. She is far too intelligent not to see through your little ploy and demand to know the real reason." They both turned to glare at her but her purpose was effected.

As soon as they stopped before the villa, Alex was out of the car and rushing into the house ahead of them. "Sonya!" he called, bursting in. "I've just had a great idea—Sonya, where are you?"

The noise of their entrance brought Rosa out of the kitchen. "The young signora is not here," she said. "She go out. She say for you to wait for her. You have lunch now? It is almost ready."

"Yes, we may as well," Penny said, looking for confirmation at the two men looming over her.

"Where could she have gone?" Alex was puzzled. He swung around to the maid who was just about to go back into the kitchen. "Did the signora say where she was going?"

Rosa looked over at Toby and said in Italian, "No, she just asked for a screwdriver and pliers and she went out—oh, maybe one hour since."

The look of concern on Toby's face deepened. "I see, well, thank you, Rosa, that will be all." Without another word he strode off into the study and when he returned moments later he growled, "One of the flashlights is gone. She may be down in the catacomb—though what the hell the screwdriver and pliers are about I have *no* idea." The two men sauntered casually out into the garden and then quickened their pace when they were out of sight of the house. But the entrance to the catacomb was shut. To make sure, Toby quickly opened it to Alex's silent amazement, then ran down to the first level. Alex could hear faint echoes as he called her name. Toby

134

came up and closed the entrance. "She's not down there. I have another idea." But a quick inspection of the sealed door behind the gardener's shed revealed nothing. "Damn!" Toby exploded. "Where the hell can she have got to?"

They walked in somber silence back to the house, where Rosa was bringing the luncheon dishes into the dining room. "Can you remember anything else the signora said or did?" Toby asked.

She screwed up her face in thought. "The only other thing was when I came in with the shopping . . . the signora had a paper in her hand and I saw funny writing on it—but that was all. Is something the matter?"

"No nothing, but thank you," he muttered.

She went out as Penny came in looking exasperated. "I've just tried to get Andrew again, but no one seems to know where he is. Any luck?"

"None," they said in unison.

"Well, we may as well eat," she said, trying to calm her own growing unease. "No use standing around fretting." And lunch was eaten in a concerned silence.

The sound of the front doorbell brought them all to their feet and they went rushing out into the hall. Toby flung open the door and let out a groan of frustration as a wretched-faced Andrew was revealed. "I have some terrible news," he announced.

"About Margo? We've already heard," Penny snapped in her own disappointment. "Come in, Andrew, we have a lot of talking to do."

They abandoned their half-eaten lunch and went into the living room. "Sit down," she commanded. "We are all as shocked by this as you are, but this is no time for breastbeating or 'what ifs,' we have to get on with it. Have you seen her?"

He nodded, his vivid eyes full of pain. "They wanted me to confirm the identification and to make a statement."

"How was she dressed?" she demanded.

"Still in her party dress," he gulped, fighting for control. "But her shoes were gone."

"What state was the dress in?"

"A bit torn and dirty."

"How torn and how dirty?"

"The police thought initially it was blood because it was a sort of dark reddish stain, but it turned out to be earth stains, and the chiffon had been torn in several places."

"The topsoil in both gardens is a light brownish gray," Toby observed to no one in particular.

"The police have changed their minds about the suicide," Andrew continued. "I told them about Margo's absolute aversion to pill popping and they confirmed it with her own doctor in L.A. She would *never* have taken barbiturates—not of her own freewill. She wasn't drowned, you see—it was the combination of alcohol and drugs that killed her."

"And it must have happened shortly after the party?" Penny put in.

"They can't be very exact, but by the blood gases they put it sometime early on the day following the party," Andrew said wretchedly. "Naturally they wanted to talk to Paul, so I'm not exactly popular with them."

"How come?" she asked.

"Because I shipped him back to New York yesterday," he confessed. He looked at them with haggard eyes. "I suppose you have already deduced for yourselves that I thought Margo was pulling one of her stunts. Paul was so upset after he sobered up that I confided in him and, rather predictably, he got on his high horse and said in that case he wanted no part in it; he had his own career to think of. I told him if he felt like that, he had better take off. How wrong can you be? Now the police suspect both of us—him because of the row they had that night and me because, since of course he was gone by last night, someone else must have put her body in the Tiber.

Luckily, I had an alibi of sorts, which they are now checking, but if they aren't satisfied they may pull me in again."

Toby, who had been ruminating in worried silence, spoke up. "Andrew, it is absolutely imperative that we go to the Villa Scorsi right away. I have my own ideas about how Margo vanished so quickly and completely, but I have to check them out in the villa. We have an added complication - or, at least, I fear we have. My daughter is missing and I have an uneasy feeling she may have had the same idea. She may be there now."

Alex let out a stifled exclamation as Andrew looked dazedly at Toby. "I'm afraid I can be of no help to you there." He let out a mirthless laugh. "In fact it is one of the reasons I'm here, because I find what has just happened so incredible! When I got back to my hotel after seeing the police, I found all of Margo's personal effects, together with this note. . . ." He pulled it from his breast pocket and held it out with a shaking hand. Penny took it and read it aloud: "'Count Scorsi regrets the tragic event, about which he has just been notified, and presents his condolences. Since you will have no further use for the villa, he has taken the liberty of removing Miss Demerest's effects in their entirety and encloses a check for the balance of the rental, which he thinks is only fair in the circumstances. One key is still outstanding, so if it is in your possession he requests an immediate return since he will be making other arrangements for the occupation of the villa.'" It was signed by Pietro Vanni. "Then you *do* still have a key!" she said eagerly.

"No, I don't. I gave mine to Paul and he told me at the airport he had left it behind in the house," Andrew said. "I've no idea who has the missing key—maybe the absent Carmella? But don't you see what all this means? Margo was right about that damned count! He must have been keeping a close watch on us all along. Otherwise how the hell did he know Paul wasn't still in the villa? How did he know so quickly about

Margo? It's not even in the papers yet." He buried his face in his hands. "Oh, if only I'd *believed* her!"

Toby got up and towered over him. "Pull yourself together. There is no time for 'if onlys.' Yes, it is obvious to *us* that he has to be heavily involved in what is going on and it's time the police knew as well. We have to take immediate action. Sonya's been gone over two hours now and I am taking no more chances, I'm through playing games." He began to stalk from the room.

"What are you going to do?" Penny queried in dismay.

"I'm going to call Cicco and tell him the whole bloody story," Toby boomed.

"Isn't he the homicide man?" Alex said, his voice strained.

Toby turned on him. "Who else? We've already had two homicides—please God it won't be three. . . ."

Chapter 13

Things had not gone quite as they had anticipated. Penny, who had witnessed Toby in a towering rage in several languages and too many times to count in English, was now chalking up another first as he tongue-lashed Inspector Cicco in Italian. For once she was totally in sympathy with him: she only wished she could vent the frustration that had been building up in her by doing some yelling and screaming herself, for the sight of her son's distraught face was almost more than she could bear.

Initially, Cicco had been difficult to contact and Toby had categorically—and rightly—refused to talk to any policeman of lesser rank. It had resulted in a delay of several hours, during which there had been no sign or word of Sonya and their nerves had frazzled with their mounting fear. And when Cicco did show up at last he was no longer the smilingly amiable policeman she recalled from Giovanni's murder, but somberly glowering and evidently impatient as Toby related their increasingly complex tale.

At the end of it Cicco snorted and threw up his hands. "Bah!" he exploded. "All this mystification you make, all these accusations you hurl at a man of high position like

Count Scorsi—and not an *atom* of proof! All you have is suppositions, suspicions. Is it that you are so idle, with so much time on your hands that you have to dream up all this . . . this . . . folderol? True, the medical examiner has ruled out suicide for this oh-so-famous but oh-so-erratic film star, but the *facts* of the case to me are simple. *Fact*—after a drunken orgy the deceased and her husband have a terrible row. *Fact*—when she disappears after this he does not call in the police. *Fact*—he flees the country before the body is discovered. Though *you* claim he was concerned about her disappearance, is that the action of a *concerned* man? *Fact*—it is in the interest of this American movie company to hide these sordid doings, so they delay the finding of the body until he is safely away. But now they have the great publicity, eh? Now they can make much money from this movie, eh?"

"But . . ." they started to protest in unison, but he held up a commanding hand. "You have had your say, so let me finish! What do I think these facts add up to? A simple, sordid crime of passion. Goaded beyond endurance the drunken husband feeds the drunken wife pills in her drinks. Then, when she dies and he sobers up, he is panic-stricken. He hides the body. He calls this director. Together they flimflam you, whom this crazy woman has already taken in with her weird tales, and you, who so obviously enjoy your little mysteries go along with it all the way. It makes you feel important—no?—to solve all these great mysteries while the foolish policemen just run around in puzzlement?"

It was at that juncture that Toby blew up. "You numbskull, you have sex crimes on the brain!" he yelled. "First Giovanni Lippi is killed and that is your answer; now Margo Demerest is killed and it is still your answer. You have got nowhere on Lippi's murder and if you continue to bury your head in the sand, you'll get nowhere on this one either. By God, if all of you think this way, no wonder the Fascists and the Nazis are on the rise again in Italy! At this rate they'll be back in control before you know it! If everyone has your one-track mind they should have a clear field. Are you too blind to see that *something* much bigger is going on? It is not just a question of two murders, there are two disappearances to explain as well— how about Carmella? How about my daughter? That is why I ask, no, I demand entrance to the Villa Scorsi. It may already be too late for Carmella, but for my daughter there may still be time if I can get in there."

"We have no evidence that the maid did not leave of her own free will," Cicco yelled back. "As to your daughter, *I* can think of another very likely explanation. I have learned from Rosa Lippi of the note in strange handwriting. *You* explain that by saying your daughter makes notes in Russian in the Cyrillic fashion, but what if the note in Russian was from her compatriots? It would not be the first time a Russian defector has gone back to Russia after finding life in America is not all that wonderful, or being married to an American is all that great—look at Stalin's daughter! She could well be on her way back to Russia by now."

White-faced, Alex surged to his feet, his fists clenched. "Sonya is an *American*," he roared. "And very happy to be so, and happy in our marriage. And do you seriously suggest, you stupid pipsqueak, that she defected carrying *only* a screw-driver, a pair of pliers and a flashlight? With no money, no papers—nothing? How do you explain *that?*"

Penny decided it was time to intervene before they came to blows. "We want to know what you are proposing to *do* about all this, inspector. For something has to be done, and quickly, and if *you* will not satisfy us then we will have to go to higher authorities."

The small man wheeled on her, his face working. "Then I will tell you what I will *do*. I will hand in my report on the death of Margo Demerest, which will contain the *facts* I have enumerated. Since all evidence at the presumed scene of the crime has vanished; since the perpetrator is no longer in Italy, and since there is no solid evidence of conspiracy against his accomplices, and also, since our authorities are now involved with more important matters, I doubt whether they will seek extradition for Paul Warner. I imagine they will accept my report and leave it at that. I will put out a missing person's report on Carmella Dossi, and if Sonya Spring has not returned in another twenty-four hours I will file a missing person's report on her. I shall contact Inspector Morelli, whose department it is, and pass along what I consider to be your totally unfounded accusations against Count Scorsi and Signor Krantz. I will tell him what *I* think of those, and then it will be up to him to take further action he sees fit. *That* is what I will do."

"But, for God's sake, at least come with us and let us examine the grounds of the Villa Scorsi!" Toby said desperately.

"Out of the question," Cicco snapped. "We have already examined the house and grounds. But, since both were cleaned up by a firm of commercial cleaners in the aftermath of that drunken party, and since all the deceased's effects had already been removed, there was nothing to find. We have talked with the cleanup crew and they reported noticing nothing unusual during the cleanup. As I see it, Count Scorsi has been extremely cooperative, and has only been very unfortunate in having such an incident take place on his property. The villa is his private property and I see no reason whatsoever to disturb him further."

"Then you leave us no recourse but to take this higher," Toby roared.

"You may take it where you damn well please," Cicco snarled as he slammed out.

"Well, at least we know where we stand with him," Penny said wearily. "Now what?"

"I'm off to the British Embassy," Toby announced, still seething with fury. "I'm getting Barham Young in on this— by God! he owes me, and now it's time to collect."

"Barham Young?" Alex queried.

"The head of British Intelligence," his mother said quietly. "He was helpful about Sonya before."

"I see—then I think I'll head back to the American Embassy and see what I can stir up there," he said, getting up. "You coming along?"

"No, I think I'll try to get hold of Andrew and see what's going on with him. Maybe he can bring some pressure to bear also," Penny muttered without much conviction.

They went about their business, leaving her sitting in deep gloom. The door opened to admit an apprehensive-looking Rosa, who sidled up to her. "I hope I did not say anything wrong to the Inspectore," she ventured. "I only tell what I tell you. Did I do wrong?"

"No, you told the truth and that is always best," Penny sighed.

"You will eat here tonight? I get nice dinner," Rosa said eagerly.

"Yes. Just something very simple. I don't think any of us feels much like eating."

Rosa went to the door then hesitated, looking back at her in mute appeal. "Was there something else?" Penny said sharply.

"No, signora, I no wish to bother you now," Rosa said, and went out.

Penny pulled herself together and went to the phone. After several abortive tries, she finally located Andrew, who sounded as miserable as she was feeling. "We've just had a very unpleasant go-around with Inspector Cicco," she said. "Though, if it is of any comfort to you, he seems to be determined to wash his hands of the whole thing as quickly as possible, having settled on poor Paul as the culprit, with you as unprovable, number one accomplice, but with no intention of pursuing it. But that isn't why I called. I'd just like to know what the position is with you and whether we can count on you for some help. My daughter-in-law, Toby's daughter, has definitely disappeared."

"Dear God! How I wish I had never dragged you into all this," he groaned. "Well, things are pretty hectic here, as you can imagine. The producers have decided to pull the company back to Hollywood immediately and to see if we have enough footage to put a complete film together." He gave another of his mirthless laughs. "They figure, with the publicity surrounding Margo's death, the movie will have to be a smash hit anyway, whether it makes any sense or not. Ironic, isn't it? I'll be staying behind for a while. In the first place the police haven't finished with me—or so they say. And then . . ." his voice faltered, ". . . as soon as they release Margo's body, I'll see to its shipment back to California. Again the producers are not about to miss out on a mass-media event that a funeral there will provide." He fell silent for a moment, then continued, "In one respect I feel a little better in that my first suspicions were not so wide of the mark after all. One of our better PR people came to me and confessed that at the party Margo had been sounding her out about the value of publicity stunts nowadays."

"Would she be a small dark woman?" Penny put in.

"Yes, did you meet her?"

"I saw them talking at the party and the discussion didn't seem to be going too well," she said.

"Yes, that's just about how it went. Not that it makes one *damn* bit of difference now." His tone was desolate.

"It may make a difference though about Carmella's disappearance," she pointed out. "If only we could locate that girl!"

"To get back to your question—naturally I'll be only too glad to help as long as I am here. What did you have in mind?" he asked.

"We have simply *got* to get something solid in the way of facts about Scorsi and Krantz. As Cicco pointed out we have nothing in the way of real evidence as yet. Scorsi seems to be unreachable, so my idea is to zero in on Krantz. If we can prove he is up to something and can tie him in with Scorsi and

144

his merry band the police may start listening to us. The worst of it is that Krantz knows me now, but he doesn't know *you.* So, when you are free and are up to it, I thought we might do some heavy snooping on him and his movements."

"I'm shipping the company out tonight on a special charter, so after that I'll be relatively free—that is, if the Italian police leave me alone. And, yes, I'm game for it. I'd give anything to see the devils who killed Margo get what's coming to them. . . ." His voice broke.

"You loved her very much, didn't you, Andrew?" Penny said softly.

"Was it that obvious? Yes, I adored her—but the feeling was not reciprocated, as you no doubt noticed. I'm not very lucky in love, am I?" he confided.

"No, you most certainly are not," she agreed. "Look, since you're a hard man to track down would you call me here tomorrow morning sometime and we can make definite plans?"

"Unless the police change their minds and pull me in, I'll do that.

Their conversation left her feeling somewhat more optimistic and this was enforced when Alex and Toby returned, both a lot calmer and both reporting that their respective embassies were moving into action.

The action was not long in coming, for they had scarcely finished their hasty dinner when the front doorbell summoned and Rosa escorted in their visitor. "Inspector Morelli," she announced and again shot a look of hurt reproach at Penny.

In contrast to the small, round Cicco, this policeman was tall and lean to the point of emaciation, his face long-jawed and beetle-browed, and his unusual greenish eyes proclaimed his Northern Italian origin. "Inspector Enrico Morelli of the anti-terrorist division," he announced in excellent English as they eyed him warily. "I understand you have some information for me?"

"You have spoken with Inspector Cicco," Toby stated.

"Yes, but may I say that, although he made his views on all this clear to me, as no doubt he has already done to you, in the present circumstances I am very much interested in what you have to say and what you think may be developing."

To Penny's surprise, the story Toby related this time was very different from the one he had previously presented to Cicco: the emphasis had changed entirely. "I am convinced that the key to all that has happened so far lies in the catacomb that runs beneath the villas. *What* I have no idea—it could be antique-looting, it could be drug smuggling, it could be terrorist activity, but I think Lippi was in on it from the outset and that our arrival here upset the initial plan, which was to use *this* area of the catacomb during the absence of the Redditches and with *his* collusion. When he could not produce what he had promised I think he was of no further use to them and so was liquidated, and the activity was then transferred to the catacomb next door."

He produced a sheaf of papers from his pocket and handed them to the attentive inspector. "If you examine this timetable of events I have drawn up, you will see that the odd happenings reported by the late Margo Demerest start up shortly after our arrival, and that the disappearance of the maid Carmella, shortly followed by the disappearance and murder of Miss Demerest, are all tied in with those events. Unfortunately, at that party Miss Demerest disclosed my own investigations, that had been stimulated by the, to me, extraordinary and unwarranted antagonistic behavior of Count Scorsi. She may even have returned to the area I had indicated later that night—as witness the scrap of her dress we found there—and may have seen or heard something she was not supposed to, and so was then abducted and killed. Now my daughter is missing, and I greatly fear she may also have gone to the villa to investigate this herself. So, I beg of you, please use your authority to let me in there. I *know* I can find the other entrance to the catacomb, and she may still be there."

The inspector looked up from the papers, his face grave. "Yes, from these you make a good case, even though, as Cicco says, there are few corroborative facts. But I feel you may well be right. We have been expecting some attempt to disrupt this upcoming conference in Roma. There have been countless rumors, but nothing concrete we could follow up on. One fact that Cicco did not confide in you, and which he did *not* follow up on, was that Lippi had recently been well supplied with money and had been in the company of members of *rightist* groups who would gladly see this conference end in chaos."

"That's what I don't really understand," Penny interrupted. "Why should the conference be of such importance to them?"

"For one thing it would put a strong dent in their own totalitarian aims," Morelli said. "A Federation of European States would immeasurably strengthen the democratic governments now in power and even the more liberal-thinking communist governments. Either way the rightists would lose out. For another, many of these rightist groups are strongly linked with terrorist groups from the Moslem world, who again would be unhappy with and hard hit by—particularly financially—a stronger Europe. This is a very complex business and it would take too long to explain, but terrorism thrives on weakness, division and indecision. So, I for one, am prepared to take your fears and suspicions seriously."

"Then you will help me get into the Villa Scorsi?" Toby said eagerly.

"I will do my best to get a search warrant," Morelli said. "But I warn you, since we are dealing with an aristocrat—however shady of reputation—it will not be easy. It may take a while."

"How long?"

"Perhaps as much as three days, which would bring us almost up to the opening day of the conference," the inspector said grimly.

A groan of exasperation burst from Toby and Alex. "But Sonya's life may be in jeopardy!" the latter protested. "Doesn't that count?"

Inspector Morelli eyed him. "I know it is a hard thing for you to accept, but she may already be dead. These terrorists spare no one who stands in their way. Our one faint hope is that they may feel they have some use for her—say as a hostage—and also that, for the moment, they are feeling secure enough to proceed with their plans. Once those plans are accomplished, however, I cannot honestly say that I think there will be *any* hope. So, first, I tell you what I do. I encourage Cicco to give out his version of the Demerest murder to the media—that should lull them into thinking all is well. Second, I urge you to keep a very low profile while we hunt for Carmella and your daughter. Third, you say you think you may find another way into the catacomb from this side. If you can, and we find something in the other catacomb, well, then we could move against Scorsi."

"Would it help at all to prove Krantz *is* Kreitzer?" Penny put in.

"It would help even more if we could establish a definite link between him and Scorsi in the *present* situation. But anything that would enable us to investigate him actively would help," Morelli agreed. "So long as you understand it could lead to Sonya Spring's death—if they have not already killed her." It was of small comfort to them but his grim words held the ring of truth. He got up. "Be assured I will do everything I can to help you find your daughter, but, I repeat, do nothing to draw attention to yourselves until the situation is clearer. I must go now, for there is much to do."

"What do you think?" Penny said, as soon as he had gone. "Have we just been handed a placebo or will he do anything?"

Toby shrugged, "He seems genuine enough, although he isn't telling us everything. I got hold of Barham and he admitted to me that they are very concerned because of the *location* of all this. He did not spell it out, but I gather one of the major hush-hush mini-conferences of heads of state that includes the British Prime Minister had been slated to take place somewhere along the Antica. He fears that all this may be connected with that. In any case our first priority is Sonya. Tomorrow first thing, I am going to have another go at the catacomb."

"May I help you?" Alex said.

They both looked at him. "I thought you were claustrophobic," his mother said.

"Not when my wife is missing," he returned grimly. "If I don't do something active I'll go crazy."

"Then yes, by all means." Toby collected a bottle of brandy and a glass and headed for the door. "Now I am going to turn in and drink myself into oblivion. I would advise you to do likewise and we will get at the catacomb early."

"Not sound medically, but in this case I'm with you all the way," Alex said. He collected a bottle of Scotch and went out with him. "Good night, Ma."

Penny went around turning out lights and testing windows, something nagging at her weary mind. She felt she had left something undone that should have been done, but could not bring it to the surface. She paused before Angela's wedding photo on the piano and wondered if, on the morrow, she should confide what had been going on to their hosts. Then it hit her. "Good grief—what a fool I am!" she muttered. "No wonder Rosa was looking glum. Why didn't the silly creature tell me? It's two days beyond her payday and I forgot all about it! I distinctly remember *getting* the money, now what the hell did I do with it?" Finally, after much rummaging, she came up with the pay packet and put some more notes in a smaller envelope. "A hefty tip plus an apology should make up for it."

She went out into the hall and over to the kitchen and listened. She could still hear Rosa's television in the little suite that led into a living room and bedroom. "May as well give it to her tonight and soothe her down." She made her way through the darkened, immaculately clean kitchen to the living room door beyond, rapped on it and opened it up. The volume of the television was on so loud that her entrance went unnoticed. Two ancient winged armchairs were ranged in front of the expensive set, their backs to her. Rosa's dark head was visible in one, her feet in carpet slippers propped comfortably up on a padded footstool; the top of another dark head was visible in the other.

"Rosa!" Penny said loudly, "I forgot your wages, I am *so* sorry. Here they are, and a little something extra for all the additional bother you've had with us."

Two startled faces peered around the wings of the chairs; Rosa's face visibly paled as she saw who it was. The other, younger face, so like her own, was visibly frightened—it was Carmella.

Chapter 14

It had not helped when both women burst into loud sobs and lamentations at the sight of her. Penny, after the exhaustions of the day, felt far too groggy to cope with two hysterical women, so after stern exhortations to calm down and go to bed and that all would be resolved on the morrow, she tottered off to bed herself. Her last conscious thought as she sank into sleep was "Right under our noses the whole time and we never even suspected—we *must* be slipping!"

By the time she surfaced both men had breakfasted and disappeared—presumably into the depths of the catacomb—and she was quietly thankful, for it gave her breathing space to collect her thoughts. Although she realized she would need Toby's verbal expertise for the final showdown with the two women, she felt that now her main task was to soothe the visibly frightened Rosa so that, when that happened, they would not be faced with further hysteria.

"Look, Rosa," she said, as the maid put her breakfast before her with trembling hands, "there is no need for you to be upset. It is all right. We are going to have to hear the whole story when Sir Tobias and my son get back, but Carmella is welcome here and she is *safe* here and you must tell her that.

Now that I have seen you together it is obvious that you are related in some way. Do you want to tell me about that now? The rest can wait until later."

Rosa looked at her imploringly, her work-roughened hands plucking at her apron. "Oh, signora, yes. She is my *nipote*— my niece, the daughter of my oldest sister who has many, many children. In Calabria there is little work, so three years since when Carmella is fifteen they ask if I can find something for her here in Roma. Giovanni, he say they need servants next door, so she go there and work for Gabriella Vanni. Carmella like her very much. But then, when Gabriella go back to the Palazzo Carmella must stay in the villa alone. That she do not like so much, but is better when the *straniera*—the American lady—come. Then Giovanni is killed and she becomes very frightened. She run away to me, her aunt."

"Why on earth didn't you *tell* us?" Penny said. "We would have understood."

Rosa avoided her gaze. "We were frightened, so I hide her," she repeated.

"But you couldn't have hidden her here forever—what were your plans?"

Rosa spread her hands wide in resignation. "I was going to send her home, but I spend all my money on Giovanni's funeral—so I have to wait for my wages. Now I can send her."

So it was that simple, Penny thought with grim amusement. "Not until Carmella has told us everything she knows about what went on next door," she said firmly. "Do you realize the police are hunting for her as a missing person? We thought she may have been murdered like the American lady! It is very important that she tells us *everything*."

The terrified look was back on Rosa's face. "What will the *polizia* do to her?" she whispered.

"Nothing, if she has done nothing wrong." Penny was thinking furiously, and a possible course of action occurred to her. "In fact we may not even tell them she is found—at least, not just yet. You must go on as usual for the moment while I try to get hold of Sir Tobias, for it will be easier for Carmella to talk to him in Italian. Once she has made her statement and signed it, then probably it will be all right—in fact it might be better and safer—if she *does* go back to Calabria."

"*O, mille grazie, signora*," Rosa mumbled. "I have been so worried. I go tell her now. She also is very upset."

As soon as Rosa was safely out of the way, Penny slipped out of the house and down to the garden. When she got to the cistern she called down the opening, "Toby, Alex!—If you're down there, come up. Something very important. I need you right away."

After a small interval Toby's silver head appeared and he climbed out, looking like a thundercloud. He was closely followed by a disconsolate Alex, sweat beading his brow and running down his face. As he reached ground level he let out a quivering sigh of relief. "Any luck?" she demanded.

"Not a bloody thing," Toby growled. "But it *has* to be there, it just *has* to be. What do you want? What's so damned urgent?"

"It's Carmella—she's here. She was right under our noses the whole time. I need you to get a statement from her."

They gaped at her. "Incredible!" Toby exploded. "Have you told the police?"

"No, and I don't think I'm going to either until we've heard what she has to say," she said firmly. "It occurs to me that she may be our ace in the hole. If Scorsi and Company are mixed up in this and have Sonya, we may be able to use Carmella as a lever to make them let Sonya go, or at least keep her alive until we can come up with something else. So let's get to it!"

They hurried back to the house and crowded into the kitchen. "If the phone rings or anyone arrives, Alex, you can run interference for us," his mother said. "It's important we are not disturbed, so, if summoned, you don't know anything about anything, right?"

"Right," he agreed.

They settled around the kitchen table with the two women, who looked at them with awe-stricken expectancy. "You tell the milord *inglese* everything," Rosa prompted in a whisper. "He understands us very well."

Carmella's rosy cheeks became even redder as they gazed at her, and she began to talk rapidly. Her accent was even thicker than her aunt's and Penny could only make out the occasional recognizable word as she gabbled on. Toby calmly took notes and from time to time interjected a question. Finally, the stream of confidences faltered and stopped, and Carmella gazed at them wide-eyed.

"Well?" Penny demanded of the grim-faced Toby, who gathered up his notes and cleared his throat. "It gives us something, but not quite what we anticipated," he said maddeningly. "I'll give you the outline and then if you can think of any questions, I'll put them to her. Although I think she understands English well enough, she just can't communicate in it too well."

"Do get on with it!"

"All right, all right! I'm trying to put it chronologically," he growled. "She was hired by Pietro Vanni three years ago. Gabriella Vanni was living at the villa with him and there was a cook and two other maids, Carmella being the low maid on the totem pole in the servant hierarchy. The count used to visit Gabriella there every day. For a short period of time—presumably after the contessa moved out—he actually stayed at the villa. Then, last summer they all cleared out back to the palazzo. The cook was fired, but the maids went with them. He rented the villa for six months to some rich South Americans who brought their own staff. Gabriella came back after they left, bringing Carmella and another maid, but she only breakfasted there and had her other meals at the palazzo. According to Carmella, she was furious with Pietro and Scorsi when the villa was rented out to Margo Demerest and she had to move out again. This time Carmella was left behind as maid-of-all-work. . . ."

"I don't see the point of all this," Penny said fretfully.

"You will in a minute if you'll just let me get on with it," Toby snapped. "I've gone into all this detail because Giovanni's part in this is interesting. He apparently had a thing going with the cook. . . ." He glanced apologetically at the impassive Rosa. "So while she was still there, he was always hanging around and, since the cook was a great gossip, knew all that was going on in the Scorsi family. When the cook was fired, they no longer saw him, not even when they returned to the villa. Then, just before Gabriella moved out for Margo, he started to hang around again; this time apparently very much in company with Pietro Vanni, who spent a lot of time with him *in* the garden, where Carmella thought Giovanni was picking up some extra money by moonlighting as a gardener. And it was at this time she noticed her uncle-by-marriage was not using the front gate but was coming in by the door between the gardens." He looked significantly at Penny.

At that juncture the phone rang and Alex quietly got up and went out. "And on two occasions Carmella saw Pietro coming in through that gate from this side," Toby went on. "Now this continued right up to the time of our arrival. Then she did not see Giovanni again. But here is where it really gets interesting. *After* Margo had been here several weeks and just after Giovanni stopped his visits, Gabriella made a special trip to the villa to see Carmella. She questioned her closely about Margo's timetable and habits and seemed disturbed when Carmella reported that Margo was not in the habit of taking sleeping pills. Gabriella then confided in her that she hoped to have a secret rendezvous with someone she cared greatly about at night in the villa and did not want anyone to know about this. She asked Carmella to help her. It is evident the girl is devoted to her, so she was flattered by this and said yes.

Her part, initially, was purely passive—if she heard or saw anyone in the house or grounds she just had to turn a deaf ear and a blind eye. This she did."

He paused to light up his pipe. "But then Gabriella came again—always, I may add, when Margo was away—and spun Carmella another tale about how she was terrified that Margo might find out about her assignations and tell Count Scorsi. This. . ." he consulted his notes, "was *after* Margo had made her panic-stricken night call to the count. She then asked Carmella to feed Margo sleeping pills in the cup of tea she always took before retiring to ensure her silence. Carmella was scared by this but she did agree, as Gabriella promised her that after Margo left Carmella would be her own personal maid from then on. Gabriella gave her this large bottle of sleeping pills with instructions for their use and that is the last time Carmella saw her. However, when it came to *giving* Margo the pills in the tea, Carmella was too frightened to do so, and she just took the right number of pills out each day and flushed them down the sink. She says she could not see the sense of it, because she did not hear the noises in the house at night anymore so concluded Gabriella was meeting her lover elsewhere. Besides, she liked Margo and was afraid of harming her. . . ."

Alex came back in and they looked enquiringly at him, but he shook his head and said, "Later . . . go on, Toby."

"We then come to Giovanni's murder and I think that when she heard of that Carmella started to put two and two together and became really frightened. The day we visited, while Margo and Andrew and I went over the house, she apparently eavesdropped on you and Margo and, when she heard Margo's version, became even more alarmed at what she might be mixed up in. She was later even more confused when Margo came to her—they did not communicate too well—and said if *she* was not around for a few days Carmella should not be worried, but then told her her husband was due to arrive. Now this Carmella did not understand at all, and was further upset when Pietro paid her a visit very early one morning, demanded the sleeping pills, which he checked carefully, and seemed very displeased with her. So, after he left, she decided she was too scared to stay at the villa, packed her things and just came around here to her aunt." He stopped and looked meaningfully at Penny. "Obviously there are further things to discuss, but not here and now. Have you any further questions for her?"

Penny was quietly dismayed, for it was not at all what she had hoped for. "Yes—three. One—was there anyone besides Pietro and Gabriella who came to the villa in Margo's absence or had anything to do with Giovanni there?"

Toby rapidly translated and Carmella answered just as quickly. "There was one man who came several times when Giovanni was there. She did not know who he was."

"Describe Krantz and ask if it was he," Penny said eagerly, but again she was disappointed. "No, she thought he was a workman of some kind. He always came in a gray panel truck, but she thought it strange he did not park by the kitchen as other workmen did. He always parked in front of the house and seemed very familiar with Pietro Vanni."

"The bald man with the beard I saw at Krantz's place!" Penny exclaimed. "Ask her." And this time the answer was yes. She let out a sigh of relief. "At least that's a link. Second, did she ever sneak back to the villa after she had come here?" This time the answer was no.

"And the third?" Toby queried.

"The key, of course! She *has* to have that other key."

"By God, yes!" His face lit up as he turned back to Carmella, who nodded timidly and undid the top button of her blouse and lifted a key on a thin metal chain from around her neck. She handed it to him and he shot a triumphant look at Alex. *"Now* we are getting somewhere—though we'll have to wait for nightfall to be on the safe side."

"There's one other thing I don't understand," Penny said slowly. "Why didn't she attend Giovanni's funeral or come to the wake here afterwards?"

This time it was Rosa who spoke up. "I tell you that. Is why she got more frightened and *I* got frightened for her. The count he call her and say she not to go. That he no want it known she kin of man who gets murdered. Bad for family name. If she go he threaten to fire her without reference—and that very bad here."

Penny felt a little surge of triumph. "So the count is on the scene at last," she breathed. "It's not much, but it's something."

"Anything else?" Toby was getting impatient.

She thought for a minute. "Yes. Ask her if she knows where Gabriella has her hair done, how often and at what time."

The men gaped at her as if she had gone out of her mind, but Carmella muttered at Rosa, who said, "She go to Salvatore in the Piazza di Spagna, Wednesday and Friday, usually at 10 AM. If something special, she go other times too."

"In the name of heaven, what on earth do you want to know that for?" Toby spluttered.

"Oh, I was thinking it is time I had my hair done," Penny said blandly.

He got up with a snort and collected his notes. "I'll have to get this statement typed up for Carmella to sign." He sighed heavily. "For once I wish Ada Phipps were here; it will take me forever."

"I'll type if you dictate," Alex volunteered with a faint grin. "One of my many skills—if you don't mind a few typos here and there."

"Good man!" his father-in-law approved.

"Just a moment." Penny interrupted their exodus. "I think we should make some plans about Carmella first." She looked over at Rosa. "On second thought, I am not sure that sending her back home just now is such a good idea. If this is as serious as we think it is and the people at the palazzo know where she is from, her home might not be all that safe. How about your aunt in Naples? Could she put her up for a time until this thing is resolved? We would be glad to pay for the trip and her board."

Rosa looked at her with a worried frown. "You think it very serious then?"

"Yes, I do. In fact I think Carmella saved her own life when she got out of the villa, or she may have suffered the same fate as Margo Demerest. Giovanni knew too much about their business and I'm certain that's why he was killed. Now *she* knows too much."

"Then I fix it with my aunt," Rosa said grimly. "She is all alone so will be glad of the company, but we accept the fare—*grazie,* signora. And you no tell the *polizia?*"

"Not just yet—later. And I'm sure her statement will be all they care about." Penny reassured her. "So you go ahead and make the arrangements and, when she has signed the statement and we all have witnessed it, I think *you* should take her and stay a few days yourself. All right?" The men went out.

"You can manage here?" Rosa said doubtfully.

"We'll manage. You telephone me here in two days' time and we can make other arrangements then." Penny was relieved that there would be one less person to worry about. "By the way, were *you* aware of any of this—about Giovanni, I mean?"

Rosa looked down and shrugged. "A little. He tell me he get good job on the side and to cover for him if the Redditches ask. But as long as he did his work here, they no ask." She colored. "He buy me nice big television and other things I want, so I no question him. I did not know about next door until Carmella say it."

"When he was gone over that period when the Redditches

left and we arrived, did you have any idea where he was? Was he next door then?"

Rosa's color deepened but she shook her head. "No, I ask Carmella but she say no. I thought he was off with some woman. It had happened before. Now I think maybe he go somewhere out of Roma, because I look everywhere. He very excited when he get back, but then *multo agitato* about you. For many days he very upset, then, just before he get killed, he seemed very pleased about something. He say we get more money very soon."

"I see, well, thank you, Rosa." The phone began to ring and she jumped up. "I'll get it."

It was Andrew. "I'm all free and clear. When do we start?"

In the excitements of the morning she had forgotten all about him. "Goodness, well, fine! But I'm going to be tied up here for a while." She thought quickly. "I tell you what. Would you be free to take me out to Albano, say early this evening about seven? I could show you Krantz's place and I could fill you in on the way as to what's been happening."

"Sure thing," he agreed. "I've kept one of the company cars, and there are still a few things I have to clear up, so that will be fine. See you at seven."

The men returned with the statement, which Carmella, looking very pleased with her own importance, signed laboriously and they all signed as witnesses. "Shouldn't we at least tell Morelli that she's been found?" the law-abiding Toby said, when aunt and niece had gone off to pack and Alex had gone in search of a copying machine to make duplicates.

"No, not yet," and Penny told him what she had in mind.

"Perhaps you're right. I've no desire to get further involved with him, at least not until Alex and I have had a crack at the catacomb next door tonight." He seemed relieved. "You realize that her statement, while involving the Vannis to some extent, still does not give us anything *concrete* on Scorsi?"

"Only too well. Which is why I thought I'd have a crack at

Gabriella as soon as I can. Hence the hairdresser's—I can't think of any other way of getting at her by herself. This really is the most confounded situation, where we can't even get *near* our suspects to question them!"

"But that might affect Sonya! Have you considered that?" he said in alarm.

"Of course I have. But it may take some time to bring this about, and I imagine your exploration tonight might give us some idea of what happened to her." They looked at each other in grim silence.

"Yes, I'm afraid it might," he said heavily. "Very much afraid . . ."

Chapter 15

As Andrew drove through the deepening twilight towards the still discernible outlines for the Alban Hills, Penny relaxed a little as she described the events of her hectic day. While she had been seeing off Carmella and her aunt at the station, Toby and Alex, now with the villa all to themselves, and to while away the time before dark and their assault on the Villa Scorsi, had made another sortie into the catacomb. This time they—or rather Alex—had made a very unexpected discovery; one that had confused the situation even further.

To keep his claustrophobia within bounds he found it best to take a break every fifteen minutes and go back to the opening for a breath of fresh air. During one of such breaks he had been moodily kicking at the red earth beside the narrow stairway when, suddenly, a section had crumbled to reveal a gaping dark hole beyond. Toby had been hastily summoned and they had cleared away an opening big enough to crawl through. Their lights had revealed a narrow passage dug through the soft tufa that ended abruptly ten yards beyond the staircase. There was nothing in the passage or its encompassing walls.

"What the hell!" Toby had exploded in exasperation. "This

can't be part of the original catacomb, it is a *recent* tunnel, but why, in God's name, is it going in *this* direction, away from the villas? We must be just about under the wall that divides us from whatever lies on the *other* side, but I haven't the faintest idea of what that is. I suppose it's not that important because this thing doesn't go anywhere, but we'd better find out all the same."

"If we had a long enough ladder, we could look over the wall," Alex had suggested.

They could only find a short ladder, but it had been enough to allow Alex, who topped Toby's six feet by two inches, to peer over the top of the wall into what lay beyond. All it revealed was more dense shrubbery and the sight of a very large red-roofed villa at some distance beyond.

"We'd better find out who owns that," Toby had said grumpily. "Not that it probably matters a damn, but at least it is something else to show Morelli eventually to prove the catacomb *was* being used for some kind of covert activity."

They had closed up the entrance and taken a stroll along the Antica, but their only reward was another pair of massive iron gates with an untenanted gatehouse beyond. "Hmmph," Toby sniffed, gazing at the heraldic shields that surmounted the gates. "For what it's worth, those are Borgese arms—not that that means necessarily this is still Borgese property. Anyway, it's not worth bothering about now; we've more important things to think about." And they had returned to the villa to make preparations for their clandestine exploration.

None of this, as Penny related it, made much impression on the preoccupied Andrew, but when it came to Carmella's revelations his interest was aroused, and he listened absorbedly until she had to interrupt her recital to direct him through Albano to the Krantz villa. As before, they parked at the lookout at the crater's edge. "Now what?" Andrew demanded.

"Now nothing," she rejoined. "I'm afraid this is going to be a pretty dull job for you, but I wouldn't ask if I didn't think it was important. I don't think it's any use trying to tackle Krantz directly, unless you can think of some brilliant cover story—which I confess I can't. But it would be useful to know who comes to the villa and, if Krantz goes out, to follow him and see where he goes."

"Won't I stick out if I park here for hours on end?"

"I've thought of that, but unless someone is actually at the gates you can't see this spot from the villa, and by day there are a lot of tourists coming and going. But I thought, as extra cover, you might want to bring along a camera or a sketchpad and pretend to be taking in the view. He's the only one who is likely to notice you, and I've described him so if he does pick up on you, you can always drive around a bit and come back. Is any of your company left here who could spell you?"

"I could probably get hold of some of the Italian extras who were on the movie. They've been laid off, so they'd be glad of any extra money. Anyway, for the moment I'm fine, let's see how it breaks." He was restive. "Finish what you were telling me about Carmella and the villa."

At the end of her story he sat in silence for some time. Finally he broke his silence, his voice heavy with grief. "Everything about this has been so *damned* ironic. If Carmella had not been so considerate of Margo and had fed her those sleeping pills as ordered, Margo might still be alive."

"How so?" Penny was astonished at this response.

"Because there was a very good reason why she *didn't* take pills of any kind: she reacted violently to them. So if she *had* been fed a couple, we would have known at once that something very odd was going on. It probably would have put her in the hospital. In fact, being unaware of this, they may not have meant to kill her at all, just to keep her quiet. But even a couple of barbiturates on top of all the alcohol she had that night at the party may have been enough to kill her."

"How dreadful!" she murmured, as Andrew choked up and

she could see the glint of tears on his cheeks in the light of the newly risen moon.

"Margo was a great believer in Fate, you know," he went on after a while. "She was always going on about it—one thing for sure, the Fates were certainly all against her this time." He heaved a quivering sigh and said in a more controlled voice, "What you've just told me puts a few dents in your own theory, doesn't it?"

"How do you mean?"

"I'd say it lets the count off the hook. What if Gabriella was telling the truth? What if she was meeting someone—a lover—at the villa, and that's what all the flim-flam was about? It wouldn't be the first time a young attractive mistress cheated on an older, rich man—it's one of the tritest themes in the movies."

"But who? And how about Pietro? He's involved also."

"You may have a joker in the deck—Mr. X. And you said yourself Pietro had pimped her once before, maybe he was at it again."

"No, that doesn't make sense," Penny said firmly. "There are too many other things. . . ."

He gripped her arm suddenly. "Look! There's something coming down the drive of the villa." And she looked up to see two bright headlights illuminating the gates and a shadowy figure opening them.

"Whoever it is, we'll follow them," she breathed. "Start the car, but don't follow too closely."

When the car swung out of the gates, she could see it was the white Lamborghini. "That's Scorsi's car!" she said excitedly. "If it goes to the Palazzo, we'll know we're on to something. We have to see who's driving it."

They followed at a discreet distance as it swung onto the Via Appia Nuova and sped back towards Rome. "Well, thank God it's not headed for the Villa Scorsi!" she said. "Is there any way you can cut through and get to the Palazzo Scorsi ahead of it?"

"I can give it a damn good try," Andrew replied and accelerated to a breakneck speed. They got to the Corso, which was already lively with its usual nighttime bustle, but miraculously found a parking spot in a side street half a block from the palazzo and scurried off towards it. The white car was already before the wooden gates of the palace, its horn honking, and as they approached, the massive gates swung open and it drove into the courtyard. Before the gates shut they caught a glimpse of the driver—it was Gabriella.

"How about Krantz for Mr. X?" Andrew enquired.

"Unless she has a penchant for sadists, I'd think that would be highly unlikely," Penny sniffed. "I'm sure her business with him has nothing to do with affairs of the heart; more likely she was acting as go-between for the count."

"So we're back to the count again. Well, what now? I don't know about you, but I'm starved, I haven't had dinner yet. Since we're downtown, how about joining me and then I'll drop you off at the villa and go on back to my vigil," Andrew said.

"I did have a bite earlier, but I can always eat," she said, and they sought out a nearby taverna and settled at a table.

"How long should I stand guard?" he asked, after they had ordered.

"Oh, *I* don't know." Penny was fretful. "I feel as if I'm wading through molasses on this one; nothing seems to be breaking as it should. If nothing happens out there before midnight I should pack it in and start again in the morning. It would help, though, if you could find someone to spell you, so that we get a continual surveillance going."

"I can try to work something out tomorrow. I should be able to hang on here for three or four more days. Then it's back to Tinsel Town for me."

She cheered slightly as an appetizing *spaghetti vongole* was placed before her and Andrew poured her a glass of Chianti. "Well, let's hope Toby and Alex will turn up something positive tonight. I wonder how they are getting on. . . ."

To Sir Tobias Glendower it had seemed as if darkness would never come as, preparations complete, his son-in-law paced restlessly up and down like a hungry tiger. "Shouldn't we take some kind of weapons along?" Alex asked. "If by some miracle Sonya is still there and alive, wouldn't they have someone on guard?"

"I'm not much of a weapons man myself," Toby returned. "But if it would make you feel better, we could take a wrench and a tire iron from the tool kit in the car."

He had managed to restrain his anxious companion until the dim street lights of the Antica had been on for a full half-hour when he deemed it dark enough to make a start, and they slipped through the shadows by the wall until they reached the villa's iron gates. There was no light at the gate, as Toby opened it with the precious key, nor in the driveway beyond. To be on the safe side, like his daughter before him, Toby ducked into the bushes and illumined their path with a penlight. They advanced cautiously until they were in sight of the villa which stood in absolute darkness, not so much as a chink of light showing through its shuttered windows.

Toby straightened up with a relieved sigh. "Looks deserted, thank God! Still, we may as well keep to the bushes as long as possible." He shined the penlight down again and Alex grabbed his arm. "Look there!" Imprinted in the soft earth was the outline of a pair of woman's high-heeled shoes. "You think those are Sonya's?" Toby asked.

"I'm damned sure of it." Alex's voice was choked. "Who but a crazy Russian ballerina would go exploring a catacomb in high heels?"

They skirted the dog pen and then ventured on to the narrow pathway that ran to the bottom of the garden. Toby extinguished the penlight, for the moon had just risen and there was enough light to make their way by. The line of statues awaited them like a silent phalanx of sentinels as they advanced on the greenhouse. Toby tried the door, but it was locked. "Damn!" he sighed. "We'll just have to break in. Here, hold the light while I pry it open with the tire iron."

"No, let me. I think if I put my shoulder to it I can bust it in," Alex declared and proceeded to hurl himself at it. The flimsy lock gave with a crack that sounded like the Trumpet of Doom, and they waited for several seconds, their ears straining to find if it had aroused a living sentinel; but there was nothing.

Toby went in first and shined the light around, kicking aside burlap bags that were scattered about the earthen floor. "Ah!" he exclaimed, as the flagstone with its iron rings was revealed. "Just as I expected."

As Alex focused the penlight, he heaved away at the two iron rings: nothing happened. They swopped places, but while Alex heaved with all his young might still there was no sign of movement from the stone. "Damnation," Toby muttered. "There must be some trick to this just like the one next door, but what can it be?" They searched the greenhouse for a clue but there was nothing. Toby shined the light around the whole perimeter of the stone and pondered. Finally he said, "Let's try it another way. If you stand on the side here, take the rings and lift them *towards* you. If it's anything like the one next door it will require a sharp jerk."

Alex bent down and did his bidding: noiselessly the stone lifted on its long side and stood upright, and the thin beam of light revealed a larger, but otherwise identical, staircase that led into the lower blackness. Toby heaved a sigh of relief. "Well, stage one complete. Keep your eyes peeled now; stage two may be ticklish if there is anyone down there, because we'll have to use the bigger light. I'll lead the way. . . ." He launched himself down the steps. Alex took a deep breath and followed after him.

At the bottom of the steps Toby shined the flashlight back towards the Redditch villa and it showed a passage lined by sealed tombs and ended in an identical monument to the one backed up to it on the other side. He turned it in the opposite direction and here the passage, again lined by sealed tombs, continued on into darkness. He focused the beam on the floor and pointed silently—it was a maze of overlapping footprints.

Alex knelt down and examined them anxiously. "It doesn't look as if Sonya got this far," he muttered. "No sign of high heels."

Toby forbore to point out the obvious ominous explanation, moving ahead along the passage instead. A black opening to the left was revealed as a small chapel with an altar and some wall paintings much eroded by damp, but no sign of occupancy. Then the end of the passage disappeared into a wider area of blackness and they hurried forward until their lights illumined a much larger chamber with decorated walls which, while disappointingly empty of life, showed evident signs of recent habitation. There was a carboy of water in one corner and several open, empty wooden boxes standing on the marble tabletop in the center that was surrounded by stone benches. Toby hurried on towards a wider flight of stairs in a small atrium beyond and shined his light upward. "The main entrance," he breathed. "And, damn it to hell, it's blocked, and long ago by the looks of it!" for the light revealed a jumble of masonry and crumbled cement blocks halfway up the stairs. But Alex's light discovered another smaller staircase beyond the main one that led in a counter-direction downwards. Toby made for it, but Alex said in a voice choked with bitter disappointment, "She's not here. I've got to get some air," and he fled back towards the opening.

The narrow stairway was long, and Toby deduced that it led all the way from the first to the third level and must therefore be a later addition to the original catacomb. When he reached the passage, it, too, revealed sealed tombs on either side but after some twenty yards the bunklike tiers yawned empty and untenanted. On the floor were more footprints and the impression in the deep dust of more boxes. Skirting the footprints carefully, he shined his light into the untenanted tiers, dread choking him, but to his intense relief they revealed nothing. He reached the end of the passage where a simple and lidless marble sarcophagus was backed up to the red earth wall. As he shined the light within, something glinted and he picked it out—it was a deep purple rhinestone attached to a scrap of silver leather. He closed his eyes for a second, conjuring up a mental image, then let out a breath of relief. "The shoes . . ." he murmured. "Margo's silver sandals. They were decorated with purple stones." Sadly he stored his find away in one of the glassine envelopes he had brought with him and made his way slowly back as he examined the floor. Just at the base of the stair something grayish-white stood out against the red earth and he picked it up and peered at it. "Part of a fuse?" he queried, and stowed that away also.

He entered the big chamber just as Alex came in from the other side. "Anything?" the latter asked huskily.

"No sign of Sonya, no," Toby evaded.

Alex slumped onto a stone bench and buried his face in his hands. "Oh, God, what can they have done with her? Where can she be?"

Toby's hand hovered over his shoulder and then drew back. "No use giving up like this. We have to search this place thoroughly," he said. "We may find some clue. You take the right side and I'll take the left, but if you find anything don't touch it, just call me."

The young man stumbled obediently to his feet and they separated. Toby's search quickly yielded some cigarette butts which he stowed away, a scrap of newspaper and some wisps of packing straw, but he was interrupted by an exclamation

170

from Alex, who was in the corner opposite the carboy of water. "Here!" he summoned. "Sonya *was* here—look!"

Toby looked at what his trembling finger indicated—almost covered by the dust were two fine black hairpins. "She sheds them like porcupine quills wherever she goes," Alex quavered. Toby gingerly picked them up and his quick eye picked up white residue on the prongs of one. He looked at it, then at the white plaster wall behind, decorated with a repetitive design of foliage, floral garlands and doves. He let out a soft exclamation and bent closer to the white band that ran between the floor and the design. "And, by the Lord, she's left a message of sorts—bless her clever little heart!" He whipped out his notebook and started to copy down the faint scratches, as Alex looked dazedly at him. "Her hands were evidently tied so she did not have much control."

"What does it say?" Alex muttered, gazing at the apparently meaningless graffiti Toby was scribbling down.

"Well, it begins with D and G in Russian. I suppose she did not dare try an S for Sonya or Spring because it is the same as ours and they might have noticed it. The D for Danirova, the G for Glendower. Then it looks like she scratched two crenellated towers, though one is very faint, and then . . ." his voice deepened in puzzlement, ". . . a minus sign, a stick figure of a man, and the initial P in Russian and what looks like a solid V with a halo over it and between them two semi-circles. . . ."

"Could it be PV—Pietro Vanni?" Alex hazarded.

"Possibly, but I don't *think* so," Toby said thoughtfully. "She could more easily have put Pietro into Russian. No, I'll have to think about this. It may be connected with the other notes she and I were going over previously." He looked at Alex's ashen face. "We've got enough, I think. Let's get out of here."

They made their way out, resealed the catacomb and covered their tracks in the greenhouse. "Even if they spot the broken lock, they may think we couldn't find our way in," Toby muttered as he re-strewed the bags over the floor. "But I doubt whether they'll be back here. It looks to me as if they've packed it in and moved their operations elsewhere. The big question is where. If I can only figure out what Sonya was trying to tell us maybe that will give us a lead."

As they hurried back through the garden, this time with Alex in the lead, Toby glanced over at the villa and stifled an exclamation. Light showed through a chink in the shutter of the far corner room of the second story—Margo's bedroom! Just as he looked, the light went out. He picked up his pace and came abreast of Alex, but decided to say nothing about it: in Alex's desperate frame of mind he would be likely to go storming into the villa and that, Toby knew, would not help the situation. Once outside with the gate relocked he relaxed slightly. "We'll get right back to those notes," he informed his tense companion. "Perhaps we can crack this thing tonight."

But as they entered the wooden door of the villa, the front door flew open and Penny ran towards them, her hair wild, her pixie-like face contorted with worry. "Oh, Toby," she gasped. "A man phoned for you some twenty minutes ago. I did not recognize the voice and he would not talk to me. He kept repeating that it has to be you and you only, and he said that, if you know what's good for you and yours, you will wait by the phone for his next call—he said it was about Sonya."

Chapter 16

The deep voice on the phone was muffled. "You listen, Sir Tobias Glendower, and you will do *exactly* what I tell you if you want your daughter back alive. You and all your party will leave Italy immediately. You will say nothing to anyone. You will proceed to Zurich. There you will stay at the Hotel du Lac and you will arrange to have fifty thousand pounds transferred to you in Switzerland. You will be contacted at the hotel with a number of an account in the Bank of Zurich on the Banhof Strasse and will deposit the money there. Once that is done your daughter will be released unharmed somewhere along the Italo-Swiss border. You will be told where. You or any of your party will *not* return to Italy. Do you understand me?"

Toby's blue eyes were like chips of ice as he listened. "I understand you all too well," he growled. "But if you think you can disguise your real designs with the pretense of a kidnapping for ransom you are much mistaken, and much too late. Now *you* listen to me. We have Carmella Dossi in a safe place, and a full statement from her that implicates you and your co-conspirators. We know about the new tunnel and the explosives. We know about the German and Arab connec-

tions. We know about the murders. In short, your whole plot
is blown wide open. So, now I tell *you* what I will do. If my
daughter is released unharmed in the next twelve hours I will
withhold this evidence from the police for sufficient time to
allow you and your accomplices to get out of Italy. It will be
no use going after me or my companions, because a full statement has already been lodged with the British Embassy, naming names *with* proof, and it has also been faxed through to
our Foreign Office in London. In other words, the jig is up,
and if you have any sense at all you will let my daughter go
and get out while you can. Furthermore, if the *least* harm
should come to her, I can assure you it will not be a question
of a mere fifty thousand pounds ransom, for I will pledge the
whole of my not inconsiderable fortune to the cause of tracking all of you down to the ends of the earth if need be and seeing you get what you so richly deserve for your crimes—and I
don't mean imprisonment; that would be much too good for
the likes of you."

There was silence at the other end and he held his breath,
praying his bluff would work, but when the man again spoke,
although there was little reassurance in his words, his voice
held far less certainty. "If that's your last word, you'll regret
it. I don't believe you and if you should carry out *any* of those
threats your daughter is a dead woman. But we will give you
some time to reconsider and be back in touch." The line went
dead.

Penny was staring at him, horror in her mild hazel eyes, for
she had heard only his end of the conversation. "Oh, Toby,
how could you?" she gasped. "To bluff at a time like this? To
let them know all the things we have discovered but for which
we have no proof? Wouldn't it have been better to play along
with them—to do what they say and then, once Sonya is safe,
to take it from there?"

He shook his head, his own eyes stricken. "No. You heard
Morelli on the subject of terrorists and I agree with him abso-

lutely. You cannot *bargain* with terrorists. If I had said yes, it would have only been the beginning of their demands, not the end, and there would still have been no guarantee of Sonya's safety. In fact, we have to face the unpleasant possibility she may already be dead. They did not waste much time getting rid of Margo, did they?"

"But, as Andrew said, that *could* have been an unforeseen accident," she spluttered.

Toby ignored that and went on. "I am banking on the fact that Sonya is *not* dead. I feel that she isn't, though that may be wishful thinking on my part. And if she isn't, well, now it is in their best interests to keep her alive for use as a bargaining tool. They wanted us out of Italy and completely off the scene: that means they haven't given up their plans and may still have had hopes of using the villas. We are *not* leaving the scene, so they'll have to alter their plans—whatever those were. We have just got to find out where she is before they put those plans into action." He picked up the phone again.

"Who are you calling now?" she said in alarm.

"Morelli—I won't tell him the whole thing, but I *have* to tell him some of it," Toby said grimly. "Especially about that tunnel. Then I'll call Barham directly. *He* should know everything, just in case they really don't believe me and go after us anyway—they might, you know." He cocked a silver eyebrow at her. "Would you like to get out and take Alex with you? I can manage and it might be safer."

"Oh, don't be utterly absurd! Of course I'm staying! And do you think wild horses would drag Alex away with Sonya in peril?" she cried, then pulled herself together with an effort. "However . . . I don't think we'd better tell him about the substance of that phone call. It would only further upset him. Maybe I'd better go and see how he's getting on."

"Good idea. Better you than me," he said and started to dial.

She went back to the study, where they all had been going

through the notes for clues to Sonya's graffiti. She found her son gazing fixedly ahead of him in despondent contemplation. "Any luck?" she enquired brightly. He roused with a guilty start. "No, nothing. Can't make head nor tail of it."

Penny went around to his side of the desk and placed a comforting hand on his broad shoulder. "You know it's absolutely no *use* brooding and worrying about this, darling. It's not helping Sonya one little bit," she said softly. "You have to have more faith in her. Sonya is a very clever girl and a born survivor, in my judgment. She's been in some tight spots before and wriggled out of them, as we well know. We know she's alive and is doing all *she* can to help."

"That's the most damnable part," he groaned. "*Do* we know that?"

"According to that phone call she is," she said, hoping it was true. "So let's get back to work on the graffiti."

But he made no move to do so. He looked up at her. "Ma, I know you and Toby have been in some very tight spots and you've become used to it, but this is something very new to me. It's true I battle with death every single day in my work, but that is in my own setting and on terms with which I'm familiar. This isn't. How do you manage to handle it so well?"

"Well, by getting on with whatever *can* be got on with to get us out of the fix is the main thing and, when the going gets really tough—and this may come as a surprise to you—I pray a lot," she said drily. "I find that very helpful."

This elicited a grim chuckle. "Yes, that does surprise me." He picked up some papers. "So, in short, I'd better quit stalling and get on with my homework—right?"

"Right," she smiled.

Toby rejoined them looking somewhat relieved. "I talked to Barham and Morelli is on his way over," he announced. "Any progress?"

Penny had been scanning her copy of the graffiti, her face wrinkled up in thought. "I've had an idea about those last two

176

figures. She's indicating a man whose name begins with P, but who you don't believe can be Pietro Vanni, and I agree with your thinking. So suppose those last two scratches are not what they seem, but an effort on her part, granted her restricted movement, to indicate what the man was *like*."

"I don't follow you," Toby said.

"Just suppose that solid V is not a V at all and the halo not a halo. Suppose it is this. . . ." She hastily sketched what she had in mind and held it up to them. She had drawn a face with a black beard and a bald head. "And we know such a man is involved—the man I saw with Krantz, the man with the gray panel truck, whom we know from Carmella was also connected with the Villa Scorsi."

"And those two semi-circles would be her attempt to indicate a face? Hmm, could be," Toby mused. "Though it's stretching things a bit."

"You don't suppose she was trying to indicate St. Paul?" Alex put in, for he had been fully indoctrinated by his mother as to the significance of the portraits from the catacomb.

Penny's face lit up with excitement. "That's it!" she exclaimed. "Pietro and Paulo! That's who the third man must be. It all makes a heap of sense. The *third* Vanni—the brother Cordelia didn't know anything about, Paulo Vanni. I did see a resemblance but I couldn't place it. But, damn it, he *is* something like Pietro."

"You may have something there, though I'm not sure where that gets us . . ." Toby began, when the phone summoned again and with an exclamation of annoyance he went to answer it. In a moment he was back. "Andrew—for you," he announced to Penny and she hurried out.

"I hit on something last night, but it was so late by the time I finished I didn't want to bother you." Andrew sounded excited. "A large dark car—I've got the number—came to the villa. The driver was a gray-haired man. When he left there was another man in the passenger seat that I think was Krantz.

I followed them back to Rome and they went into the Libyan Embassy. They drove into the courtyard so I still couldn't see clearly who they were. I waited until—oh, well after midnight—and was just about to pack it in when the car left and I followed it back to Krantz's place. Any good?"

"Yes, great; something to pass on to Morelli, who is due here any second. He can trace the number of the car and can find out who the gray-haired man is. Pity you can't say positively it was Krantz, but a clandestine after-hours visit to an embassy we know is hostile to the Western powers should be enough to spark Morelli's interest. Are you back at Albano now?"

"No, I got hold of a couple of extras I know who live near Albano, and they've agreed to keep an eye on things and spell me. They're good guys. All I told them was we thought Krantz might be a Nazi war criminal with modern Fascist leanings, so that interested them—one's a Christian Democrat and the other's a Communist, so neither are very fond of the Fascists. They are going to note the comings and goings and do the following bit if necessary. Any luck on Sonya?"

"A little. She wasn't next door, but we're pretty sure she's alive and are working on where she might be now. Want to come around here later and I'll fill you in?"

"I don't know when I'll be free." His exuberance was gone. "They are releasing Margo's body to me today, so I'll be tied up making arrangements for shipping the casket back to California. I'll call you back when I'm through."

The doorbell pealed. "Yes, do that. I have to go," Penny said hastily. "Morelli has just arrived."

The saturnine countenance of the tall inspector was a complex of emotions; anger and concern struggling with excited interest, as she opened the door to him and ushered him through to the study. "Sir Tobias," he rasped, "I must see that tunnel immediately. You have no idea how serious this matter has become. We will discuss your other findings later."

"You realize there is nothing *in* the tunnel except foot-prints, nor does it go anywhere," Toby said mildly as he led them down the garden. "But, if the footprints are of interest to you, we did try to disturb them as little as possible."

Morelli's only answer was a preoccupied grunt. As Toby opened up the entrance, Alex said, "I think I'll pass on this one if you don't need me. I'll go back to the house and ride herd on the phone."

"I'll stay up here too," Penny added, "I've sort of lost track but I think this is the gardener's day to come and so I'll steer him away from here if he does."

It was Toby's turn to grunt as he turned on the big flash-light and the two tall figures disappeared into the bowels of the earth. They crawled through the low opening and Toby shined the light on the solid walls and then the end of the pas-sage. "See, nothing," he murmured.

"I think you may have missed something," Morelli said tightly and stalked to the end. "Shine the light upwards." Toby did so and let out an exclamation, "By Jove, you're right!" for there was an opening carved out of the rock leading up from the tunnel.

"Just as I feared," Morelli said. "We are now standing un-der the garden of the villa belonging to Prince Borgese. I imagine there are only a few inches to break through at the end of that opening. A few minutes' work and they'd have had a clear shot at the villa. There's little doubt about it now; we are dealing with terrorists—terrorists who are terrifyingly well informed."

"How does Prince Borgese come into this?" Toby was puzzled.

"He doesn't directly, but this was supposedly one of the deepest secrets of the upcoming conference: the prince put his villa at the disposition of the heads of state of Italy, France, Germany and the United Kingdom for the duration of the con-ference. They are scheduled to have their first unofficial meeting here in two days' time. Naturally, we were all set to guard the gates and the perimeter, and there would have been a couple of guards on the outer door of the villa itself but, since these mini-conferences are supposed to be so hush-hush, the heads of state wanted all this kept to a minimum for obvious reasons. Hah!" He gave a mirthless bark of laughter. "They'd have been in and out of the villa right under our noses. We owe you a great debt, Sir Tobias, you appear to have been right all along. And but for your unexpected presence here they would have accomplished their object."

"But all this is academic now," Toby protested. "They've obviously given up on it—they cleared out of here, presumably after Giovanni's murder, and now they have cleared out of the Scorsi villa, as I informed you."

"Have they?" Morelli's tone was doom-laden. "I doubt it. If they can't use this tunnel, they will undoubtedly try it some other way. Unless we can round them up first."

"Are you going to?" Toby demanded, his heart sinking.

"How can we without further proof? This is a democracy, remember? We can certainly keep a close eye on the Vannis, Scorsi and Krantz, and that might put a crimp in their activities, but we've no real idea how big their organization is, so it still might not stop them."

"If we could find my abducted daughter, that would give you the proof you need to haul them in," Toby said quietly. "Kidnapping is a major crime."

"Unfortunately, on that we have made no progress and haven't the faintest lead," Morelli returned.

"Ah, but *we* have, and I suggest we get back to the house and I'll show you what we have and what we have deduced thus far. You may be able to pinpoint her location right off the bat."

"If they have not already killed her and disposed of the body," Morelli pointed out grimly.

"I told you of the phone call. I believe there is still hope."

"And I hope you're right—let's go. But you realize that even if we find out where she is, at the first sign of movement on our part they still might kill her," Morelli said as they made their way back to the house.

"Or use her to barter their way out."

"You know as well as I do that we cannot do that—we don't barter with terrorists."

"Then I will just have to get to her first," Toby stated. "I think you owe us that much. If she is found, to let us have the time to get her out or at least to substitute myself as a hostage."

"And get yourself killed also?" Morelli snorted. "Time enough to discuss all this *if* we find her."

Toby showed him a copy of the graffiti and Morelli's strong brows knitted in perplexity as he muttered to himself in Italian, *"Uno castello? Una fortezza? Due torri?"*

"God, what a fool I am! That's it, that's probably what she heard, *'due torri'*," Toby exclaimed, making for a gazetteer of Italy. But, while an examination of its pages yielded several Due Torri, not one of them was in striking distance of Rome.

"There is a via delle Due Torri in greater Rome," Morelli volunteered. "It is just off the via Casalina going out into the countryside on the way to Forsinone." They looked at each other in sudden hope.

"Could you find out if any of the principals involved have any property there?" Toby demanded.

"Yes, come back with me to my office and we'll start checking—I have to make some arrangements to keep the Vannis under surveillance."

"My son-in-law should be in on this," Toby said firmly. "After all it was he who discovered the tunnel."

"If you insist, but he would be more useful here. I am going to send in one of my more trusted men to look at those footprints, to see if we can get a line on how many there were and their approximate sizes and so on. Your son-in-law could show him the way in and point out your footprints to him."

"Well, all right," Toby assented doubtfully, and hunting up Alex he explained Morelli's needs, omitting the new lead in the interests of speed. Penny was found in the garden communing with the aged gardener, and was explained to in her turn, and Morelli peremptorily insisted the gardener be paid off for the day. "You may return and finish your work here in two days' time," he said to the startled old man. "Police business concerning the murder of Giovanni Lippi."

"Shall I come along?" Penny asked.

"No, you stay here and get the phone. They may well call back," Toby replied. "This may be just a wild goose chase, but it's worth a try."

There was a short delay while Morelli located his technician and, after he had arrived, explained what was needed. The men departed in their several directions leaving Penny to her own devices. She wandered disconsolately back to the study and looked at Sonya's message again. *"Due torri,"* she murmured. "But what the hell could that minus sign mean? Near? Before?" She was electrified when she heard the front door open, and for a moment sat transfixed, her heart thudding. Finally, she nerved herself to get up and peer around the door into the hall: Rosa was bringing in two suitcases. "Rosa! What on earth are you doing back here?" she cried.

The dumpy little woman started with fright and gasped, "Oh, signora, I saw the car gone and thought you were all out. I come back. My place is here."

"But why didn't you call? And what about Carmella? This is not good." Penny was exasperated.

"Carmella is very well. She stay with my aunt and already my aunt find her a good job. She work for American Navy captain and his family—*multo simpatico, multo gentile,"* Rosa enthused. "No ask references. They not need me down there so I come back."

"But I told you it is not very safe here! The same people who killed Giovanni may strike again."

"Is why I came," Rosa said simply. "My Giovanni was not a very good man or a good husband, but he was mine, and they should not have killed him. You try and find out things about that and bad things happen to you, and now the poor young signora is missing. So I come back to help. You will tell me what to do?"

There was no point in sending her back now, Penny thought resignedly. "Oh, very well. I'm afraid you'll find things in a mess. We've been so busy."

"No problem." Rosa's face lit up. "I put my things away and go right to work. You no worry about the house, I do everything."

Penny was thinking fast. "Rosa, does the name *'Due Torri'* mean anything to you? Did Giovanni ever mention a name like that?"

Rosa looked blank for a second then brightened. "Ah, *Due Torri—si!* Not real name! Is . . ." Her English failed her, ". . . *nomignolo.*"

"*Nomignolo?*" Penny reached for her pocket dictionary, and her own face brightened. "Oh, it's a *nickname*—for what?"

"*Uno piccolo villagio sulla mare—Santa Maria di Alitura—in vicino Ostia Antica,*" Rosa gabbled. "Giovanni he go there sometimes for *la pesca*—fishing. I go there with him one time, oh, long ago."

"Was he there recently?"

"Two months ago he go for a little, but come back soon. No fish he said."

Penny was having a quiet brainstorm. "When you could not find him in Rome that time we talked about—could he have been there?"

Rosa shrugged. "Perhaps—I do not think of that. But why should he go there? He no take his fishing things."

"That's what we're going to find out." Penny was getting excited. "Would you show me the way? And have you a picture of Giovanni you could show around when we get there? This may be important, very important—it may help us find the young *signora*."

Rosa's dark eyes were bright with anticipation. "I fetch pictures—we go now?"

"Right away—we'll take the other car. I'll write a note to Sir Tobias while you get ready. *Santa Maria di Alitura* was it?"

"*Si*. I go." Rosa bustled away with her cases and came back clutching two photos—a wedding picture of the handsome young Giovanni and a thin, pretty Rosa peeking out under a white veil, and another more recent snapshot of Giovanni in the garden of the villa. "What we do with these?" she demanded.

"When we get there, you'll have to do the talking," Penny explained. "You say you look for him because he has disappeared. We'll try to find out who he knew in the village and where he stayed. We can make up some story to explain it all on the way. Are you sure you want to do this?"

"Very sure," Rosa said, her mouth set in a firm line. "We go after those bastards who kill him, eh?"

Chapter 17

The village of Santa Maria di Alitura did not live up to its mellifluous name, for it consisted of an unplanned huddle of fishermen's cottages down by the water, a couple of larger farmhouses standing at some remove from the village and several other buildings, either smaller farmhouses or more prosperous fishermen's cottages, that stood closer to the water, several sprouting their own little wooden piers. If the church of Santa Maria had given the village its name, it had long since disappeared, leaving behind the ruins of a bell tower in the middle of a field, and the only evidence of antiquity was the small two-towered fortress that stood dangerously close to the sea and on the side of the coast nearer to Ostia Antica. The whole of the hinterland was flat and marshy, and even the sandy beach had an eroded and unappetizing look to it.

"So we find it!" Rosa said brightly. This had not been without difficulty, for her memories of the route had been vague in the extreme and Penny had had to resort to the map that Alex had providentially left in the car. "What do we do first?"

"Maybe we should look at the fortress before we go into the village," Penny said, for she had spotted a sandy track winding off through the coarse marsh grass that led to it. They bumped down it as she remarked, "The village does not look very old."

"Oh, is very, very old," Rosa contradicted. "But many, many years was deserted. Malaria very bad here, Giovanni say. Then Mussolini he drain the marshes here, Ostia Antica, many, many places and then the people come back. No malaria here now."

As they drew up before the towers it was evident that the fortress was deserted; a huge rusted padlock sealed its weathered wooden gates and a faded wooden board on them warned that it was private property and trespassers would be prosecuted. Carved into the stone lintel above the door was an heraldic shield that elicited a flash of interest from Penny, for it bore a cardinal's hat that surmounted a field of Barberini bees, and this put her in mind of Lucia Scorsi. But it was obvious that the captive Sonya had not indicated this moldering ruin: the minus sign had to mean something else—the big question was what.

"Nothing here, so we'll get on to the village." Penny turned the car in the sandy expanse before the fortress, noting as she did so that there were no signs of any other car tracks. "Now, you must be very careful about what you say," she warned Rosa. "I won't be able to take any part in this."

"Oh, I think of very good story, you'll see." Rosa was visibly excited.

"Shall I stay in the car or come with you?"

"Oh, you come! I explain you very well." They drew up in what served as the center of town, an irregular expansion of the road that led down to the beach and which boasted a *taverna,* a tiny *groceria* and an even tinier *frutteria.* Penny noted with quiet relief that there appeared to be no news store, for the uneasy thought had come to her en route that the villagers might have seen the Roman papers and so were already aware that Giovanni was no longer in the land of the living.

Rosa, schooled by long years of looking for her husband, got out of the car and made straight for the taverna.

Pushing aside the multi-colored curtain of plastic strips that masked the open door, they walked into its dusky, wine-laden coolness, and as their eyes adjusted to the dimness they made out two patrons hunched over a checkerboard at one of the small plastic tables. The proprietor, heavily mustached and blank-eyed, stood stolidly behind the bar polishing glasses, and a frowzy-looking peroxide blonde leaned against the bar, her jaws moving rhythmically as she chewed gum and stared off into space. Rosa advanced purposefully to the bar, ordered a white Frascati for Penny and a Galliano for herself and then, leaning confidingly towards the proprietor, started her spiel. Luckily for Penny, the man was apparently deaf and also had almost as much trouble with Rosa's accent as she had herself, because he kept saying *"Che?"* and *"Come?"*, forcing Rosa to slow down and speak up, so that Penny could follow most of what was said and was duly amazed at Rosa's ready powers of invention, as she produced the photos and showed them to the barman.

The story as it unfolded was an ingenious one: her husband and she had had a terrible quarrel more than a month ago and he had gone off in a rage, and good riddance she had said at the time, but now there had arrived from America this widow of his uncle, who had died and left her Giovanni a legacy—a tidy sum. She had this big problem now, this aunt-in-law, who knew no Italian, had been instructed to give the money to him and no one else. She was a very suspicious woman, this aunt, so he had to be found. Could the barkeeper help her? If he could find her husband there would be something in it for him.

The barkeeper was evidently a man of slow thought, for he chewed on one end of his mustache and pondered over the picture. Yes, he admitted, he had seen this man, in fact he had stayed at the taverna. He had been fishing at Due Torri.

"Yes, yes—when?" Rosa said eagerly. But the taverna stay had been several months ago, and Penny's heart sank.

"But . . ." the man resumed, "he was here a month ago. Several nights he was here—a good customer, very."

"Where did he stay?" Rosa demanded.

"Not here," the man said stolidly. The barmaid, who had been following the conversation, had edged around to the inside of the bar and had sidled up to the proprietor. After inspecting Rosa from top to toe, her loose-lipped mouth curled in a sneer. She nudged the proprietor and whispered in his ear, then rolled up her eyes, giggled and turned away. "Maria here knows," he reported. "She says if you make it worth her while, she'll tell you."

Rosa did not miss a beat. "*Quanto?*—how much?" she demanded.

More whispering before he said, "Ask the American to give her forty dollars and she will tell."

"Twenty," Rosa said promptly. Maria turned to face her and nodded. Straight-faced, Rosa turned to Penny and said in English, "This girl say if you give her twenty dollars she will tell where Giovanni is—you may take it from his inheritance."

"He is here then?" Penny played along, opening her bag and grudgingly extracting a twenty-dollar bill, which she hung on to. "She will show us where?"

Rosa repeated what she had said, and something like alarm came into Maria's blank eyes as she said to Rosa. "I can only tell you where he was staying. I do not know if he is still there. For a month I do not see him."

Rosa eyed her suspiciously, plucked the bill from Penny's fingers and held it out to her but did not give up her hold on it. "You will tell us all you know and this is yours," she said.

"He stayed with Paulo Venturi—I show you the house," Maria gulped.

"Who is he?"

"*Uno artista commerciale,*" the proprietor put in. He

waved a proud hand at a garish poster behind the bar that showed a scantily clad blonde on an upturned boat and quaffing a Cinzano. "He did that for me, especially."

Maria had come out from behind the bar and was eyeing them nervously. "You will show us the house," Rosa said, handing over the bill. She nodded and went over to the door; as they followed her Penny managed to whisper to Rosa, "Ask her if this Paulo drives a gray panel truck."

Outside Maria pointed a fat red finger. "See the Due Torri? Follow the beach along towards the village. There, on that drainage canal, is the house of Paulo Venturi." It was one of the medium-sized houses and stood all by itself.

Rosa asked her question and was rewarded by a vigorous nod that sent Penny's hopes soaring. "*Si,* he drives a gray panel truck, but he is not here now. See, it is not there." Indeed, apart from a small motorboat moored at the wooden pier by the house, the place looked deserted with all its windows shuttered.

Further questioning of the increasingly reluctant Maria elicited the fact that, although she had not seen Giovanni, she had seen Paulo several times during the past month and she had also seen two other men with him outside the house. One of the men had come to the taverna and bought up a big supply of liquor. "It is all I can tell you," Maria said, darting back inside.

Rosa said, "Stay here" to Penny and went after her. She emerged in a few minutes and reported. "I ask the proprietor about the other man. He say they wanted the drink for a fishing expedition and that the man's name was Carlo."

"Carlo!" Penny exclaimed. "Could it be the count? Was he small, well dressed, gray-haired?"

Rosa shook her head. "No, I ask what he look like. He was big and fat with a red face. And I find out this Paulo Venturi came to the house six months ago, and say he was an *artista.* We go to this house?"

"Let's go back to the car and think a bit. You were great in there, Rosa."

Rosa grinned widely, then sobered as they walked back to the car. "I bet that cow was one of his women," she muttered as they got back in.

Penny sat behind the wheel and thought. It all fitted so well: Paulo Venturi *had* to be Paulo Vanni, and Sonya's minus sign now made sense. Quickly she got out a notepad and made a rough sketch of the location, including the track that wound out to the deserted house. "I think," she said, "that we have done all we can safely do by ourselves. If the young signora is in that house, she will be well guarded, so we shall have to go back to Rome and get help." She looked in despair at the locale, for there was not a scrap of cover for any surprise raid on the house. If Sonya was there it would take a miracle to get her out alive. She started the car and turned it around, aware that the few patrons of the tiny stores were beginning to stare curiously at the car. "We'd better not linger here any longer."

They drove back to Rome in silence, Rosa deep in her memories, Penny struggling with the germ of an idea. By the time they drew up before the villa the idea had sprouted into a full-fledged possibility.

"I will start dinner—we will have to eat from the freezer tonight," Rosa announced as they hurried up the path. "It will be good to be back in my own kitchen. And tomorrow I will put the house to rights."

Penny hastened into the living room to find Toby pacing up and down, drink in hand. He looked relieved at the sight of her, but growled, "Where the hell have you been? I was getting worried. Morelli and I got nowhere on the via delle Due Torri lead."

"Where is Alex?" she demanded.

"Gone down to the American Embassy again to see if they can help."

"Good! I'd just as soon not get his hopes up, but I think I have found where they are holding Sonya," she said breathlessly, and related the happenings of the afternoon.

He heard her out in rapt silence. "It doesn't sound too good, does it?" he commented at the end. "It looks as if they may have cleared out and moved on."

"Oh, I don't think so. Why should they? It's a perfect hide-out. They have no idea about the message Sonya left and this Carlo laid in a large stock of liquor. The only danger now is if word gets to them that we've been making enquiries about Giovanni."

"I'd better get Morelli right back here. He was stepping up the pressure to get a search warrant for the villa Scorsi, but I think this takes priority."

"Wait a little! I've had an idea and I would like to talk it over with Andrew first," she said. "It is the only way I can think of to get a lot of strangers into that tiny village without causing our quarry to bolt or do something desperate."

"Oh, that reminds me—Andrew called about half an hour ago. He's back at his hotel. I told him to call off his surveillance of Krantz's place; the police will be dealing with that now."

"Just let me call him first and get him here—then you call Morelli. And you can fix me a drink—I need it," Penny said and went out to the phone.

As it turned out Alex was the first to arrive back; he was in an angry, bitter mood. "They were so quick to check all sources to see that Sonya had not gone, or been taken, back to Russia; they were so pleased with themselves the other day when they phoned to confirm none of this had happened, but now. . . !" He gave an angry laugh. "They feel the kidnapping is none of their affair, that the Italian police should handle it. They were even lame-brained enough to suggest we follow the kidnapper's instructions and get out of Italy. As if I would dream of doing such a thing with even the remote possibility that Sonya is still here and alive!"

Seeing him so distraught, Penny changed her mind on the spot. "Alex," she said quietly, "I think we have discovered where she is, but getting her out of there—even if we can bring off what I have in mind—will be a thousand-to-one shot. Are you up for that?"

He looked down at her, his hazel eyes so like her own pain-filled. "Anything would be better than this hell, *any* kind of action. Where is she and what have you got in mind?" She told him.

Andrew and Morelli arrived on the doorstep at virtually the same moment, which again caused her some agonizing. She decided to tell Morelli the first part and see his reaction to that before broaching her wild idea. His reaction played into her hands. He groaned and ran a hand through his dark hair until it stood up in spikes. "Now, of all times! I think you may be right, but some of the heads of state to the conference have already begun to arrive and my department is flat out—in fact the resources of our whole police department are stretched to the maximum. And from what you have described about the terrain, this will need an all-out police offensive. I realize it is dangerous to wait, but I simply *cannot* spare enough men for it. Maybe in three days or so I can. The best I can do at the moment would be to send two undercover men into the village to keep an eye on the place."

Penny glanced enquiringly at Toby who nodded a go-ahead. "Then maybe you could give us those two men and also your blessing on a wild idea I have come up with. . . ." She looked over at Andrew. "I had hoped to broach it to Signor Dale first, because it will all depend on him and how much he can do to help us. You see, the great difficulty is that there is no cover of any kind near the house, so what is needed is a large-scale diversion of some kind to enable at least a couple of men to get *into* the house and spring Sonya, if she is there. The village is nowhere tourists would ever go, so to introduce a large number of strangers there without arousing suspicion needs something very special. So this is what I have in mind. . . ."

At the end of it Andrew was grinning widely. "Fantastic!" he exclaimed. "And I'm all for it. Mind you, it might take me a while to set it up; I doubt I could be ready before the day after tomorrow, and I'll need help with special permits." He looked at Morelli. "Would you be able to help with those? From the owners of the fortress, a permit to film on a public beach and so on?"

Morelli nodded assent. "And I will make sure the local *carabinieri* give you no trouble."

"I could go in tomorrow with a few handpicked people to recruit some of the villagers as extras for the shooting." Andrew was becoming increasingly enthused as he went on. "That is usually a surefire way of getting local support. I even know where I can get hold of two or three frogmen suits. That would enable you to get some men up that canal unseen, while I am doing my thing on the beach—what a scenario!" He looked appraisingly at Alex. "You've got the looks for a leading man, but I guess you'd rather be one of the frogmen for your debut on film. I can get one of the Italian bit players to stand in for the day as hero. I'll make them all action scenes because we won't have time to do any scripting. My cover story will be that these are some extra scenes for Margo's movie the Hollywood office had dreamed up. That sound okay? Though God knows how I'm going to get the money out of them to pay for it."

"I'll take care of that," Toby said quietly. "Whatever you need—don't even bother your producers with it."

At the look of dawning hope on her son's face, Penny's heart turned over, for she knew what a very long shot this was. A glance at Toby's rigid face confirmed he was thinking precisely the same thing.

"So the idea is that, under cover of Signor Dale shooting scenes for the movie on the beach area between Due Torri and this house, the frogmen will sneak up this drainage canal to the house and break in?" Morelli asked. "And those, presumably, would be my two men and you, Dr. Spring? Can you shoot, doctor?"

"No, but in these circumstances, put a gun in my hand and I'll sure in hell learn fast," Alex assured him grimly.

Morelli transferred his attention to Penny and Toby. "And will you be in on this?"

"I don't think I dare show my face in the village again," Penny said. "I might be recognized. And the same goes for Toby, whom the kidnappers must know by sight from the papers. No, I'm afraid once this has started it will all be up to Andrew and Alex." She glanced uncomfortably at the man whose life they had once saved. "I'm sorry, Andrew, but this *will* be very dangerous for you, but you're our only hope."

"I told you before I would do *anything* to get the bastards who killed Margo, and I meant it," he said somberly. "This will be the best directing job of my life."

Morelli sighed heavily. "Well, I see I need not repeat how dangerous these people are. The fuse you picked up in the Scorsi catacomb, Sir Tobias, has been confirmed by my explosives experts as belonging to a particularly deadly new type of high explosive. If they've got it stored there and you get them cornered and do not get them under control in time, they could send themselves, you and the whole village sky-high. On the plus side, there may not be very many of them. Going by the footprints in the tunnel on this side, there were only four men involved in that, and it is Sir Tobias' impression that there may have been a couple more sets in the other catacomb. So, at maximum, you'll have half a dozen to deal with or, with luck, perhaps just a couple. We know very little of this Paulo Venturi or Vanni, if he is one and the same, but one thing for certain—to do what has been done so far, he *has* to be a fanatic. Do not forget that for a single moment."

Chapter 18

"Even if those *stronzi* go for the deal the old man wants her dead." The muttered words caused Sonya to open her eyes a cautious crack.

"The old man can spout off all he likes, it's what the boss says that matters—and he says 'hands off' until he gives the word, so don't you forget that, Carlo."

"Pity to waste a choice bit of *culo* like that. I wouldn't mind getting right into that one—looks good to me: big boobs, long legs. Yes, I can think of interesting things I'd like to do with her. Maybe the boss'll let us have a go before we finish it, eh? Sort of a bonus for all this waiting around? God, I'm pissed off—how about another bottle, Peppi? I'm dying of thirst."

"You're always dying of thirst—all I can say is you'd better keep what few wits you have about you. If Paulo finds you half-sozzled, he's liable to off you and not think twice about it—you know how he is." The voices diminished into low grumbling and she closed her eyes again.

If she had inherited certain intellectual gifts and an astounding facility for languages from her father, it was her mother's genes that were working now: a dominant will to survive and a Byzantine deviousness of mind linked with a pragmatism that arbitrated against useless worry and enabled her to relax and conserve her strength. At the moment she had done all she could do, and so there was nothing for it but to watch and wait. Realistically, she had accepted the fact that her chances for survival were the slimmest—her captors had been too cavalier about showing their faces to her and naming names and that, she realized, was a very bad sign. Only when they had transferred her to this place had they bothered to put a hood over her head.

The one thing she had going for her was that she had successfully fooled them all into believing she knew no Italian, and so, from the first, they had talked unguardedly before her. Her mobile lips curled into a sneer: it was to the two oafs outside she owed the knowledge of where she was to be taken and that had enabled her, though at that time she had been bound hand and foot and slung like a package into a corner of the catacomb, to shake loose some hairpins and scratch the message. But had it been found? She had to believe it had been, there *had* to be hope. . . .

She opened her eyes and stretched luxuriously on the narrow canvas army cot; her head rested on a thin, lumpy pillow whose striped ticking smelled of mildew and she lay on a scratchy wool army blanket. Was this what Siberia would have been like? she wondered drowsily, taking in the rough board walls, the ill-fitting door that allowed her to hear most of what took place in the room beyond; the small, grimy, salt-encrusted, barred window, one pane cracked, against which some captive flies buzzed hopelessly, and the junk-stacked walls. It had to be a storeroom, she supposed. At least this was a lot warmer than Siberia, she told herself, and certainly a lot less crowded.

In small ways she had made some progress. At first, when they had flung her in here they had kept her tied hand and foot, but this had been too bothersome for her lazy guardians, what with her vomiting and her demands to use the galvanized pail in one corner of the room that served as her sanitary arrangements. They had ascribed her vomiting to fear; in that they were wrong: she and only she knew its true cause, a secret she hugged to herself and which steeled her determination to survive.

To save themselves work they now tethered her—a wrist and an ankle bound on long ropes to iron hooks out of reach overhead—enabling her to reach the pail in the corner and to feed herself. The only times she saw them now was in the early morning and late evening when they brought in the wooden tray with food and water. The one called Peppi would just dump the tray on the bed and leave her to it with no eating utensils. Carlo, whose intentions towards her had been unmistakable from the first, tended to linger, leaning against the door and leering until she finished the food and he collected the tray. Neither of them spoke any English, so she had mimed washing her hands and face, and a small metal bowl and a pitcher of water had finally appeared: potential weapons, she reflected, when the time came—but that time was not yet.

The only other weapon she had found in investigating the junk within the limit of her shackles was a solid steel rod that she now kept hidden under the blanket. With her one free hand she had tried working on the knots that bound her; the one on her wrists, tied by Peppi, was hopeless, but the one on her ankle, tied by Carlo with much furtive fumbling in the process, held more potential and she was working on that. But again, she could not afford to act prematurely and loosen it too much in case it was discovered. Once both her strong legs were free, she dwelt with considerable satisfaction on the prospect of kicking Carlo in the place it would hurt the most.

What chiefly irked her was the fact that she had lost all track of time. They had taken away her watch, and after she had regained consciousness in the darkness of the catacomb she had no idea how much time had elapsed while they had kept her down there. Here at least she could keep track of the waxing and waning of the endless days.

By straining at her bonds she could get close enough to the window to achieve a glimpse of the outside world, but it told her little. All she could see was a sward of coarse grass, a featureless beach and the gentle waves of the Mediterranean. She had yet to see a single person on this beach, so she deduced that, wherever Due Torri was, it was certainly no resort area. The house she was in she knew was "Paulo's place," but who exactly he was and what he had in mind she had no idea. At the very thought of him she felt a thrill of anger not unmixed with fear.

It had all been so sudden, so unexpected; one minute foolishly congratulating herself as she tugged away at the entrance to the catacomb, the next her shoulder seized. As she had looked up into the blazing dark eyes of the bald-headed, bearded man they called Paulo, his fist had come up with a swift uppercut that had caught her on the point of her chin—and then blackness. With her unfettered hand she felt her chin, which still after these many days was tender. What a sight she must be, she thought drearily.

She had come to with a blinding light in her eyes and a deep voice demanding over and over in Italian how much she knew. She had feigned blank incomprehension and had spattered back in Russian, but he had slapped her around some more and switched to English, and after her senses were reeling and the pain level had become unbearable, she had finally answered in English, although she had managed to make it broken and thickly accented—so that her lack of comprehension about what he was asking would seem more feasible. The expert, vicious slapping had continued until she was semiconscious and he was satisfied—or maybe discouraged—by her meager knowledge, and he had let her be. By the time he was finished her eyes were almost swollen shut and her face had remained swollen for days, but, mercifully, that had been the end of it.

Since then she had seen but little of him. Once in the catacomb, when he had overseen the removal of the sealed boxes they had stored there: four men had been with him then, the two now outside and two others whom she thought were Arabs, for they spoke Italian with a strange guttural accent. It was them he seemed to trust more than his fellow Italians, who had been delegated the menial task of guarding her. And then it was he who had dropped that frightening hood over her head and carried her out of the catacomb to be bundled into some kind of van where she had lain uncomfortably on a jumble of equipment and jolted to her present prison, where he had seen her installed in this makeshift cell. Since then he had not checked on her, although she had heard his voice on many occasions in the next room.

For the first few days of her imprisonment she had sensed in the disjointed conversations she had managed to eavesdrop on that things were in confusion. That their original plans, whatever those were, were in the process of being changed and not without acrimony among them. Then, in the past three days, she had sensed another change, a quickening of excitement and a new purpose: last night Paulo had been here and there had been much coming and going, and she had the sinking feeling that time was running out for her.

This uncomfortable thought brought a rush of bile to her throat and she quickly staggered off the cot and retched violently into the bucket in the corner. It brought about a momentary stilling of the voices in the other room, then Carlo's voice, "She's at it again—at this rate she's never going to last until D Day. Pity that! I think it's your deal, Peppi, and make sure it's not off the bottom of the deck." Shivering a little with disgust, she wiped her chin with a burlap bag that served in place of a towel and collapsed back on the cot.

From the outset of her captivity she had rigidly kept her thoughts away from her nearest and dearest, knowing that dwelling upon them would drain her own courage. Of Alex she dared not think at all. At the time of their unlikely marriage, she had been attracted to him physically and entranced by the hope in the new life he had held out to her. But since their marriage and with all the depth of emotion of her Slavic nature she had fallen deeply in love with him. She adored him and knew that he adored her, and the thought of what he must be suffering was almost beyond endurance. With her father she was on more comfortable ground, for there the tie was far more an intellectual than an emotional bond. Almost from the start she felt she had understood this complex man, that their minds were on the same wavelength, and it was on him she had been concentrating: willing him to find her message, willing him to understand it and act; willing him to believe she was alive and could be saved; willing him to *come*. But would he be in time with the odds so stacked against him? It was this thought that brought her to the edge of despair.

The voices in the next room suddenly became loud and angry. "Fuck you, Peppi—you're cheating again! I've had enough of you, you bastard."

"I don't need to cheat, you moron. You're so sozzled you can hardly see the fucking cards, let alone know how to play 'em. Here! Where do you think you're off to?"

"I gotta get outta here. Gotta get some fresh air, or, by God, I'll be wringing your scrawny neck." There was the sound of a door opening and then a muffled exclamation from Carlo. "There's a crowd of people on the beach—here, come and have a look! Something's going on."

"Holy hell, come in, you fool!" There was the sound of scuffling. "You know we're not supposed to show ourselves, not today of all days. Want to end up like Giovanni? Shut the god damn door. We can see through the chinks in the shutters."

Noiselessly, Sonya slipped off the cot and strained towards the window: sure enough, there was a jeep parked on the beach and a couple of men in her field of vision, smoking cigarettes and gazing out to sea; if only she could attract their attention! The sound of footsteps approaching the door sent her diving back onto the cot, and she feigned sleep as the door opened. "She's out of it," Carlo announced.

"Better check. We don't want her getting any funny ideas if she hears anything outside."

Carlo came over to the cot and she could smell the sour wine on his breath as he leaned over her, one hand fumbling at her bosom. "No," he said. "She's asleep all right. White as a ghost she is, poor cunt." The door shut and she gasped with relief, but lay still until his footsteps had retreated and her queasiness had subsided.

"I don't like this!" Peppi's voice was shrill. "Not even a fucking phone so we can contact Paulo and ask him what to do; not a fucking car to take off in!"

"Calm down! He said he'd be back about noontime."

"It's after that now—what the hell is keeping him? What if it's the police out there?"

"Nah! Do they look like a bunch of flatfeet?" Carlo was scornful. "See, come here and have a look through this knot-hole. There's a couple of trucks over by the Due Torri— they've got the gates open and all. Maybe they're fixing the old place up—no, by all the saints, look! That's a movie camera they just got outta that truck. It's a fucking film crew! Well, I'll be . . . they must be making a movie! Look, they've got some of the locals in on it too—see that blonde cow over there? She's at the taverna."

"I still don't like it," Peppi repeated doggedly. "That looker who died on us was one of them movie people, wasn't she? We'd best get the guns out, just in case."

Sonya's thoughts raced with her pulse: to pick on this un-likely spot for a movie? It did seem too much of a coincidence. Could it possibly be that they knew where she was, that this was a rescue attempt? She *had* to signal her presence in some way—but with what?

She was still wearing the same unsuitable clothes in which she had set out on her ill-fated exploration, although they had taken away her shoes. She looked down at the jade-green linen suit, now much begrimed, and the blue and green patterned blouse. They were certainly eye-catching enough, but dare she shed any of them? If her captors came in, she felt that Peppi in his present state of nerves might just shoot her out of hand. Other than her outer clothes she just had her panties and a bra. She looked thoughtfully at the cracked pane and fumbled for the steel rod beneath the blanket: the bra, if only she could get out of it, would certainly be eye-catching if it could be tied to the rod and hung out that window. The thought of her bra flying like a banner brought a smile of grim amusement to her bruised lips. Once more, rod in hand, she strained towards the window, but to her disappointment, although the jeep was still there, the section of the beach was empty of people.

Well, she had to do something. With the rod she poked at the cracked pane until it gave way and fell outwards with a faint tinkle: the flies soared off into freedom and a gust of warm salt-laden air blew in. She glanced at the door in alarm, but the men were too engrossed in their own argument to hear. Returning to the cot she unbuttoned her blouse and with agonizing contortions managed to undo and wriggle out of her bra. She was bathed in sweat by the time she had finished and had to wipe her slippery hands on the coarse blanket to dry them enough to tie the bra firmly to the rod. Again she strained towards the window, and by stretching desperately to the bounds of her tethers she managed to work the rod through the gap and wedge it into one corner of the window, so that the bra was out of sight although the rod was visible. There was nothing to do about that so she prayed her guardians would be too preoccupied to notice, should they check on her further. Exhausted, she flopped back on the cot and willed herself to calm down, as the argument continued in the next room.

"If they come near the house, I'm going to run them off." This was the truculent Peppi.

"Are you crazy? There's a *carabinieri* down there—see? Talking to that man with a beard, the one with a bullhorn in his hand?"

"We've every right to be here and this is private property. They've no right to trespass."

"They're on the *beach,* you fool! Anyone has the right to go there, and if you show yourself the *carabinieri* might come snooping to see who we are. We can't risk that." Carlo was exasperated.

"What if the cunt starts to cut up in there—scream or something? Maybe we'd better gag her and tie her up good until they've all cleared off." Sonya's heart skipped a beat.

"I've an idea—why don't we wrap her in a tarp, put her in the boat and pretend as how we're going fishing? That's the story I gave in the village. We can stay out till they clear off." Carlo was eager.

"And leave all this stuff unguarded? Oh, that would be just great, that would. Paulo would have our livers out when he shows up."

"Why would they come here? There'd be no reason to. And we don't have to go far out. We could take the guns and keep an eye on everything from the boat—it would get us away from this rathole for a bit. Come on, I'm all for it!" Sonya's hopes plummeted.

"Well, I'm not, see. You're not giving the orders around here, Paulo is," said the literal-minded Peppi. "And Paulo's orders were very clear. Stay here, stay out of sight as much as possible, and guard the stuff and the girl till he's ready. I'm not taking any flaming chances, and that's that. Paulo left *me* in charge, so you just shut your face and keep an eye on what those freaks are up to out there. You'd best gag the girl, like I told you."

"If you're so fucking set on that, *you* do it—*cazzi*. I'm having a drink," Carlo growled. "I wonder what your precious Paulo would say if he knew how easily *you* panic."

Sonya hastily curled herself up again and feigned sleep as the door opened and a furious Peppi stamped in. He shook her roughly by the shoulder and when she opened her eyes motioned with the gun he was carrying for her to sit up. She pretended to be terrified at the sight of it and shrank away from him, but he pulled her towards him and produced a grimy handkerchief from his pocket. "Here, Carlo," he called. "Come and keep her covered for a sec while I get this on her," and he put the gun carefully beyond her reach.

She shook her head and mimed frantically, pretending to vomit and pointing at the pail; but it was useless, he only shrugged indifferently, and as the glowering Carlo appeared in the doorway, tied the gag firmly into place and pushed her back on the cot, testing her bonds.

"If the poor bitch chokes to death, it'll be your fault, and don't think I won't tell Paulo that," Carlo observed, as they went out and the door slammed shut.

She lay rigid with anger, tears of helpless frustration pricking her eyes: from the beach came the sound of revving engines, faint explosions and confused shouting. "Whoever you are out there," she prayed, "come. See my sign. Help me— and oh, *please* make it soon!"

Chapter 19

"How I wish we could be with them," Penny said wistfully. They had just seen Andrew and the excited Alex off to Cinecitta, where the last preparations were to be made prior to their planned descent on Santa Maria di Alitura. Since she had mooted her unlikely plan things had been hectic and there had been little time for reflection, but now that it was finally going into operation their only role would be to sit on the sidelines and wait, and this thought irked her beyond belief.

Toby had been very withdrawn and silent, his blue eyes vague and abstracted. Now he said, "I've had an idea—it's a risk, but I think it may be of some help to the lads and worth a try."

"What is it?" she demanded. "I'm game for anything at this point."

"Well, in spite of what Morelli has had to say, the more I think of it, the more it looks to me as if the only real fanatics involved in this are Krantz and Paulo Vanni. Maybe there are other fanatics in Paulo's unmerry band, about which we have no information whatsoever, but, when you consider they recruited someone like Giovanni, it seems to me that the other underlings may be more of *his* ilk—in it for the money—rather than dyed-in-the-wool fanatics. From what little we've seen of Pietro and Gabriella I'd say they were motivated more by greed than any kind of idealism, however misplaced, wouldn't you? And, besides, they and Scorsi are being closely watched."

"Okay, I'm with you thus far—so?"

"So—Morelli is also keeping close tabs on Krantz, so he is out of it as far as direct contact with Due Torri is concerned," Toby continued with deliberation. "That leaves Paulo. We know from the undercover man in the village that he was there yesterday but is not there now. My idea would be to keep him away from it until this thing is over and done with."

"Oh, great! How do you propose to do that?" She was mildly sarcastic.

"I'm assuming that Pietro must know how to contact him. So I propose to call him and tell him I'll accede to Paulo's ransom demands, but that I must see Paulo face to face or get some guarantee from him that Sonya is still alive, and also that I have another proposition for him. He has not called us back on that—which is *not* a good sign, I know, and it's a very long shot, but I think it's worth a try."

"But he'd never *go* for it! And anyway what's the point?"

"The point is this: we know he has no phone out of the cottage in Due Torri. He may wonder if I am up to something, so he'll have to stay in touch by phone with Pietro or, better yet, me. Ergo, he won't be able to do it from Due Torri. If I can keep him on a string for several hours, especially if I hint around about knowing of his *changed* plan, it may just do the trick."

"Won't Morelli be furious?"

"At this point I don't give a damn what Morelli is or does," Toby said. "It's Sonya who concerns me. Morelli could change from his present sweetness-and-light act in a second, just like Cicco did. He's not concerned about *her*—all he wants is to nab the terrorists before or during the act."

Objections were crowding in upon Penny. "What if he does set up a meeting with you and then nabs you as well? We'd be worse off than we are now! And another thing—they must still have the key to the door in the wall. What if they got us out of the house on a wild goose chase and then went in through there to use the catacomb as originally planned?"

Toby smiled grimly at her. "I rather wish they *would* try something like that, they'd be in for a nasty surprise. That explosives man of Morelli's—nice, efficient chap, by the way— and I already thought of that. He planted a very small charge down there yesterday and set it off, so the tunnel is inoperative. What's more, the charge must have jarred some stuck mechanism loose in the Tropaion and it swung open as easy as you please. I just *knew* that thing had to be a door." He was momentarily sidetracked by archaeological fervor. "It obviously was built as an escape hatch so that, in case of a raid on the catacomb, they could hop through it and out the back stairway—very ingenious." He brought himself back to the present with an effort. "Anyway, the upshot is we no longer need the search warrant to get into the other catacomb—Morelli checked through it yesterday afternoon, but he found nothing further."

"Then why doesn't he just pull in the Vannis and the count?" she cried. "Surely he has enough on them now?"

"Nothing *concrete* unfortunately. Oh, he could probably pull them in on suspicion, but they'd be out again in no time with Scorsi's connections and it might provoke Paulo into something precipitate. That's the last thing Morelli wants until he gets their cache of explosives and a clearer line on exactly who is involved. With all the police resources they have yet to spot Paulo *in* the city, and until Morelli has all his VIPs safely stowed away in their respective embassies, he just wants to keep a lid on the situation." Toby got up. "So, are you with me on this? I ought to get going."

"Why ask me? You're the one who is sticking your neck out. I don't seem to have any part in it," she grumbled.

"Oh, but you have! You'll have to hold down the phone at this end, if I have to go out to a rendezvous—that's most important," he said, looking at his watch. "What time did Andrew say they were going to start for Due Torri?"

"He hoped to be set up there and shooting by noon."

"Then there's no time to waste." He stalked out and she followed after, still grumbling. "I know I complained about all the rushing around I had to do in Hawaii, but that was a breeze compared to this set-up. I swear I've spent half my time either *on* the damn phone or waiting for it to ring. At this rate I'll develop 'telephone ear' and I've *already* developed a case of galloping frustration." She subsided into sulky mumbling as he got the palazzo and was put through to Pietro Vanni.

As she listened, she had to admire Toby's performance which was masterly. He managed to convey the impression of a man who was running very scared but who had something up his sleeve. He blustered, he cringed a little, he hinted heavily that not only would he save Pietro's skin but would see it was very much worth his while to play along with him and, like a drumbeat throughout, kept insisting that he had to speak with Paulo either face to face or on the phone. "If you know what's good for you, you'll act immediately. If you don't move within the next hour or so it will be too late. I'll be waiting here for his call," he urged and hung up.

"Did he go for it?"

"I think so," Toby said with a sigh. "Now we can only wait and see. I wonder where the hell Paulo has gone to ground. He's not at the cottage and he's not next door."

"How do you know he isn't at the villa?" she said, uneasy at the very thought.

"Because he has to be mobile and so needs transport. Now that he knows we've discovered the catacomb, he'd be too wary to drive in and out of the villa in case the police are watching it."

"I can think of at least two other places he could be."

Toby's eyebrows shot up. "Oh? Where?"

"The Libyan Embassy for one—that man who drove Krantz there the other night, didn't Morelli say he was their First Secretary?"

Toby was shaking his head. "No, the Libyans are always under surveillance, he'd never go there."

"Well then, there's the place Lucia Scorsi mentioned—the count has another estate in the Campania. He could be there."

"Good Lord! Why didn't you mention this before? I ought to tell Morelli, he could check that out." He reached for the phone.

"Because I've only just remembered it; I've had a lot of other things on my mind," she snapped.

But Morelli was unavailable, and after being shunted through several other officials, Toby slammed down the phone in disgust. "Well I tried! I dare not tie up the phone any longer."

They stared at each other in a strained silence. Penny broke it. "This waiting is hell, pure hell. How I wish we had gone with them and just kept out of sight," she repeated. "I wonder how they are getting on."

Andrew's carefully thought-out choreography had so far been working without a hitch. He had started shooting by the Due Torri itself, but had gradually been working the entire company further and further up the beach until now they were almost abreast of the shuttered house. The bit player elected to play hero-for-the-day had thrown himself heart and soul into his heady role and was out-Bonding James Bond. His enthusiasm was infectious and the villagers, along with the small band of professional extras recruited from Cinecitta, were re-

sponding to Andrew's shouted commands with the precision
of trained soldiers and as if they had been doing this all their
lives. At his right hand stood an administrative assistant, also
armed with a bullhorn, who was translating his commands
into Italian, and was one of the few who had been alerted to
the real purpose of the enterprise. It was he who noticed the
momentary opening of the door and the appearance of Carlo.
"There's somebody in there right enough," he muttered to Andrew.

"How many did you see?"

"I only caught a glimpse of one man."

"Then you can bet he'll be watching us," Andrew said and
passed on the information by the walkie-talkie he held in his
other hand. He motioned the three frogmen, who had been
standing a little apart from the rest with their rubber raft, into
action. One of them also held a walkie-talkie. They pushed the
rubber raft into the waves, piled into it, paddled a little ways
out, anchored, then swam back in to come out of the water in
back of the beleaguered hero, who immediately swung
around, shot two of them, who "died" on the sands while the
third plunged back into the water.

"We'll do this shot three times," Andrew muttered into the
walkie-talkie. "On the second shot I'm going to move you
along so you'll be almost up to the canal. After the third shot
I'll wave you away and bring the rest of them down a bit in
this direction, and when I say 'go' you go into the canal and
take off as fast as you can. I have an idea to keep our watchers
occupied while you get around the back of the house."

"Understood," the man with the walkie-talkie said. "Ready
when you are."

The frogmen made a disparate trio: both the policemen
were on the short side, so Alex towered over them. To make
his height less obvious he had hunched over, and in consequence looked like a rejected and dejected monster from the
Black Lagoon.

At the completion of the second shot that brought them out of the water at the back of the house, the shorter of the policemen grasped Alex's upper arm, gave it a warning squeeze and said, "Doctore, make it very casual, but take a look at the back of the house nearest the beach. I think it may be a signal that your wife is indeed there." There was a hint of amusement in his low voice.

Alex looked and made an instinctive lunge towards the house as he saw what it was, but was restrained by the hand on his arm. *"Calma, calma, doctore.* It is good that we know where she may be." Then to the other policeman, "Tomaso, go over to the jeep and pretend to look for something while you take a good look at that window. See if we could get in there."

Tomaso did his bidding but returned shaking his head. "No, there are bars and it is very small. Even you, *sergente,* could not squeeze through."

"Then this is what we must do." The sergeant looked at Alex. "We will swim around the moored boat and come out of the water behind it. This will cover us from the house. Tomaso will slip down and see if she is still there—if so, he will cover the door from the window and shoot anyone who enters. We do not know how many are in there so I will lead the way to the front door and kick it in. I'll go in shooting. Do not shoot unless you have to. You make for that back door and kick it in if necessary. Tomaso cannot mistake your great height so will not shoot. It will all be very fast, you understand? No matter what is happening, just take your wife and get her to the jeep and take off as fast as you can."

"What if they have her in the other room and use her as a shield?" Alex asked huskily.

"We will already know from Tomaso if that is so, and in that case he will be with me. We are both expert marksmen and one of us can take the man out. That is why I do not want *you* shooting, *doctore;* an Uzi is no respecter of persons in the

211

hands of an amateur." He turned to Tomaso as Andrew's voice summoned them for the third shot over the walkie-talkie. "Remember the inspector wants at least one of them alive. Now, as soon as the director says 'go,' we slip behind the jeep, get the guns and go into the water. You have got your knife, *doctore?*" Alex nodded, and for the third time the unlikely trio made their way into the water as the sergeant said, "Your turn to die in the sand, Tomaso, my turn for the water."

The third shot was completed and as they picked themselves up from the sand and the sergeant returned to the beach, Andrew waved them away and started shooing the rest of the cast ahead of him down the beach in the opposite direction. "Go," he said quietly into the walkie-talkie.

The trio walked casually back to the jeep, got the guns, and ducked out of sight and into the canal. They gained the shelter of the motorboat. "Now, Tomaso," the sergeant breathed, and Tomaso, bent low, scuttled to the back of the house and along its length until he was at the barred window. He peered in cautiously, gave a thumbs-up sign and flattened himself on the ground, his gun trained through the broken pane. They slipped out of the water and along the short side of the house and the sergeant peeked carefully around to the front. He swore softly, "*Sgabello!* What the hell is the director doing? Does he want us all killed?"

Alex, peering over his shoulder, saw Andrew, bullhorn in hand, slowly edging backwards towards them over the grass, while motioning his gaggle of actors to approach him. The sergeant was almost up to the front door, Alex close behind, when suddenly it opened and they flattened themselves against the wall as a man's voice yelled angrily, "*Va via*—get out! You trespass. Private property. Go!"

Andrew hesitated, turned around, looked surprised, then smiled ingratiatingly and started towards him. "Sorry, I don't understand you," he called, "speak English?"

The man stepped out, pointing a rifle at him. *"Va via!"* he called again, and Andrew's smile was replaced by a look of astonished alarm. He started to back away, his hand raised placatingly.

Unfortunately, at this juncture the *carabinieri,* who had been standing on the sidelines watching the movie-making with interest, decided to take a hand. He let out a yell of outrage and started to run towards the armed man, fumbling at the flap of his own holstered gun. "Don't, you fool! Put away that gun," he yelled. "He has the permissions. He makes a movie!"

At the sight of the policeman charging at him Peppi lost his head. He let off a wild shot that whistled over the *carabinieri's* head and then turned the gun on Andrew. The sergeant stepped away from the wall and shot him in the back, but as Peppi toppled, a last convulsive twitch of his finger on the trigger loosed another shot that caught Andrew in the arm and sent him spinning to the ground. The sergeant was at the door and inside in a flash, Alex on his heels.

Carlo, gun in hand, was already halfway towards the door in the rear, but as they tumbled in he swung around and tried to pull up his gun. The sergeant shot him dispassionately in his fat paunch and, as Carlo fell to the floor with a scream of agony, fanned the room with his gun, kicked open the other doors and then let out a shout, "Tomaso—all clear. Get in here! Only two of 'em and I got them both." Alex hurled himself towards the door in the rear, as the sergeant kicked Carlo's gun out of his reach and turned to meet his partner.

Alex almost collided with the dishevelled figure, uttering wild squeaking noises behind its gag as it hopped towards him. "Oh, my darling!" he sobbed, his hand fumbling for his knife, as he gathered her to him. When he slashed the gag away a little moan of horror escaped, as he took in the mottled mask of green, yellow and purple bruises that was the face of his beloved. With a growl of rage, he slashed the ropes that bound her and cradled her to him. "Whoever did this, I'll kill them, I'll kill them," he choked, tears streaming down his face.

"It's all right, I'm all right. It's nothing, it's over. Oh, Alex, please don't cry!" Sonya managed to get out as tears started to pour down her battered cheeks. "You're here, that's all that matters!"

He scooped her up in his arms. "And I've got to get you out of here." But his way was blocked by the sergeant at the door. "Sorry, *doctore,* but as long as your wife is unharmed we need you here for a while. Will you fix up this villain, so he doesn't die on us before he talks? And there's your friend. He's been shot—I don't know how badly. His assistant says they bring a medical kit from the movie truck."

"But I've got to get her away from here," Alex roared. "The rest of those bastards may show up at any minute."

"I'm sorry but there is no doctor in the village. I must insist. She is safe here with us for the moment and you are needed."

"Yes, darling," Sonya murmured. "I told you, I'm fine. Put me down. Go on and do as he says."

Reluctantly he lowered her onto a chair. "Doctor, doctor, save me," he muttered bitterly, as he snatched the first-aid kit from the dazed-looking *carabinieri,* who had only just been put in the picture by Tomaso and was just beginning to realize his own narrow escape from death. Alex stalked out to where Andrew still lay on the ground, propped up by the now ashen-faced hero, and surrounded by the cast. He pushed his was through and knelt by Andrew, who grinned weakly at him. "Something went awry with my scenario," he muttered through clenched teeth.

"Serves you damn well right, you could have blown the whole thing and killed us all with that damn fool stunt," Alex growled as he examined the wound with quick, expert fingers. "You're damn lucky at that. The bullet went right through and didn't damage any bone. I'll stop the bleeding and once you're in the hospital they'll fix you up in no time."

"It hurts like hell!" Andrew complained. "Can you do something for that?"

Alex looked into the kit and snorted. "Only some pain pills, no morphine. I can give you a couple of those. Otherwise you'll just have to grin and bear it." He gave him the pills, finished the bandaging and got up. "Better carry him up to the jeep, the other one will be right along," he told Andrew's assistant, who had been busy dispersing the villagers to their homes and getting the cast to pack up and get back to the trucks. "And wait for me."

Alex went back inside and knelt down beside the writhing Carlo. "Hmm, he's gut shot, so I can't give him anything by mouth for the pain and I don't have any hypos. The bullet's still in him. All I can do is patch the wound until you get him to the hospital—and the sooner the better if you want him alive. Andrew Dale is being carried to the jeep—that okay?" He was bandaging the wound as he spoke. "Better put this one in a blanket to carry him, and keep him wrapped in it. He may go into shock if he's jolted too much."

The sergeant nodded at Tomaso, who collected the blanket off Sonya's cot and he and the *carabinieri* carried away the groaning Carlo. "Tomaso will drive them in the jeep to the nearest hospital. I have to stay here and phone from the taverna—the only phone in this benighted place—with a report. I suggest you take your wife in the truck with the movie people back to Cinecitta, and they'll send you back in a car from there. You'd better hang on to your gun for the present. I'm afraid it's far from over." His face was grim.

"What do you mean?" Sonya and Alex said simultaneously.

"Look for yourself!" The sergeant strode over to another door and flung it open to reveal a pile of wooden boxes, their covers wrenched off. "These were sealed and I've opened them all—and, but for one box of explosives that would have been sufficient to blow *this* place to hell, they were all empty. It's a dummy cache those two clowns were guarding. Paulo must have shifted the main cache elsewhere on the quiet. And until we find it, nothing is over."

Chapter 20

On the way back to Rome the reunited lovers had a spirited argument: Alex was all for rushing Sonya off to the American Hospital for a thorough checkup; she had other, very definite ideas. "We go to the villa and I sit in a lovely hot bath full of bubbles and perfume for a long, long time, I wash my hair, I have a big, big meal and I tell you all about everything that happens to me," she declared. "What's the use of being married to a doctor, if he won't look after me? I don't need a hospital. I hate hospitals. I won't go."

"But I need their facilities to check you and see you're okay," he protested. "Darling, be reasonable! I need X rays, blood tests. . . ."

"No X rays, no, no, no!" she cried in alarm. "I hate X rays. Definitely not! You take me home, I'm fine." As usual, she got her way.

Their parents were so overwhelmed at the sight of them that all they could do, after the initial fervent embraces, was to gaze raptly at them and utter inanities like, "Well, well, well—this is great," and "Jolly good show!" although when he took in what had been done to his daughter's face, Toby punctuated his inanities with little growls of fury, like some dyspeptic bear.

A surprised and delighted Rosa was summoned and rushed off to prepare a meal worthy of the happy reunion, and Sonya, having announced her number-one priority, went off to take her luxurious bath. Alex rapidly filled them in on the details of the rescue, but was obviously so anxious to be with his beloved that his mother ended his misery by saying, "Why don't you go and keep an eye on Sonya? Obviously, from what you've told us, the police think she may still be in some danger." He was out the door in a flash.

She heaved a huge sigh of relief. "Well, thank God that's over! And they came out of it in one piece, although poor Andrew is somewhat the worse for wear." Toby was still uttering his little growls as he foraged in the wine bin for the choicest vintages to go with Rosa's proposed feast. When he surfaced from the bin, he observed, "I think we can anticipate a visit from Morelli shortly. I only hope we can hear Sonya's account of what happened before he gets here." He cleared his throat. "I don't think we need mention my long-shot of this morning."

"Since it didn't work there's no point in bringing it up," Penny returned, for there had been no phone call from either Pietro or Paulo.

"Hmpf! Well, we'll have to tell him about the count's estate," Toby fussed.

"Fine! But then I think we should bug out of this whole deal. I'm all for quitting while we're ahead," she stated flatly.

Toby looked shocked. "But we can't—we're too much involved, whether we like it or not. You heard Alex—Paulo and some of his men are still roaming around out there with enough explosives to take out half the conference. He has to be stopped! I agree with you up to a point. Once Sonya has made her statement, I feel that—much as we shall miss them—they should get right out of here and out of Italy.

Sonya knows too much and so is still a target. I'm sure with all the problems Morelli has on his hands, he'll agree with me and let her go."

"Fine! But I still feel we've done our bit and we can leave the rest to the police." They continued to bicker amiably until Sonya reappeared, clean and glowing, in a fresh new outfit: she was fussing at the adoring Alex, "Are you sure you didn't find my shoes?"

"I told you—the sergeant searched the whole cottage and found no sign of them, and they certainly weren't in the catacomb, were they?" he appealed to Toby.

"Shoes?" said Toby, perking up. "What's this about shoes?"

Sonya told him. "How odd!" he muttered. "And Margo's shoes were also missing. . . ."

They settled down to hear Sonya's saga, but were interrupted halfway through by Rosa's announcement that the food was ready. They transferred the recital to the dining room where, for the first time in days, they all ate with a good appetite, to Rosa's great delight.

All went happily until Rosa produced a particularly luscious dessert, consisting of an almond cake topped with fresh raspberries and thick whipped cream. Sonya tucked into hers with little coos of delight, but she had only taken a few mouthfuls when suddenly she dropped her fork, put her hands to her mouth, and rushed out of the room, Alex pounding after her. Toby and Penny looked at each other in silent alarm, and a few minutes later Alex came back looking very determined. "Well, that settles it—she's been violently sick. I'm taking her to the American Hospital—I should have done that right away."

Sonya followed him in protesting. "Is nothing! I just ate too much, too quickly, that's all. I don't want to go." She was very white.

"Nonsense!" her father barked. "Of course you should go."

"Heaven knows what you might have picked up in those

terrible conditions you were in—it could be anything: ty-
phoid, cholera, God knows what!" Alex was adamant.

"No, is not anything," she said stubbornly and looked ap-
pealingly at Penny for help, but there was none forthcoming.
"I think it would be best to go and get it over with," Penny
said. "If it is nothing, you'll be back in no time. You know
where Salve Regina is?" she asked Alex, who nodded impatiently.

"Yes, clear across Rome, so the sooner we get there the better. I'm not taking any more of this, Sonya," he said sternly,
and pushed his protesting wife out the door. "But is not necessary, there's something I tell you . . ."

Their exit was followed hard upon by Morelli's entrance.
He was looking exhausted and far from happy. "I have been
informed of what happened at Due Torri and I need a statement from your daughter right away. Where is she?" he demanded.

"Her husband has taken her to the American Hospital for
treatment. She appears to have been badly mistreated and
beaten," Toby growled, glaring back at him.

"Oh!" Morelli was taken aback. "My men did not inform
me of this. Well, has she said anything of what happened? I
cannot afford the time to go to the hospital, so tell me what
you can and I will get her official statement later."

"She only had time to tell us some of it before she became
ill again," Penny said. "But I think it will be enough for you
to take more action than you have up to now." It came out
with more sarcasm than she had intended. "Sir Tobias can tell
you about it better than I."

Toby gave a terse account of what Sonya had related and
ended, "So it appears there *are* only four men in Paulo's outfit, two of whom your men have put out of action, and the
other two, whom she can describe for you, she thought were
Arabs—probably, in light of what else we know, Libyans.
And it is they who must have helped Paulo remove the explo-

sives and left the dummy cache behind. Although she didn't *see* any of this, since she was in another room she heard many comings and goings yesterday, which must have been when it was done. She got the impression that action was imminent and they were close to disposing of her."

"It doesn't help us as much as I had hoped," Morelli grunted.

"My God, man, what more do you want?" Toby flared. "You've enough to pull in Krantz and Paulo, *if* you can only find them. You know how many men are involved with them, and probably those other two sets of prints in the catacomb belong to Pietro Vanni and Krantz. I've no idea why they waited so long once we got on to the catacomb, but now they're on the move, so why the hell don't you *do* something?"

"I can tell you *why* they waited until now," Morelli said tightly. "They were waiting for reinforcements, which they won't be getting. Our men picked up four more Libyans who tried to come in through Milan yesterday from Germany. They are known terrorists and we got the tip-off from the West German Embassy."

"Then why not pick up Krantz?" Penny broke in.

"But she never actually *saw* him," Morelli gritted. "Not in the catacomb, not in Due Torri."

"No, but dammit, she heard him!" Toby cried. "About three days ago at Due Torri she heard a man who came there when Paulo was *not* there and who urged the guards to kill her. She heard them discussing him again today. Although they did not name him they referred to him constantly as 'the old man.' She is enough of a linguist to know he was not a native Italian, even though he spoke Italian fluently—so it isn't Scorsi. What other 'old man' is there?"

"He hasn't budged from the villa since our men have had it under surveillance," Morelli objected.

"Haven't you at least tapped his phone?" Penny queried.

Morelli withered her with a glare. "We are not allowed to use such methods. But if your daughter is confident enough to identify his voice, we may have enough to get a search warrant. Not that it will help, because the explosives cannot be there. Nothing has been brought into the villa under the noses of my men."

"They may be at the count's country estate." Penny put in. "I don't know where it is, but the Contessa Scorsi could tell you. I have her number if you want it."

"The count again!" Morelli was exasperated. "Don't you realize that not a single bit of the evidence you have provided points to him?"

"I grant you that," she retaliated. "But Pietro Vanni is his estate manager—he would have access, and when things fell apart next door, it strikes me as the most likely place to go to ground. Good God, inspector, we're not making all this up, you know. We're trying to *help*."

Morelli controlled himself. "I realize that, but aside from the maid's statement that he was seen using the door between the villas and that Paulo had visited the villa, we have nothing much to tie Pietro in with all this. We are not even sure Paulo is his brother or that they are still in contact."

Toby had evidently been having second thoughts, for he said, "I think there is not much doubt about that. I may as well confess that I called him early this morning and asked for a meeting with Paulo. Even though nothing came of it, having now heard Sonya's story, I believe I may have achieved my purpose of keeping him away from the cottage. According to her they were expecting him around noon—and he never showed up, either then or later, since you still had a man there."

Morelli glared darkly at him. "We might have nabbed him right there!"

"Not without a lot more bloodshed." Toby was firm. "They would have been five to your two, don't forget, and I was thinking not only of my daughter and son-in-law but also of all those innocent bystanders on the beach. It also strikes me that he may have had an informant in the village, who warned him off after the fracas at the cottage."

"You're right there," Morelli growled. "My sergeant told me that when he went to phone in his report from the taverna, the barmaid there was talking very excitedly to someone, but that he cut her off and put the phone out of action until I could get some back-up to him. We arrested and interrogated her, but she knows very little. She was just paid to report any activity around the cottage to this bar in a slum area near here on the Via Meropia."

"Hasn't the wounded man told you anything?" Penny asked.

"Not yet. They operated on him as soon as they got him, but the doctors say he will not be able to be questioned until late tonight. That may be too late—the opening session of the conference takes place at eight this evening in EUR. Now it is *imperative* I talk with your daughter—it's just possible she may have heard something, *anything,* that will help us pinpoint their target. The only place we know they won't try anything now is the Borgese villa next door, so that leaves the rest of Rome. God, what a nightmare!"

"Haven't you got anything on the van?" she persisted.

"Oh, yes, for what good it did us. Last night a fire was reported on a piece of waste ground by the Piazza Federico Lante near here. By the time the firemen put it out the van involved was gutted, but it fits the description. They've changed vehicles, and God knows what they're in now." He got up wearily. "Call me as soon as your daughter returns or you can contact her.

"Just call my office and they'll transmit the call by radio wherever I am. I must check with the local police on the count's country estate—not that I think that will help us."

Penny followed him out. "Is there any report on Andrew Dale's condition?" she asked anxiously.

"Oh, the movie man? They gave him emergency treatment and sent him on to the American Hospital. It was only a flesh wound—he'll be all right," Morelli said as he hurried out.

Toby tried to contact Alex at the hospital but got nowhere, so they settled down to another nerve-stretching wait. "I can't stand this, I have to do something," Penny said eventually. "I think I'll start packing their things. Like it or not, they're leaving." She stamped out. Toby sought the consolation of his pipe and the brandy bottle.

The sound of the front door opening brought them both out into the hall in a flash as Sonya came in. She was looking smugly triumphant and was closely followed by a dazed-looking Alex. "You'd better come in and sit down," she said gaily. "I am fine, but there is something we have to tell you. Good news!" Behind her Alex made incoherent noises of assent, as they scuttled back to the living room and sat looking expectantly at her.

Sonya sat down and beamed at them. "I am going to have babies—two of them."

They gaped at her. "Twins!" her father roared, looking accusingly at Penny. "There are no twins in *my* family."

"Nor in mine," Penny gasped. "Are you sure?"

"Oh, yes. Three months gone—which is why I get the morning sickness now, which often happens."

"But why didn't you tell us? You must have known!" they chorused.

"I did not tell anyone, not even Alex." She smiled up at his dazed face. "I did not want to spoil our honeymoon and I knew he would fuss. About the two babies I did not know, but the ultra-sound showed them. It's good, one for each of you so no need to fight. They think a girl and a boy, but that is not certain. In my mother's family are many, many twins. I am very happy. Will be born in late December—Capricorns, just like you!" she smiled at her astounded father.

"Well, we're delighted of course." Penny pulled herself together and went over and kissed both of them. "Aren't we, Toby?"

"Eh, what? Oh, yes, certainly." He came out of his trance with a start. "Now, you fill them in on what's happening and I'll get Morelli back here and then we'll get you out of here. No more risks!" And he rushed out muttering, "Twins?"

Penny explained what Morelli wanted from Sonya, who nodded serenely and curled up on the sofa. "I will think very hard," she declared and closed her eyes. "Get me a drink, darling."

Alex came out of his daze. "It's not good for you."

"A little wine will not hurt," she murmured. "Good for my stomach."

"Get me one too while you're at it," Penny said. "And don't fuss." He sighed and did as he was told.

Morelli was not long in answering the summons. When he came in and saw Sonya's face, he looked duly shocked and was at his gentlest with the young couple. "My apologies, signora, when you have been through so much already, but this is vital," he stammered. "Have you thought of anything at all that may help us?"

"I have been thinking very hard," Sonya reproved. "And yes, I remember some strange things. In the catacomb, the fat man, Carlo, he complained constantly about the place and Peppi says to him, 'You should be used to it, it's why you're here, you are used to'—and he uses a word I do not know . . .'" She looked for help from Toby. "He says, 'you are a rat who always works in a dark place, in a *fogna.*'"

"A sewer," her father translated and looked at Morelli, who nodded excitedly. "Yes, yes! We've got some background on Carlo now. He was a municipal employee in the water and sewer department until he got fired and did some time for petty theft. Go on!" he urged.

"The only other thing I hear and do not understand was yesterday. Carlo, he says, 'The flags should be flying soon' and Peppi says, 'They can't fly soon enough for me—then we get our pay-off when it is done. The first was better than this. I'm fed up with this delay.' Does that help?" Sonya gazed around at them.

An image rose in Penny's mind. "The conference center," she breathed. "The big place in EUR with all those flagpoles in front of it. Are the flags flying, inspector?"

Morelli was already on his feet and on his way out the door. "They will be hoisted in one hour when the floodlights go on and before the conference begins. We went over the center inch by inch—but, by God, we never thought about the sewers! Please God, let me be in time!" And he was gone.

"Well, that was easy enough," Sonya said happily. "Now, let's go on to something really important. What shall we name the babies?"

Chapter 21

The opening session of the conference of the Federation of European States got underway with due pomp, if a little behind schedule: the flushed excited faces of the lesser delegates—who had been well wined and dined at a long drawn-out reception at the Farnese Palace—were in somewhat marked contrast to their respective heads of state, all of whom exhibited a certain amount of strain. It was to their eternal credit, however, that not one of them developed a diplomatic illness at the last minute but, to the man and woman, soldiered bravely on.

Unlike their juniors they, perforce, had been apprised of the true situation, and Morelli for one, would not have blamed them for a more craven reaction, since his men, burrowing like moles in the complex sewer system beneath the great conference hall, had already unearthed and deactivated three separate caches of explosives. The terrifying thought that drove them all desperately onwards was that there were probably more to come, although the vital areas, which would have brought the vast dome tumbling down on the crowded arena had already been cleared.

That they had scotched the snake not killed it, was evident when reports came in of bomb explosions within the West German, Russian and American Embassies; in all cases they were from the sewer system. Although there was some structural damage, because of the tight security in all the embassies, there was no internal loss of life or even injury, although one unfortunate Japanese tourist, who happened to be strolling down the Via Veneto when the American Embassy bomb went off, was decapitated by a flying manhole cover. Tragic as this was—particularly for the tourist—to Morelli, so acutely aware of what the carnage *could* have been and still on tenterhooks for the lives of his own men, it seemed a token price.

But the toll was not yet complete. While the plenary session was still in progress, a municipal truck was stopped at one of the many road blocks that had been unobtrusively set up in a wide perimeter around the hall. The men in the driver's seat tried to argue with the *carabinieri* that they were on an emergency call to Residential Gardens Hotel, an exclusive apartment hotel near the arena. A bright *carabinieri* phoned the hotel surreptitiously and found no such call had been made. The men were ordered out of the truck. Instead they opened fire, leaving two policemen dead, two others wounded, and sped away into the night. But it was a fatal mistake. The *Guarda Mobile,* with their quarry finally pinpointed, went after them in full force, and the desperate chase headed back towards Rome. It was a chase that could have only one ending. After screaming down the wide Viale Guglielmo Marconi and gaining the Lungotevere di San Paulo alongside the Tiber, the truck, trapped by police cars coming towards it and those closely following behind, disappeared in a blinding sheet of flame: there was not enough of it or its occupants to discover how many men it had carried. The two men who had been seen at the roadblock answered Sonya's descriptions of the Arabs; the big question was whether Paulo Vanni had also been on board.

228

During all this turmoil in Rome, a small squad of armed men, armed also with a search warrant, had descended upon the quieter purlieus of Albano and had stormed the Krantz villa. The old man had not taken this intrusion lightly, but had set the Doberman on them and fired off several shots with his rifle before being winged in the arm and overpowered. Screaming his hatred, he had been hauled off to the hospital under close arrest. A search of the villa revealed no further explosives, but, acting on a suggestion Toby had made earlier to Morelli which had caused that much tried man to exclaim in horrified disgust, they had made a careful search of the house and in a cupboard had come upon a cache that confirmed Toby's imaginative guess, firmly tying Krantz to murder and the terrorists. The cupboard contained several hundred pairs of women's shoes—some moldering and of styles that dated back all the way to World War II. All were in separate plastic bags and neatly labeled with names and dates. But it was not these that mainly interested the Italian police. Their focus was on two pairs of shoes that had not yet been encased or added to this gruesome collection: one, a pair of silver leather evening sandals studded with purple rhinestones and missing a small scrap; the other, a pair of black leather high-heeled pumps. In this case Krantz had been a little too precipitate in his fetish: Sonya was alive to identify and reclaim her shoes.

The task delegated to the residents of the Redditch villa was the guarding of this vital witness. "We can't spare you a single man," Morelli had said. "But here's another revolver and Dr. Spring still has the gun issued to him. Lock both inner and outer doors to the villa and keep a constant watch until we can afford you some protection. Don't let anyone in you don't know and don't accept deliveries of any kind. Explain all this to the maid, and perhaps you should send her away for her own safety until this is over." But Rosa had indignantly refused to budge.

A surprising addition to their garrison had been Andrew

Dale, who had turned up, his arm in a sling, but otherwise in a state of high spirits, and had demanded to stand his share of guard duty. While he regaled Penny and Sonya with a blow-by-blow account of the "Battle of the Beach," Toby and Alex amused themselves by rigging up an elaborate booby trap and alarm system with pots and pans from Rosa's kitchen and a set of decorative cowbells across the door between the villas. They also wedged some two-by-fours across the bottom of the cistern to block the exit from the catacomb "just in case" and, highly pleased with themselves, rejoined the others in the living room. "Perimeter secured," Toby announced; he was beginning to fancy himself in the role of a general.

They all grinned at him and turned their attention back to the animated Andrew. "The producers are beside themselves with delight at the news of my 'injury,' he related. "I think they are going to milk it for all it's worth and are a little put out that I'm not closer to death's door. I shudder to think of the publicity they are going to put out on this; they'll probably end up with me trouncing the terrorists single-handedly à la Errol Flynn and saving the damsel in distress. And they've undoubtedly got their writers already on a derring-do script about a dashing young director saving a beautiful Russian ballerina from a fate worse than death. . . ." He grinned over at Sonya. "Although they will be certain to omit the twins and the handsome husband who patched up the dashing young director."

"More fool them," Sonya said serenely.

He turned his attention back to Toby. "Anyway, no question that they'll pick up the tab for the day's shooting and be happy to do so. What is more, they are chartering a plane to take poor injured me back tomorrow for the whole publicity bit, and I was suggesting that Sonya and Alex come along. I could drop them off in New York on the way to California. Would that be possible?"

"Sonya still has to make a complete statement for the police," Toby pointed out. "A lot depends on what happens tonight and how soon they will let her go. I'm all for it. As long as she's here and the terrorists are on the loose she'll be a target. When are you taking off?"

"About four tomorrow afternoon from Leonardo da Vinci. Why don't you all come along?" Andrew urged. "We'll have a ball."

Toby repressed a shudder. "Thank you, but Penny and I have to see this through here, and for the rest we'll just have to see what happens."

It was Rosa, at her usual TV watch, who apprised them of the attacks on the embassies and of the murders at the road block, although all mention of the aftermath of this and of the finds at the conference hall had been carefully suppressed. And it was to be the literal-minded Rosa who became the heroine of the hour on the following morning and who revealed their ongoing danger. They were still at the breakfast table when the bell to the outer gate pealed. "Probably Morelli," Toby said. "But if it isn't, don't let anyone in, Rosa."

She nodded and trotted off to the gate. "Who is it?"

"Delivery for a Rosa Lippi," a young voice answered. "A package."

"Who from?" she persisted.

"*I* don't know—I'm just the delivery man." The young man was getting impatient. "It's from Gucci's—leastways it's a Gucci box."

"I order nothing from Gucci or anywhere else. You take it away and ask, and you bring it back tomorrow if it's for me. I don't open this door today," Rosa announced.

"Oh, come on, don't be stupid, lady! I gotta have it signed for!"

"Too bad. Come back tomorrow and I sign," Rosa said and

stamped back up the path, as the man yelled and cursed at her from behind the closed door. She was in the process of describing all this at the breakfast table when there was the dull crump of an explosion that set the windows rattling. "I'll take a look," Alex said tightly, gathering up his Uzi.

"Oh, do be careful, darling," Sonya called after him anxiously. When he reappeared a few minutes later he was grim-faced. "An explosion by the Villa Scorsi. A small delivery van and the car behind it. We'd better call Morelli—it must have been a time bomb."

Rosa was gazing at him open-mouthed. *"Dio mio!"* she whispered. "It was meant for *me?* If I had brought it in . . ."

"Then we'd all have gone up with it," Penny said. "Thank you, Rosa. You just saved our lives—and yours."

The news of this latest outrage brought Morelli from the bed into which he had collapsed in the early hours of the morning. He was haggard and unshaven but his brief respite had driven the desperation from his eyes and there was a new air of confidence about him. This time he did not arrive alone but with a considerable entourage, including the sergeant from Due Torri, a police stenographer and—amazingly—a policeman carrying videocam recording equipment. "A new technique for us," he announced to Andrew with some pride, as he waved at the camera. "We take the witnessed statement from Signora Spring on film in the presence of a uniformed officer and this will stand in our courts should it come to that—although in this case I do not think it will."

Sonya and Alex departed to the study with the cameraman and the stenographer to make their statements and the rest settled down to a mini-conference where Morelli filled them in on the actual events of the previous night. At Penny's firm insistence Rosa was included, and Morelli took her further statement about the incident at the gate.

At the end of it he sighed and shook his head. "I am afraid this confirms my worst fears—Paulo could not have been in the van last night. The package was handed in to the delivery service at eight this morning for immediate delivery—and he is the only one left unaccounted for."

"How about the other Vannis?" Penny said. "It was a Gucci box and that immediately put me in mind of Gabriella."

He looked at her with a slight smile. "I'm afraid that is out of the question. In all that turmoil last night, a complaint was received at police headquarters from Count Carlo Scorsi to the effect that he had been robbed. Pietro and Gabriella have taken off, but not empty-handed. According to him they have taken a considerable amount of money, a car and several valuable paintings from his country estate. Reportedly he was beside himself with rage."

"But weren't they being watched?" Toby protested.

Morelli's face tightened. "Supposedly. Cicco's men were on that detail and the inspector will have a lot to answer for on this and on other things he so conveniently did not do. The Vannis got out of the palazzo and past them somehow and are on the run." He paused and brightened. "But they won't get far. The alert is out throughout Italy and Interpol has been notified. We'll get them. But they could not have been responsible for the package bomb."

"So Scorsi is now trying to wriggle out of this whole thing." Penny was glum.

"The Scorsis have always had a knack for that," he returned. "And, as I've said all along, we have nothing concrete against him. One thing for sure, this whole affair has left him a lot poorer—maybe even a little wiser."

"So where does that leave us?" Toby said impatiently. "In these circumstances I am more anxious that ever to see my daughter out of this."

"I agree with you, in fact I strongly urge Dr. and Signora Spring to leave with Signor Dale this afternoon. We will even provide an escort to the airport. Not that I think Paulo will try anything else. If he follows the usual pattern, he himself is now trying to get out and save his own skin. There is nothing more of consequence he can do: his men are all dead or in custody; Krantz is taken and the Vannis are on the run. If we get lucky we may still catch him, but these mystery men of the terrorist world are as elusive as shifting shadows over the face of the earth. The important thing is that he has failed in his main task—thanks in large measure to *your* discoveries."

"But surely Paulo is pretty distinctive? He should not be that difficult to spot!" Penny cried.

Morelli chuckled grimly. "By this time he is probably clean shaven, with a full head of hair and a brand-new identity."

"Hasn't Carlo done any talking? Given you any idea of what their ongoing plans were?" she persisted.

He shrugged. "Oh, yes. Now he talks to save his skin, but mainly it has only confirmed what we had already deduced." He glanced at Rosa. "He claims to have had no hand in the murders. It was Selim, one of the Arabs, who knifed your husband on Paulo's orders. And, as Signor Dale here suggested, Signora Demerest's death was not intended—they were trying to keep her quiet until their business was done. Although, myself, I think Krantz would have had her killed eventually. That dirty murdering swine! Death would be too easy a penalty for him. Some of the shoes in that locked cupboard belonged to Italian women in our Resistance during the war. . . ."

The return of the honeymooners abruptly ended the conference and from then on it was a frantic flurry of activity to get them and Andrew packed, ready and out to the airport in time for the chartered plane. "Well, it is certainly not a honeymoon we are ever likely to forget," Alex grinned as he kissed his mother goodbye. "May we expect you when the twins arrive?"

"Wild horses couldn't keep me away," she assured them, and after much hugging and kissing all around she and Toby waved them into the plane. Andrew was the last one to board. As he hugged Penny he whispered, "You're the only woman who has ever been lucky for me—oh, if you were only thirty years younger!" She grinned and cuffed him amiably across the ear.

Morelli's escort insisted on seeing them back to the villa, and when they were at last alone Toby looked enquiringly at her doleful face. "Well, what do you want to do now? For what it's worth, I think it's over."

"What an unsatisfactory business this has been right from the start!" she sighed. "I feel that we were scrabbling around on the outside the whole time. I mean, you never even *saw* Paulo or Krantz. We met the Vannis precisely twice, the count once, and we didn't get in on *any* of the action."

Toby chuckled. "But we got the job done, didn't we? The murders solved, the terrorists spotted—what more do you want? And you haven't answered my question."

She paced moodily up and down. "This place seems so empty without Sonya and Alex," she complained. "And I sure in hell don't want to go back to sightseeing—I've had quite enough of that."

Toby looked knowingly at her. "I have a suggestion. Let's get out of here. I'd like to get all this information on the catacomb up to Fittipaldi. I think it has so many unusual features that he'll get it scheduled properly now, which should bring joy to your heart for that will infuriate Scorsi. Why don't we drive up to Florence for a couple of days and then head for home? I could certainly use some peace and quiet after all this."

She brightened. "Yes, Oxford in vacation time has a lot to be said for it. I'll go and talk it over with Rosa to see if she's willing to look after the place, and then I'll call the Redditches and tell them they are damn lucky to have her."

"Then I'll call Fittipaldi and fix it up." Toby headed for the phone and she made for the kitchen.

After she had explained their plans to Rosa, who was in another minor frenzy of baking, she looked anxiously at her for her reaction. "Will you be all right, coping with all this on your own?"

"Oh, no problem. We manage," Rosa assured her.

"We?" Penny queried.

"Enrico—the new gardener, and me." Rosa slid her a sly glance. "He is very good man, I think. Quiet. No drinking, no smoking, no women—is a widower. Two big children, one granddaughter—*una bella bambina!* He tell me his troubles, he like my cooking."

"I see." Penny was quietly amused.

Rosa grinned suddenly at her. "I think you do. Who knows? It would be good for him, good for me."

"But what will happen when the Redditches leave?"

"Oh, I belong here. They go, others come—I stay." Rosa was serene. "I am very good at what I do—no problem."

"Well, *we* certainly have appreciated you," Penny said. "And we'll miss you."

"And I you, signora," Rosa said firmly. "You are *multo sympatica.* You help me and Carmella. I am satisfied—the man who kill my Giovanni is dead. You go now and be happy. I take care of everything—after I bake this cake."

Highly tickled, Penny went off to pack and phone the Redditches.

As they loaded up the car and locked the fatal garage for the last time she felt a sense of overwhelming relief. "You know, I have had the most terrible thought," Toby said, climbing in beside her and starting the car.

She tensed again. "Oh? What?"

"What if the twins should look like *us?*" he demanded dolefully.

She burst out laughing. "Oh, really, Toby! Think positive! With any luck they'll look exactly like their parents. And what's wrong with us, I'd like to know? We may not be pretty, but who can resist us?"

He joined in her laughter, and chuckling they drove for the last time down the Appia Antica heading for new horizons.